Kingdom of Pershee

Double Trouble

Alex Lee Davis

Purple Rose publishing

ISBN:
978-19999152-3-0 (Paperback)
978-19999152-4-7 (Kindle)
978-19999152-5-4 (Hardback)

Cover Design by Big JayArt

Dedication

Dedicated to Malia, Judah and Tyler.

Kingdom of Pershee – Double Trouble

"From the first line to the final paragraph, this story had me hooked.
The characters and storylines will live on in my head for a long time. I very much hope there will be another book in the series soon."

Sue Johnson – poet, short story writer and novelist

Chapter 1

Break In

The early evening sun dimmed its gaze. Tall buildings cast lazy shadows across pavements, quiet alleyways, and busy streets. Fortunately, this made breaking into the library a lot easier for Tia and Lisa. They had sneaked out of their martial arts lesson to execute their plan to return to Sanguel.

Now in the alleyway beside the library, they used the large industrial bins and skip to conceal their movements.

"Keep looking out."

"I am," Lisa said. She peeked out from behind a large rusty skip overflowing with bricks, rubble, empty paint tins and timber from the library renovation.

"There's no one there. Well… just passers-by and they're not looking in this direction, too busy nattering. Although, I could have sworn I saw Adrian."

"You're always visualising lover boy. I think you need your glasses," Tia giggled. Tia found a few planks of wood to secure the lid of an adjacent industrial bin in an open position. She hoped it would provide a sufficient shield from onlookers. She clambered on top of a large black recycling bin.

"This is so exciting. And by the way, I only need my glasses for reading," Lisa said, her eyes darting frantically about the alley, hoping she wouldn't see a rat. "Ben will never guess that we're going back to Sanguel." She felt smug that she had outwitted her brother. Her school rucksack housed her martial arts kit and smaller rucksack that Arabella had given them from their previous visit to Sanguel; it contained her slimline sleeping bag, tuber - for protection, water canister, torch, and cloaking device necklace. She had followed Tia's instructions and it had all gone smoothly, so far.

"It doesn't smell of rotting rubbish. Thought it would with all these bins. Smells of… paint and…" With a deep intake of breath, Lisa continued, "Wood and something else…"

"They're recycling bins not food bins," Tia said, carefully levering the window above her head and securing a plank of wood between the bottom frame and the window to wedge it open. Old paint flaked about her fingers.

"It's a good thing the cars are making so much noise," Lisa said.

Tia threw her rucksack through the opening onto the toilet floor. "I'm going in." She grinned down at Lisa, "Start making your way up. Stay clear of this." She pointed to the plank of wood that held the awning window open. Tia went head-first onto the window ledge, her box braids tied into a ponytail, keeping her body low not to hit the window above her head or knock the plank out of place. Once through, she slowly pivoted her body around so that her legs dangled in the direction of the pile of boxes beneath her. Her hands tentatively held the flaky windowsill, her feet met with the first box whilst she managed to steady her hands and body against the wall. She quickly stepped down, although the boxes shook, she made her footing sure, glad she had prepared the boxes earlier. Once on the ground, she looked up for Lisa's appearance.

Lisa's head came into view, she looked down at Tia, "It's further than I thought."

"Bag first." Tia lowered her voice, signalling for Lisa to throw in her rucksack. "Remember steady, down slowly." Tia could see Lisa struggling with taking the rucksack off her back, something she said she would have done whilst being the look out. The rucksack tumbled to the ground with Lisa close behind, landing in a sprawl on the floor.

"Are you ok?" Tia helped her up. "I should have warned you about the boxes, they're a bit shaky."

"Fine. Glad no one saw me - so embarrassing!" Lisa swept her brown hair from her face and sat up.

Tia giggled, "It was funny."

Lisa laughed. "I can live it down if only you know about it. Please don't tell Ben, he'll tease me endlessly!"

"Don't worry I know what you two are like - siblings at war, but I think you love each other really," Tia said.

A sharp bang made them both snap their heads towards the window. The plank of wood had fallen from the ledge, the window flapped back against the weakened frame.

"I thought someone was coming in!" Lisa sighed with relief. "I can't believe you managed all this in your lesson."

"I told you; Miss Pugh didn't suspect a thing. She was too busy putting the books in the secure room. I begged so hard to go to the toilet; she had no choice. Who can resist my innocent act? Anyway, the window latch was painted shut and the boxes were all in that cupboard."

Lisa said, "I didn't think that door could be opened. Believe me I tried."

"I released the latch with the tuber," Tia said, proudly.

"I thought the tubers would only work in Sanguel!"

"Same here! Anyway, the boxes were okay, they contain toilet rolls and fancy bins."

"How do you know that?"

"Look, silly." Tia laughed and pointed at the labels. "I thought someone was going to catch me as I pushed the heavier ones to the walls. But the work men started drilling. It helped to cover me."

"Imagine, if you hadn't done this, we wouldn't have been able to get in here. Mr Evans told us the book exchange scheme for Year 7s will finish this week, cos the library will have to be totally closed until the opening."

"I didn't want to wait around till then," Tia said.

"If Arabella was still here, she would have left it open, never mind health and safety rules." Lisa retrieved her pendant from her bag. "I hope this still works." They put on their Sanguel rucksacks and shoved their larger school rucksacks in one of the toilet cubicles.

Lisa was about to open the toilet door when Tia pulled her back. "Builders."

"What about them?"

"I heard the library staff say that some of them have to start working late if they're going to get the library ready for the big re-launch."

"Who's been a little detective?" Lisa said.

"We've got to be careful. I couldn't get into the Reading Room, there were too many coming and going."

"You were going to go without me?"

"No. I was simply checking things out. I wanted to find the door."

"We didn't exactly go through a door," Lisa said.

"Ray and I did. It was in the reading room," Tia said, confidently.

Lisa wasn't so sure. She followed Tia cautiously out of the toilets. They looked up and down the corridors. There was no one present. All lights were off except the emergency exit lights. However, the narrow run of upper windows provided enough light for them to see their way.

They hurried along the short corridor into the main library. The windows had been covered to protect the stained glass.

"It looks strange and dull in here," said Tia.

"Smells like the alley." Lisa sniffed.

A section of bookshelves was cordoned off and covered with polythene sheets. Empty shelving was lined up against the wall, covered with polythene. They looked like square shadowy figures, throwing their shape across the vast space they once inhabited. Large signs stating 'keep out' or 'danger' dangled from scaffolding which supported the newly constructed mezzanine floor. Tia and Lisa tiptoed underneath. They could hear muffled discussions and hammering going on above them, shades of light emanating from that space. They hoped not to bump into any of the workers.

"This will be so amazing when it's finished," Lisa whispered.

They entered the long corridor to the Reading Room.

"I remember when Ben and I kept running along this corridor, thinking we were going to get away from Arabella. We certainly didn't. It all seems quite funny now," She chuckled, "but, back then, we were desperate to get away. Arabella was no ordinary librarian."

"So true," Tia said.

"Strange, I'm not so fearful." Lisa smiled as they hastened along the dimly lit corridor, triggering an alarm without noticing.

"The Reading Room." Tia swung the door open with glee not checking if anyone was inside.

"What's that noise?"

"Sounds like a car alarm. Come on," Tia said, eager to find the way out to Sanguel.

The Reading Room door closed behind them with a slurp. Tia had already retrieved her torch from her bag, she shone the light around the windowless room. She sighed in dismay. The room was overrun with scaffolding like a metal spider web, large floor-to-ceiling polythene strips divided the space; stage blocks and boxes looked trapped in this web of metal and plastic.

"Where on earth do we go from here?" Lisa also had her torch searching the area, "it's so confusing…, it looks so different."

"Too different," Tia said.

"Perhaps the scenery will change like last time." Lisa hoped.

"We were watching the 'enter if you dare' thing," Tia recalled.

Lisa nodded. "It got scary…when Ben and I didn't want to do what Arabella told us."

Tia hoped that what Lisa had to say would help them find the way out, so she asked, "What did Arabella tell you?"

"She said we had to follow the path."

"She told us that too. Follow the path outside this door. Do you think we went through the same door?"

"No way, we argued so much, I think she got rid of the door and gave us the open scenic route." Lisa chuckled. Tia gave in to a smile, knowing how much Ben and Lisa could argue at the drop of a hat over absolutely anything, just to disagree seemed to give them some type of enjoyment.

"Ok. Let's work from the main door. We sat around here. Yes?" Tia said, walking over to the spot occupied by groups of unopened large tins of paint.

Lisa stood beside her.

"And the stage was over there." Tia shone her torch at the dusty partitions, stage blocks and planks of wood stacked in a clumsy pile.

"So, the door would be over there." Tia's light zigzagged over to the far left of the room, stage blocks concealing the hopeful door.

"Do you think if we called Mrs M…, Arabella, she would find us?" Lisa asked.

"We could only call her Arabella in Sanguel, so I'm not sure she'll hear us."

"It's worth a try."

"You call and we'll still search," Tia said.

The girls made their way through the layers of partitions. Lisa gave up calling Arabella's name because she was frightened that the workers would eventually hear her. The dust tickled her throat, prompting a coughing fit, which wasn't easy to control or keep quiet. The coughing fit eventually subsided.

They moved carefully between the stage blocks and wall. "Here it is." Tia tugged at the door handle. When the door flew open Tia and Lisa were shocked to be met by misty skies and howling winds.

Chapter 2

Good Spot

Rafe was ecstatic because he had made it into the summer training camp for American football at a local club. He hadn't told Tia about it because he knew she was only interested in returning to Sanguel to find Meela. Tia had been uninterested and flippant in telling him he may not make the team. Now he was happy to tell her all about it when she got back from her martial arts class, he would even gloat about scoring a touchdown for the first time. He ruffled his two strand twists at the top of his head, pulling them into a top knot with a black hair band.

Rafe had stopped at the shops to buy Tia her favourite sweets, he hoped this would go some way to apologizing to her about not wanting to go back to Sanguel on the day she had suggested. Rafe flung his head back in celebration and gulped some of his canned drink. As he turned the corner, a body slammed into him.

"Sorry mate." The harassed voice squeezed out, as the person struggled to his feet.

"Ben?" Rafe gasped, shaking the spilt drink off his new team shirt.

Ben glanced up through his fringe, relieved to see Rafe; his words tumbled out as he repositioned his rucksack on his back, “Rafe…soz. Fresh fade, nice!”

Rafe smoothed the side of his head with a smile, a nod to the compliment.

Ben quickly continued, “I was looking for you. The girls have gone!”

Rafe placed his hand on Ben’s shoulder. “Slow down.”

Ben stopped wide-eyed with excitement, took a deep breath. “I was looking for you. Your mom said you were at football.” Ben furrowed his brow, confused at the American football team shirt Rafe was wearing rather than his school football team shirt.

Rafe nodded with a big grin. “I made the team.”

“But you’re already in the team?”

“Not the American football team for year 11s.” Rafe proudly smoothed the shirt down, in preparation to tell the detailed story about the try outs, but Ben got in before him.

“The girls have gone to the library. We might just catch them. I knew they were up to something; that Lisa can’t hide a thing from me, you wait until…”

“But the library is closed. It’s after five and it’s not a day when the public can have a nose round.” Rafe finished his drink, stopped short of a bin, took up a basketball aim and shot the can in the bin. As he was about to celebrate, Ben grabbed his arm to hurry him along, "I saw them messing around the skips."

Rafe's heart sank, and at the same time he gathered a spring in his steps. "Gross!"

"That's what I thought."

"Why didn't you stop them?" Rafe's footsteps quickened. "You're dressed like a ninja."

Ben smiled at the compliment. He made sure he wore dark clothing to follow Lisa and carried his Sanguel rucksack just in case. "I couldn't. You know what Lisa's like when she gets something in her head."

"This isn't Lisa's doing, it's Tia's," Rafe said, speeding up to a jog.

"Tia?"

"Yes. She's been going on about, well, hearing Meela crying."

"How? - I mean we didn't meet Meela. Alamo told me his sister had been taken to the kingdom of …" Ben frowned, keeping up with the increasing pace, "so how would she know what Meela's voice sound like?"

Rafe didn't reply.

They passed the road that led to the library.

Ben stopped, "The library's that way."

“I’m not going anywhere without a shower and change of clothes.”

“You’re fine.”

“You got something wrong with your nose bruv.”

They ran the short distance to Rafe and Tia’s home.

Chapter 3

It's Never Easy

Tia and Lisa huddled against the closed door, shielded from the turbulent scene they had just observed.

"Are we really on the edge of a cliff?" Lisa trembled; glad the door was firmly shut.

"We must have the wrong door."

"Perhaps the wrong scene," Tia said. "All this work around here may have shaken things up a bit."

Lisa's eyes widened, "You mean, like when we ripped the book, and our pendants didn't work properly?"

"Weeee. Didn't.... rip.... the book! You and Ben did. Aaanyway...," Tia said, not wanting to dwell on the consequences of Ben and Lisa's past squabble. "I'm going to try again. See what happens. I'll open the door more slowly. I think there was a ledge we could shimmy out on, look for a way down, across... or something."

"Jump on a cloud?" Lisa said.

Tia ignored Lisa's comment but thought she would jump on a cloud if she had to. She put her ear against the door.

"What are you doing?" Lisa asked.

"Listening to the wind. Once it dies down, we'll try again."

Lisa listened too.

Silence.

"Can you hear an alarm?" Tia asked.

"Sounds like it's coming from the library, not out there." Lisa faced the door.

They glanced at each other to confirm that they were about to exit. Tia slowly cracked the door, peeked through the gap, and felt the burst of fresh cold air.

"What's it like?" Lisa whispered, not wanting to look, as she felt the wind rush through the gap in whimpering ripples.

Tia slammed the door, touched her necklace, zipped her hooded jacket, secured her hood and rucksack, "We've got to go down, stay close to the wall," she said. Lisa zipped and secured her belongings too.

"It's never easy," Lisa sighed.

"Where's the fun in that." Tia chuckled, knowing her friend well enough to know that Lisa would love the adventure even if she complained.

"I hope my jeans won't get ruined, these are new, got them on Saturday, mom'll throw a wobbly if I ruin them."

"Come on, tell her it's the new fashion, holes and rips are in."

"True."

"Call it riptastic." Tia chimed and stepped cautiously out onto the stony ledge; white mist swirled about them. With their backs against the rugged wall, they inched their way down, the curve of the library's outer wall served as a guide and support. The bitter wind pushed them along.

Lisa repeated, "riptastic style," to help her make good the uncertain descent through the patchy mist that only revealed a stony slope, slippery in places. A deep, earthy smell rose to meet them as they made their descent.

"It's so difficult to see further than a few metres." Lisa grumbled.

"Hopefully, the mist disappears soon. It makes all the shapes look quite scary; I can't see anything familiar," Tia said. "Like the crossroads, or the path, let's not forget the tree Ben fell out of."

"Don't remind me." Lisa cracked into a giggle remembering Ben's plight, only that at the time she didn't find it so funny.

The wind subsided. Glimmers of hazy sunlight against a grey sky revealed itself in patches. They were able to make out a sequence of dilapidated stone steps through the veil of clouds leading into a rugged area. The steps eventually disappeared into a wide uneven pathway.

"Tia, what are those things?"

“Trees, I think.”

The trees looked like ghostly figures enticing them to advance through the mist. Even though the mist was still evident, they could see the dark soil gradually give way to yellow sandy ground. Tia was heartened. A large tree came into view, the mist hung on its outer limbs like a draping Christmas decoration.

“Look. The post.”

They ran towards the familiar black and white post.

“I can remember it growing out of the ground.” Tia gave the post a welcome tap and looked up. “That’s new.”

They stood back to view the silver plaques which served as direction arrows at the top of the post, black italics inscribed the name of the destinations. They followed the Sanguel direction as they didn’t recognise any of the other places.

*

“At least we know we’re going in the right direction.” Lisa sighed with a happy demeanour.

“If we move quickly, we should get there in no time. The path is easy to see even with this mist,” Tia said.

They happily chatted away not noticing something travelling behind them, gaining ground quickly. The faint, yet growing rumbling still didn't distract them until it was upon them, shrill snorting, clatter of hooves and screeching wheels. It moved so swiftly, the dust made them cough and their eyes burned with unwanted tears, the curtain of mist burst apart,

"Get out of the way, get out of the way!" A voice boomed.

Chapter 4

Trapped

Traffic slowed as tired commuters honked their horns, trying to get home from work. Rafe was dressed in dark clothing, his Sanguel rucksack strapped tightly across his back, he and Ben dodged into the library alley way, their trainers muffled their urgent steps. Rafe looked up at the building, a flashing blue light and faded bleep came from the box high up on the wall.

"The alarm," Rafe said, in dismay.

"Bet they set it off," Ben smiled.

"Well, if they have, security or the police may come to check it out. We best be quick." Rafe wasn't convinced with the way Ben was going to enter the building. Ben had hoisted himself up on the bin towards the window, he was glad to find it was open. He quickly peered in, threw in his rucksack, his movements were quick with little regard for what he was going to meet on the other side. Ben missed his footing and almost hit his head against the wash basin as he fell. Some of the boxes collapsed but cushioned his fall. Ben was sprawled across the floor.

Rafe opened the toilet door. "Why are you on the floor?"

"How did you get in?"

"The side door was open. These shoulders need more room," Rafe said, with an air of nonchalance as he pulled Ben to his feet.

Ben had already spotted something familiar from under the stall door, "I told you. Look there's the evidence." Ben snatched Lisa's bag from the cubicle, her martial arts kit spilled out as he shook it.

"I did believe you Ben."

"Let's see if we can catch up with them." Ben dragged his rucksack from under the fallen boxes.

"I think you'd best put your sister's things back in that bag, or…"

"What's she going to do?" Ben chuckled, "She's not here."

Rafe raised his eyebrow.

Ben thought again, so instead of throwing the bag on top of the kit he pushed the kit in the bag and threw the bag back where he found it. "Let's see if we can catch up with them or find a short cut."

"I'm not so sure. When Tia's ready she's like a puma."

They left the toilets without checking to see if anyone was around. The alarm had stopped but its blue light flashed every few seconds. They stopped for a moment taking in the changes in the main area. They had failed to spot the guard on the mezzanine floor, who had caught sight of them seconds after they entered the main area.

"STOP. YOU VANDALS!" His torch light caught their feet in flight.

Rafe and Ben dodged under the scaffolding and weaved their way around to the reading room. Once there, with horror and excitement, they crouched down and moved stealthily behind piles of boxes, partitions and finally settled behind the stage blocks in a darkened corner of the room. The guard eventually shot into the room, breathing heavily he said, "No use running, the cops are on the way." He beamed his light across the room. Ben and Rafe slowed their breath and crouched even closer to the blocks.

The guard laughed.

"There's no way out of here." He pulled the keys for the premises from his back pocket and jangled them in front of him. "You can have a great night's sleep in here or I can call it in as a false alarm."

He paused; they could hear him catching his breath. "So, you fancy a night in?" His torch swept the ground in a criss-cross fashion and crawled along the boxes towards the stage blocks, Rafe lowered his head, hoping his top knot wouldn't reveal their hiding place.

Heavy footsteps were heard heading into the room.

"Winston, Winston? You got them?"

"Yep. They want to stay overnight," Winston said, "looks like kids."

"Come on. Jack's getting the first round in. We can swing back and let them out before our shift's over, the police will be here by then."

"Yep, the cops'll teach them a lesson they won't forget." He shut off his torch and slammed the door. Keys secured their fate.

Chapter 5

Changes

The man on the cart yanked at the reins. Tia and Lisa tumbled out of the way. The horses hurtled off the path into an unsettled halt. A man dressed in a colourful cotton top, which should have been loose fitting, tucked into brown trousers; his waistline heaving and sighing at each breath. Lisa was amazed to see how quickly the cart driver jumped down from the carriage on to the grassy area and strutted over to the dirt track, to see if they were alright. His familiar frame and the mopping of his brow prompted Lisa's and Tia's recognition of him.

"Mr Peri!"

He assisted them to their feet.

Lisa said, "Didn't you see us?" When she really wanted to sarcastically say 'try and hurt us, why don't you!'

"Well, well, well. My little travellers." He smiled and rubbed his sweaty brow. "I'm so sorry, so sorry. I was in a rush, a rush you see, I didn't see you, came out of the fog." Lisa wasn't impressed.

"I'm ok," Tia said, as she tentatively stretched her arms and legs.

"I hope I haven't hampered your wonderful skills, WON…derful skills."

Tia smiled up at him. "Don't worry, I'm fine. Think I've just knocked my arm."

Lisa gave him a hard stare to indicate he was missing the point, but Mr Peri was none the wiser, so Lisa turned her more positive attentions to Tia. "Have you broken it?"

"Well let's see." Tia knew Lisa wasn't fond of Mr Peri and tended to exaggerate his mistakes. "It's not broken, just a little strange, I'm fine."

"I'll check the horses." Mr Peri hobbled off to the horses, now grazing.

"You do that." Lisa gave a fake smile and turned to assist Tia who needed no help.

"He's not changed. Idiot!"

Tia suppressed a chuckle, slowly rotated her arm. "Don't be so hard on him. It's difficult to see through all this mist."

Lisa whispered, "You didn't stay with him, like Rafc and I did." She raised her eyes to the heavens. "He's a right idiot!"

"Hush, he'll hear you," Tia giggled. "He's not that bad."

*

Mr Peri set about explaining to Tia and Lisa what had happened in Sanguel while they were away. The temperature warmed as they sat next to Mr Peri, wedged in on the cart seat. The large barrels on the cart clunked together, releasing a sweet smell that reminded the girls of strawberry jam.

"So, you see, Evan and Alamo are doing a great job, great job. I'm so proud of them."

"We know. We know," Lisa said. Mr Peri nodded, unaware of Lisa's sarcasm.

"I'm sure Mrs Peri is proud of them too," She added.

"Does the council take up a lot of their time?" Tia asked.

"Yes, of course. They have enooormous responsibility, to speak on behalf of the young people who were trapped and are now free from the mines. They are ammmbassaadors, ammmbassaadors, I tell you." He puffed up his chest even further, one hand flying in the air above his head to emphasise the grand nature of his sons' titles.

Lisa nudged Tia and rolled her eyes as she mouthed '*ammmbassadors*', the way Mr Peri had exaggerated the word.

"What about Meela? Has she returned home?" Tia asked.

Mr Peri suddenly seemed uncomfortable and broke into a coughing fit; his bald patch oozed a sudden flow of sweat. He snatched at the cloth in his trouser pocket and patted feverishly. Lisa contemplated tapping his back to help alleviate the coughing, but as she noticed the large patch of sweat seep through his top, she changed her mind. But she did ask, “Are you okay?” with as much care as she could feign.

“Water.” He pointed to a spot under Tia’s seat. Tia pulled out a wooden water bottle, released the bottle cork and handed the bottle to Mr Peri. He slurped at it. As he spoke water seeped from the edges of his mouth. “Yes, yes.” He managed; the coughing fit abated. An uncomfortable silence lingered.

Mr Peri cleared his throat with a final loud cough and gulp. “The games still exist, but for positive reasons. It’s for celebration. Even the adults get involved. It’s so entertaining, so entertaining.” He laughed harder than he needed to.

“Do you take part?” Lisa let out a giggle. Tia nudged her. Before Mr Peri could reply, Tia asked, “Is Meela back in Sanguel?”

Mr Peri’s voice lowered, “No… she prefers to remain where she is.”

“We’re going to visit her,” Tia announced.

Lisa added. “Last we heard she was in the Kingdom of Clover,”

Mr Peri hesitated, "…Pershee."

"Pershee?" Tia was surprised. Lisa flashed a suspicious glance at Mr Peri.

"Yes." Mr Peri mopped his, now dry, brow.

"Well, that's where we're going," Lisa said.

Mr Peri hesitated before he continued. He elevated his tone with confidence, "And how are you going to get there?"

"We're going to ask Arabella," Lisa said.

"No need to do that." Mr Peri was hasty in his response. His little bubble of confidence burst, then slowed his pace and said, "You can see her as soon as you get to Sanguel. I can sort you out with transport and you can be back before night fall." He tried to sound convincing.

"Sounds good to me," Tia said.

Mr Peri wasted no time in continuing his chatter about the changes in Sanguel.

They knew all too well how Mr Peri loved the sound of his own voice, but the fact that he was relaying enlightening and entertaining information made them willing to listen.

*

They entered the large open gates of Sanguel. A guard greeted them, wearing a brown turban, bronzed breastplate over matching blue tunic and trousers, a sword harnessed to his back, and brown boots. Where once the courtyard had ruined statues and sparse drying vegetation, it now brimmed over with foliage. The statues were renewed; the bronzed statue of a robed man carrying a yoke now had silver-coloured chains holding the buckets on either end, water ran through the holes in the bottom of the buckets. A new statue stood in the position of the remains of the previous half-crumbled feet. Red vines with pink and violet flowers curled around the arms of the statue as though they were a shawl slipped around its dark shoulders. A new well had been constructed, large wooden buckets encased by copper strips sat around its base.

Lisa whispered to Tia, “It’s so beautiful.”

“Yes. Yes. Very beautiful indeed,”

“You really shouldn’t listen in on other peoples’ conversations,” Lisa said.

Mr Peri chuckled, “I believed you were speaking to us.”

“Mr Peri…what happened to Evelyn?” Tia asked.

“He’s imprisoned and will be there for a long, long, long time. No need to worry about him.” His tone carried a hint of disappointment for someone he thought was once a great leader.

The horses trotted steadily towards the stables, undisturbed by the mechagribea coming towards them. Tia and Lisa froze as they saw the large, orange, furry beast stride towards them. They were expecting it to attack, instead it calmly ambled past, its triangular shaped ears rotated like sails, its metal teeth concealed inside a large jaw and white snout. A cart was strapped to its back, containing two large, empty barrels.

The girls couldn't see the three children trailing behind the cart until they came alongside them. The children smiled and ran up to the mechagribea, patted its hind legs and ran off playfully. Tia and Lisa couldn't believe what they were seeing.

"How is that possible?" Tia gasped.

"Why isn't that beast agitated?" Lisa continued to stare at the scene over her shoulder.

Mr Peri said, "The little lad programmed them to help us."

"Do you mean, Rowhan?" Tia asked.

"Yes. Yes. He made them helpful. Plough the fields, pump water, it's such a sight, such a sight to behold."

"Where? Can we see it?" Tia was fascinated, Lisa wanted to see it too, yet both still held a sense of fear about the damage those beasts could do.

"Well, because you want to visit Meela, I suggest you take the quickest means possible." Mr Peri steered the horses towards a small enclosure, “You can see all that when you get back.” The horses came to a halt.

“We might as well see Arabella before we leave,” Tia said.

“And say a quick hello to the others,” Lisa added.

Mr Peri hoisted his large frame to the ground and helped Tia and Lisa from the cart, he said, “If you go now, you will have time to see them when you get back. Like I said, they are all in council meetings. No point wasting time. No point at all. You’ll be back in no time. No time.” He inhaled, “Most important. I know Meela is there now. And will be leaving tomorrow for a trip …”

Tia was compelled to follow his direction although she felt it wasn’t genuine. He hurried them into his workshop area of the stables after securing the horses.

*

The contraption looked magnificent in this section of the stables. The outer structure which formed the horse’s body was made of bronze. Its metal shone in the dim quarters. Two horses’ heads and necks formed the front of the contraption, their bodies joined together to create a circular cabin large enough to seat four people comfortably. The breast of the sculpture contained the majority of the mechanism to provide movement; this section engaged with the undercarriage which housed the additional tubes and wires connecting the torso and hinged legs. When the contraption was in motion, the upper half of the two horses would bob up and down, the legs would rotate along with concealed wheels to allow the contraption to move swiftly and smoothly.

Mr Peri smiled with admiration "One of my greatest achievements." His chest extended; it looked as though he was going to burst out of his clothes at any moment. Tia and Lisa tried not to laugh at Mr Peri's demeanour, he hurried around to the breast plate, opened it, muttered to himself as he fiddled with the mechanism.

Finally, he said, "Well," he hurried to the contraption door, wiped the window section, which was already spotless, with his sleeve, "you will be quite comfortable in there." He opened the door, "I've made a few changes, polished all the wood myself." He leant forward and smoothed his hands over the wooden flooring and side panels, grabbed a cloth hanging from a nearby hook and rubbed at a non-existent spot. He pulled out a small wooden step.

"Passengers can see out as they travel." He flashed the cloth at the eye level circular glass. "Whatever you do don't touch this lever." He pointed towards the metal ceiling. They could see a grey, oblong button beside a square indent. “If you accidentally hit it, the ceiling will open. You don’t want that if it’s raining or worse, windy, windy is no good.” He swirled his finger above his head to indicate turmoil, the girls got the message, and chuckled as he continued to twirl his finger next to his temple, towards them and back to his temple. He placed the cloth back on its resting place.

He held the door open for Lisa and Tia to get in, they sat side by side on the firm yet comfortable seating. They could see a small slot that gave a limited view of the way ahead. It was occupied by the backs of the horses’ metal heads. It looked as though it was only there to provide a portrait of the horses, but Mr Peri pointed out its true purpose.

“Ventilation, ventilation,” Mr Peri said cheerily, and placed their rucksacks beside them.

“This is so soft,” Tia said. She brushed the red velvet fabric as though stroking a cat. The fabric covered the seating and ran up the panel, above their heads.

“All down to my wife. Wonderful. Wonderful, wife.” A wide grin complemented his face before he hurried off to the far section of the stables, where he had his workstation for repairs, rest, and meals. He came back with a medium-sized brown cotton sack, a string tied around its top. He handed it to Tia.

"A few provisions." He smiled.

Tia took his smile as a sign of relief.

"Thank you," They both said, without looking at what was inside.

"You'll be quite safe. This will stop right at the end of the track, which is the Pershee end, the red hills. Once there, follow the signposts. It's a straight walk to the Palace, not far. You can't miss it. Everyone, everyone, is friendly, they'll show you where it is if you get lost. But you won't get lost," he said hastily, pleased with himself.

Before they could respond to him, he flipped the step back in place, slammed the door and pulled the lever behind the contraption to release it from its station. He marched swiftly to the front of the contraption and patted the horse heads as though they could feel his touch. He tugged on a rope above his head, and the gates opened with a plume of dust. Some of the dust filtered into the ventilation slot. The girls fanned it away.

The contraption rocked back and forth, the horses' heads dipped and rose with the rocking motion. It slowed and slowly rocked backwards, shunted, and lurched forward. Tia and Lisa were flung backwards against the back of the seat, grateful for the soft finish. The sack Mr Peri had given them fell against their feet along with their rucksacks. They grabbed onto the leather straps beside them. A sharp, shearing metal against metal sound could be heard from beneath the carriage as the mechanism rolled forwards onto iron under-soil runners. They heard the fading cheers of Mr Peri as they left the large gates. The contraption gathered pace and began to shoot through the woods. Tia and Lisa eventually let go of the straps and settled back.

"He seemed happy to get rid of us." Tia mused.

"Yes, and he lied," Lisa said. "Alamo told us this thing was created by Evelyn - silent horses, that's what they called it."

"Not so silent now," Tia said, as they heard a gentle knocking sound rise in the undercarriage, reverberating into the heart of the contraption.

"As for him making alterations, well can we believe that he did it all on his own, or did evil Evelyn have something to do with it?" Lisa asked.

"We can find out when we get back. Feels like a train ride." Tia rocked along with the motion.

Lisa looked down at the sack. "Do you think there's something nasty in there?"

"That's a stretch!"

"Well, we can't believe him."

Tia picked up the sack and held it open so they could both see.

"Slices of cake, biscuits and a bottle." Lisa lifted out the container. "It's a drink of some sort," she said, as she shook the bottle. Tia gave her a look of 'I'd never have guessed it'

"It all smells great, like ginger and vanilla," Tia said, "I wonder if Mrs Peri baked them."

"Her food is delicious." Lisa reflected. "I wonder if Mr Peri can cook now."

Tia giggled, "I doubt it."

"Did I tell you he wanted me to do all those chores and things and Rafe to practice for the games? I wasn't going to do that!"

"If he's on the council, why wasn't he at the meeting?" Tia asked.

"I bet they chucked him out." Lisa studied the biscuits lovingly, wondering whether to bite into the one with currants or the other one with chocolate looking bits.

"Why didn't we ask him? He was on the board when last we heard. And he wanted us to go. I mean, He really wanted us out of the way," Tia said.

Lisa nodded, but Tia felt that Lisa's reaction was more in response to how much she was enjoying the biscuit.

"Do you think he was trying to get rid of us?" Tia asked.

Lisa stopped chewing.

"Do you think he was trying to get rid of us?" Tia repeated.

"Of course! He gave us his snacks."

"Be serious."

"I am." Lisa swallowed. "He loves his grub, and he certainly wouldn't normally give it away. But he has no reason to get rid of us. We were going anyway."

"But not quick enough." Tia thought for a moment, watched the view whizzing past in the circular window. "Perhaps he didn't want us to see Arabella…," Tia said. "I bet he's up to something."

Lisa swallowed with a gulp, "Let's go back."

Tia sighed, "Too late. This contraption is only going one way."

Chapter 6

Old Friends/Old Enemy

"Why didn't you grab me?" Ben yelled.

"How could I grab you? I was falling too!"

Rafe and Ben staggered to their feet.

"Besides, I thought that door led to the path." Rafe shook his head and tied his hair up. "I was as shocked as you when I saw the mist."

"Now I know what it feels like to fall through the sky."

"Bizarre."

"Exciting." Ben grinned, shaking debris from his hair and clothes.

"Now I understand the 'look before you leap' thing. - I'm glad our landing wasn't bad. Thankfully that grassy spot broke our fall," Rafe looked up towards the area he and Ben had landed and then rolled out of control to their present position, "a few metres to the right and we wouldn't be walking away."

Ben said, "If anyone had seen us, they would think we've just dropped from the sky, like aliens or something."

"We did fall from on high, I'm not so sure about aliens though... We need to work out where we are." Rafe squinted hoping his eyes could decipher the shadows in the mist. He managed to make out clusters of trees. “Doesn’t seem familiar.”

The hilly area was splattered with trees and rugged soil.

“Where do we go?” Ben asked.

“My first thought is the crossroads. I can remember my way to Sanguel from there, but this fog’s disorientating,” Rafe said.

“Well, let’s just put our best foot forward,” Ben said, trying to be optimistic.

“What does that really mean?”

Ben shrugged, “Let’s go that way.” Ben looked at Rafe, saw him raise his eyebrow and changed his mind. “That way then.”

“Let’s listen for a moment. Can we hear anything?”

“Why? I can’t…”

Rafe put his finger to his lips. Ben stopped talking and listened. There was a stomping sound echoing in the distance.

“We’ll follow that sound.”

“What if it’s a monster or something?”

“We’ll find out what it is when we get there.” Rafe jogged off towards the sound. Ben reluctantly followed.

“Tubers to the ready,” Rafe shouted over his shoulder.

This sparked Ben's excitement; he was eager to use his tuber as he hadn't had a chance to fight with it as the others had done on their adventure in Sanguel.
They weaved through a sparse wood, the patchy mist turning yellow as they went. The clinks and thuds drew them in deeper and deeper. The misty trees bounced curious sounds around them; they had to stop a few times to get their bearings. The mist grew thinner the closer they got to the strange sounds. They slowed their pace as the noise became clearer. They stopped as they saw a group of young people dressed in denim dungarees and an assortment of different coloured tops, hammering wooden stakes into the ground, others hammering planks and securing wires across the stakes to create a barrier. The groups worked in pairs along a ten-metre stretch. A large tent was set with refreshments for the workers. Horses meandered in an enclosure next to the tent along with the carts that carried tools and materials.

Rafe and Ben hooked their tubers onto their belts. Rafe nodded to Ben, to indicate that he would engage with the group. Ben would hold back should anything go wrong.

Four of the young people stopped working and eyed Rafe as he approached them. He stopped a slight distance, enough for him to be heard and run if necessary.

"I'm a bit lost. I'm looking for the way to Sanguel."

A girl dressed in dungarees and a blue top used her hammer to point in the direction of the parting between the trees on the opposite side.

"Thanks." Rafe smiled, turned to head where Ben was situated.

"Rafe!"

Rafe turned to see Sam, his cornrows much longer, trailed in the wind as he ran towards him with a big grin of surprise. Ben sprinted out from his hiding place.

"Sam!" Rafe gave him a fist bump. Ben followed suit and said, "We're glad to see you."

"What are you two doing here?"

"Looking for Tia and Lisa," Rafe replied.

"They're not here," Sam said, running his hands over his cornrows.

"They were heading to Sanguel," Ben said.

"They were going to visit Meela." Rafe struggled to hide the anxiety from his voice.

Sam looked puzzled.

Rafe quickly explained, "Tia wanted to find Meela. She kept saying she thought she was in danger."

Ben added, "And Lisa said she wanted to visit Evan and Alamo, to see if they had found her. So, we assumed they would be here."

Rafe raised an eyebrow as if to say I'm not sure about that.

"I can tell you; Meela is not in Sanguel. She's in Pershee," Sam said.

"Is she okay?" Ben asked.

"As far as we know, why would Tia be worried?"

"I don't know." Rafe felt embarrassed. "I think it could be down to losing her mom. Well, that's what I kept telling her, but she denied it. Well, I think that's why she left without me. I was too sceptical."

Ben tapped Rafe on the shoulder. "Welcome to my world. It's like telling Lisa not to do something, then, we both end up in trouble because she doesn't listen."

"We'll see if we can catch them at Sanguel. They may be seeking Arabella's help. Wait here," Sam said. Sam ran off and came back on horseback with another horse and rider. "Thought I'd bring along one of your friends."

Ben gave Rafe an obvious nudge.

"Rafe, nice to see you again." The rider, whose familiar curly black hair, worn in a ponytail spoke warmly.

"Pleasure is all mine." Rafe couldn't stop his broad grin.

“Hi Izzy,” Ben chimed. Izzy smiled, but her attention was firmly on Rafe.

“I guess I’m riding with you.” Ben went over to Sam, “We’ll leave the love birds together.”

Sam gave Ben a hand as he hoisted himself on to Sam’s horse.

Rafe and Izzy were too busy admiring each other and getting reacquainted, they didn’t hear Ben’s teasing and Sam’s raucous laughter.

“Sorry to break up the getting-to-know-you session, but if you want to catch Lisa and Tia, we’d better get going,” Sam said. He waited for a few minutes until Rafe finally got on the horse with Izzy. Sam wasted no time galloping back to Sanguel, Izzy and Rafe happily trailing.

*

Once back in Sanguel they headed straight to Hill House. A new wlde bridge had been erected over the, now, water filled moat. A steady flow of people moved about. They left their horses at the Hill House stables and went to meet with Arabella. However, Arabella was in a meeting, so Sam and Izzy gave Rafe and Ben a guided tour of the improvements made to the Royal House.

“We closed off the mines not long after you left, but disagreements on the council have made it difficult to come to a resolution on what to do with them.” Izzy explained.

Just being at the entrance of the mines reminded Rafe and Ben of the awful conditions that children had to work in; dusty, cold, cramped conditions, with limited breaks. Now the area was much brighter, the dust had settled so it was much easier to breathe.

“The orbs are still used,” Ben said, and tried to jump up and catch hold of the cord that held the balloon-like lighting for the mines. Rafe reflected on how he and Lisa caught the spores to make the lighting orbs for the mines, little did they know at the time what trouble they were going to get into.

Sam explained, “They’re still the most effective way of seeing and breathing down here.”

Rafe inhaled. “Is that mint?”

“Yes.” Sam pointed to small bunches of green shoots along the passageways. A faint wind released the aroma. “Introduced by Arabella, the fragrance takes away that awful death smell.”

Ben nodded in agreement. “I can smell roast lamb.” He grinned.

Sam continued to explain what areas of the mines were still open. “The cells are still in use for obvious reasons.

Evelyn is the only person in that part of the mine. He's awaiting a move to a more secure prison. He created so many problems with his fake defenders it was very difficult to deprogram them."

"So, they had to be separated. Deprogramming is going well, without Evelyn." Izzy clarified.

"Let's see what he says when he sees us." Ben grinned.

"Don't play up to him," Izzy warned, "He deserves everything he gets."

"I won't," Ben said.

"I'm interested too." Rafe looked at Izzy.

"He's still a creep!" Izzy said and stopped as the others walked on. "I'll see you all later. I really do care about the company I keep. Besides, I need to get back to help the others. See you later Rafe."

Rafe called after her, "What were you guys doing out there?"

"You're asking that now?" Ben aimed at Rafe. Rafe returned a hard stare.

Ben gave a fake cough and said, "I meant you came all this way on horseback and …"

"Don't try it, Ben. I'm not embarrassed. Izzy and I had more important things to discuss."

"Like what?" For a moment Ben caught a glimpse of bashfulness flutter across Rafe's face, which Rafe finally hid with a chuckle.

Rafe tapped his nose.

Sam watched all this with some amusement.

Izzy offered an answer. "We're creating new quadrants for crops and grazing ground for new cattle. See you later." She smiled at Rafe and jogged to the exit. Rafe watched her go as Sam and Ben continued to the cells.

"You coming big man?... Or you got something better to do?" Sam joked without turning around.

"I'm here." Rafe caught up with them and mirrored their stride.

*

Two guards flanked the large metal door, dressed in the regal defender's garments: dark jumpsuit, trouser legs tucked into calf length black boots, hands gloved, and hoods pulled forward obscuring their faces. Blue stripes ran around their hoods and edge of the wide cuffs. They greeted them.

One of the guards opened the metal door to the cell area.

"This door is new. It does a good job of eliminating Evelyn's calls and taunts. When he realised that we no longer pandered to his whims, his attitude got much better. But be careful, he's still a trickster." Sam warned. The gate gave a sharp clunk behind them.

They heard Evelyn before they saw him. "I have visitors and it sounds as if they are not from here." His tone was calm and light-hearted.

They walked past three empty cells before they saw Evelyn behind the bars in a long grey robe and sandals, a stark difference to his previous elaborate dress or feigned humble attire. His greying hair untidy, not kept in its neat central braid. He was stood on a wooden table, hands behind his back, staring out of a small cell window. Rafe kept his face neutral; Ben couldn't help but have a wide grin, happy that Evelyn was locked up for all the horrible things he had done.

They waited in silence.

Evelyn turned to view his visitors; his eyes lit up with mischief as he viewed them. His beard was groomed with beading, separating into two points, with which he would play, shifting the coloured beads around.

Ben broke the silence, "You're lucky, this cell is better than the one you flung us in."

"I did no such thing."

Evelyn produced his crooked, stretched lips that they presumed was his smile.

"Rafe - Ben."

"You remembered our names," Ben said, proudly.

"Of course - how could I forget half the quartet that bought disaster to my kingdom?"

"We made it better." Rafe gave a satisfactory grin knowing it would irk Evelyn even more.

"How so?" The weird smile had dropped, and a wicked sneer crept across his mouth.

"We exposed you for who you were." Ben pulled over a stool to sit in front of the bars. He composed himself like a journalist ready to fire questions.

Rafe and Sam kept a safe distance away and watched the exchange.

Evelyn stepped off the table onto his small bed; neatly adorned with grey bed linen, a pillow propped up against the wall where he had been reading, the book on the floor.

"The games brought much wealth to Sanguel. Parents…, their families gained great lavish rewards. What more could they have asked for? I created the games to provide them with all that they desired, all that they have now!"

"It wasn't for them. It was all for you and your greedy, despicable means," Ben said, his tone steady and firm.

Evelyn whipped his head in Rafe's direction like a snake ready to attack, pausing, he sat comfortably on the bed with crossed legs, and calmly asked, "What do you say Rafe?"

Rafe sighed. "There really isn't much to say."

Evelyn laughed a derisive laugh, "A man of little words."

"He doesn't want to waste them on you!" Sam snapped.

"Thank you, Senior Defender Samuel Stoic." Evelyn turned his attention back to Ben. "Where is that meddling sister of yours?"

Rafe didn't like the way he said it and really didn't want Ben to respond. However, Ben replied, "You haven't seen her?"

"So, she's in Sanguel." Evelyn nodded thoughtfully. "And that must mean Tia is here too."

"Leave Tia out of this!"

"Always to her rescue." Evelyn gave a satisfactory grin. "What do you want from Sanguel? Again?"

Neither of them responded.

Evelyn laughed to himself and responded as though he really didn't want them to hear his comment. "Your kingdom must be boring." He used his fingers like a comb to run through his hair.

"It's fine actually." Ben raised his voice. "Better than you think."

"Yet you found your way here again, even though it was made more difficult."

"What do you mean, more difficult?" Rafe asked. "And what's that got to do with you?'

One of the guards called Sam away. Evelyn ignored Sam's departure.

"The library still stands?" He shook his hair as though a cool breeze was blowing through the cell.

"Of course. It's being renovated," Ben replied.

"Don't say anymore Ben. I think it's time for us to go," Rafe said.

"I'm sure it won't be standing for too long." Evelyn's stare went from Rafe to Ben.

Ben was annoyed with Evelyn's smug persona. "The library will be as good as new. In fact, it'll be better. All sorts will be in it. Schools will benefit and..."

"Come on. Let's go," Rafe said

"Before you depart. What school do you attend?"

"Don't tell him," Rafe said, and turned to walk away.

Evelyn glanced at Rafe, connected again with Ben.

Ben got up but didn't make a move towards the exit. "What harm can you do?" Ben sneered, "Hillfield Academy, Year 8!"

"He's far too big to be in year 8," Evelyn said.

"Rafe's not in Year 8 he's older, year -"

"It's none of his business," Rafe shot back.

"Sounds idyllic. But you can't be learning much." Evelyn stood up and stretched his limbs as though he didn't care.

Rafe stood at the gate and beckoned to Ben to leave.

"It's perfect 'cos you're not there. Now, keep out of trouble!" Ben taunted and wagged his finger at Evelyn like a teacher admonishing a pupil. Evelyn slowly sat on his bed, then in one swoop he laid back, his hands clasped behind his head. "That I'll try." He grinned. "Best conversation I've had in days."

As they left Rafe said, "There is something about him that doesn't feel right. It's as if he's up to something."

"What can he do? He can't go anywhere. He's just full of the smelly, brown stuff." Ben chortled.

They met Sam on the way out. "Arabella will see you now. She's quite excited to know that you're here."

*

Arabella was waiting in a room set off the main hall in Hill House. It was a cosy room with comfortable chairs and a small table engraved with a woodland scene. A large window flooded the small room with afternoon light.

"Rafe, Ben, welcome to my private quarters." Arabella opened her arms and embraced them as they entered. Her flowing purple gown made her look far more regal than they had remembered, but her dishevelled hair soon reminded them of her inconsistencies.

"Duty calls." Sam left the room.

Arabella said, "How was your meeting with Evelyn?"

"Uneventful," Rafe shrugged.

"He's where he's supposed to be. Good riddance." Ben looked around, and his eyes lit up as he saw the side table festooned with food and drink. "Is this your reboot space?"

Arabella looked baffled.

"A place to relax," Rafe said.

Arabella smiled, "Come, sit, have what you like."

Ben wasted no time in lifting the silver platters one after another to reveal the heated, delicious food, the aroma filling the room. Ben helped himself heartily. Arabella handed Rafe a plain cloth package held together by a brown cord tied into bow which he placed directly in his rucksack. Rafe hadn't seen where this package had come from, but he recognised

Arabella's urgency when handing it over, asking questions would not be permitted, she winked at Rafe and said, "Please, help yourself."
Rafe got up as Ben settled on a chair opposite Arabella to start devouring the food.

"I see you still have a healthy appetite." Arabella smiled generously.

Ben nodded his mouth was too full for him to answer.

Rafe sat next to Ben. Before he started to eat, he said, "I'm sorry to get straight to it, but have you seen Tia or Lisa?"

Arabella sipped a glass of red juice, "I believed them to be at the stables with Mr Peri."

This news relaxed Rafe. He enjoyed the meal as they listened to Arabella's views on the way forward for Sanguel since she had taken her rightful place as ruler. Especially that they wanted to broker better working relationships with the other kingdoms, particularly the kingdoms of Clover and Pershee.

"What is Pershee like?" Ben asked.

Arabella paused for a moment, then she said, "I'll try to help it make sense to you… All the kingdoms are like Sanguel, people of different hues and backgrounds getting on with their lives. However, as you discovered in Sanguel there is always someone seeking to disrupt the status quo for their own ends. Pershee is no different. However, their royalty deems it their duty to work well with other kingdoms." She hesitated. "I know that Tia is concerned about Meela," Arabella said.

"How -"

"Before you continue Rafe, I am always aware, but, as you know, I can't always tell you everything."

Ben nodded again, knowing all too well that he didn't want to say anything that would irritate Arabella.

"It's for your own good. When you speak with Lisa and Tia, let them know they must tread carefully. The Lanquis of the Kingdom of Pershee is -"

"Lanquis?" Rafe asked. He had finished his meal and wondered how Arabella's meals always tasted so satisfying.

"It's the King of Pershee. The Queen is the Languin, the Prince the Lanquint and the Princess Languinette, which Meela will eventually become."

"So, she's really marrying a prince," Ben eventually said, as he wiped what tasted like raspberry juice from his chin.

"It's difficult becoming a Languinette, Meela has to prove herself first. After all, Mr Peri organised this marriage as part of the kingdoms coming together, in the time when Evelyn was ruler. Meela will be the true judge of whether she wants to go through with it. My concern is that the Lanquis, Levi, Languin and Lanquint are all on a peace keeping mission to Kingdoms across the seas. And there has been some talk of an unsettling change in Pershee. I'm not too sure of all the details. However, the Languin's mother is in command. Elleba is her name, and she shares the same title as her daughter. So, please warn Tia and Lisa to be careful, I know her to be a very prickly character." Arabella's concern was evident on her face.

"We will," Ben said, eagerly, wanting to impress on Arabella that he had become responsible.

"I have something for you." Arabella became more upbeat, went over to the large window, and tapped the wall beneath the window, the wall slipped down to reveal a secret nook. Rafe and Ben craned their necks to get a better view, but Arabella made sure to keep the section she was dealing with out of their view. She tapped the wall again and the entrance sealed up. She turned to face them, holding four curved metal strips, 10 centimetres in length.

"These are for you," with a generous smile she said, "Place them on the bottom end of your tubers."

"What does it do?" Rafe asked.

Arabella chuckled. "They will take you far above what you can imagine."

"That's it?" Ben said, not wanting to sound rude or get into any trouble, as he tended to do with Arabella.

"Remember to place it at the bottom section of the tuber," She instructed firmly. Rafe had already started to connect the metal strip to his tuber after placing Tia's carefully in his rucksack. Ben received his and Lisa's gratefully. "I'll show the girls how to connect them when I do mine."

Sam entered the room with a swift knock. He carried two tunics, one ruby with small white squares around the neckline and another, green with blue squares around the neckline. The side seams concealed the opening to access any weaponry. "You'll need these to help you blend in when you get to Pershee. I have Lisa's and Tia's here too."

Rafe and Ben took off their jackets and placed them in their rucksacks and put on the loose-fitting tunics.

"That's better. They liven up your garments. You almost look like Pershee nobles." Sam laughed.

"I like the sound of that," Ben said.

"I have another meeting and I can't be late. My life is now filled with so many meetings. I hope to take a long holiday soon. All the best. And I have all my faith in you to make sure Meela is okay," Arabella said, as she left the room.

Ben looked outside to make sure she had gone then said to Rafe, “I thought she would have explained things a bit better, but in her true style she left us with a riddle.”

“Well, I think that’s really her style. We’ll work it out. But in the meantime, let’s find out what Lisa and Tia have been up to. I can’t imagine Lisa having a great time with Mr Peri.”

“Neither can I,” Ben laughed.

Chapter 7

Malfunction

"It feels as though we've been travelling for hours," Tia said.

"Those biscuits were tasty."

"It's a good thing they were filling, you'd be quite hungry now," Tia teased, "and there are still a few left."

Lisa gave Tia a friendly shove. The contraption lurched forwards and flung the two surprised girls to the ground as it came to a halt.

"What just happened?" Lisa struggled to her feet as the contraption lurched forward again and came to a sudden stop. Tia stayed on the floor of the contraption. "I'm not getting up until this thing makes up its mind what it's doing."

"Giddy up, giddy up," Lisa yelled.

Tia laughed, "I don't think that's going to help."

"I hope it moves more smoothly now, otherwise my brain may drop out of my ear." They both started to giggle, then they heard a slow whining sound emanating from the front of the contraption. It started as a soft whine and became louder with each passing minute. They covered their ears and waited for the racket to subside. The end of the whine was accompanied by a strong smell of hot metal and burning oil. They got back onto their seat and looked out of the windows. From what they could see the contraption had stopped in a clearing.

"I can't see much," Tia said.

"Neither can I," Lisa was trying to see through the front gap, "Their heads are in the way."

"No hills. No red." Tia stepped out of the carriage, holding onto the door. "There's woodland up ahead and a post, I can't see what it says."

"Well one of us could take a look, and the other one could keep the door open to grab the other one in, just in case," Lisa said.

"Ok. I'll go."

Lisa said, "No, I'll go."

"You hate running."

"I don't hate it. I just don't like it."

"Same thing. Just yell if you feel any movements." Tia sprinted to the post.

Lisa held the door open willing Tia on.

The post was further away than Tia had anticipated. She inhaled deeply to catch her breath. The wooden post had three direction arrows: Sanguel behind them 20 miles, Clover 15 miles to the right and Pershee 17 miles ahead.

Under the directional arrows was a gold plaque which stated:

BEWARE

Travel by daylight.

Tia thought it strange, but not scary even though dusk was upon them. She believed they could be in Pershee in no time.

"Tia, Tia, Quick!"

Tia turned to see the contraption rocking on the spot. She started running, even though she wanted a few more minutes to catch her breath. As she neared the carriage, it shot forwards, then slowed. Lisa stretched her arm out as far as she could while holding onto the frame of the door. Tia ran after the carriage only a few strides behind as it slowly moved along.

"Tia!" Lisa yelled.

The contraption shot forward, throwing Lisa backward into the cabin, the door slammed shut.

Chapter 8

Stables

"You mean they are back, or they should have been back!" Rafe shouted. He was stood by Mr Peri's work bench.

"Like I said, I said, I've said it!" Mr Peri was frustrated with Rafe's stern attitude and moved away from the work bench to the set of tools hanging along the brick wall.

"You haven't really confirmed anything." Ben sauntered over to the contraption's now vacant area.

Mr Peri mopped his gleaming head with an already damp cloth. Rafe's grilling was getting to him.

"They should have returned by now. I'm really sorry, so sorry. My galloping horses is out there too. I can't imagine what's happened to it."

Rafe was the same height as Mr Peri, and he wasn't giving in. He shook his head in dismay. "You seem more concerned about that thing than Tia and Lisa."

"I'm concerned about all of them. All of them." Mr Peri went to fetch a broom.

"By the way, it's called silent horses," Ben said. Mr Peri turned away and busied himself with clearing up for the night, making more of a mess than clearing up.

Rafe was not impressed. “Mate, you’re like Marmite.”

“What? What?’

Rafe refused to explain. “Awful taste.”

“Loved... or hated... or loved.” Ben sighed in an attempt to defuse the situation.

“I was waiting for Alamo and Evan to go see what’s happened.”

“Why didn’t you go?” Rafe asked.

Mr Peri was indignant. “I have to keep this place running.”

“And?”

“It’s getting dark….”

“You thought about yourself.” Rafe’s voice was low and unaccommodating.

“No, I know they’re safe.”

“How would you know that?”

“I just do…”

“Have you got a crystal ball? Can you mind read?”

“No.” Mr Peri hung his head in shame.

“Well, you don’t know. They could be in danger!” Rafe threw his hands in the air.

Sam’s excitement, as he entered then room, lowered the anxiety in the stables, “Evan and Alamo are on their way.”

Mr Peri shouted, “Hurrah!” he dropped the brush he was making a mess with, “I’ll get you some food.” He bolted for the door, knocking Sam sideways, leaving the door wide open.

Chapter 9

What a Quandary

Tia had run as fast and as far as she could, the contraption now out of sight, the last trail of brown dust gone. She had followed the contraption's tracks for what seemed to be an hour, now surrounded by woodlands, she focused on the track ahead, and used the birdsong to move her along, which gradually faded as the night drew in. Stars brightened the inky blue sky that rolled over head. Tia was wary in these surroundings but not scared. A tremor along the ground made her aware that something was coming. Tia saw the familiar signs of a dust cloud building up ahead. She moved to the side of the track. The contraption hurtled past her, she had no time to call out to Lisa or try to get inside. As fast as it had come it flashed past her going backwards. She threw her arms up in despair she wasn't sure if Lisa was still in the contraption heading back to Sanguel. Should she go on or head back to Sanguel? Tia looked up at the darkening canopy of greenery. Fading light crept through the cracks. She wished she had taken her rucksack when she had gone to view the signpost.

Tia held her tuber in case she came upon any monsters or predators. She decided to settle in a tree whose flowers looked so familiar to her, its branches sprayed outwards leaving a flattened area to sit in. Most of all, Tia was drawn to its purple-blue flowers reminiscent of her mother's favourite Jamaican flower. Tia inhaled deeply; its aroma reminded her of gardening with her parents and grandparents. She made good her footing as she climbed up the short distance to her lookout platform. She settled down, enough to avoid any predators and see the track below. She wondered what had happened to Lisa and hoped that she had got to Pershee safely, or if not, she was back in Sanguel. Tia looked around, heard the lazy creak of tree limbs. The frenzied flight of blue birds from the surrounding bushes made her jump.

"Whatever you are, you'll see the rough side of my tuber," She whispered. She held her tuber poised for anything and hoped her pendant would work, being invisible would be great about now she thought. Then she heard words that made her feel a surge of relief.

"Tia, Tia?"

"Up here."

Lisa scrambled up the tree, grateful it wasn't too far to get to Tia, with one rucksack on her back the other in her hand, along with the food sack.

"I'm so glad to see you!" Tia said.

"Me too!"

Lisa was out of breath; she spoke between gulps of air. "The stupid thing - kept stopping - starting." She flopped beside Tia. Tia took the sack hoping Lisa hadn't finished all the goodies inside.

"Then it went backwards. Stopped. When it started rocking, I got out. I'm so sorry I couldn't pull you in."

"Doesn't matter, we're still heading in the right direction."

"I don't fancy walking around in the dark." Lisa shuddered. "And for the first time I think I'm glad to be in a tree."

"Most of it's mushy."

"Sorry. It wasn't me; the contraption threw it around. I didn't eat anything more, just drank from my water bottle, not the one Mr Peri provided, not sure where that ended up."

"Oh well, better than nothing." Tia managed to fish out fragments of biscuits into her hands and enjoyed each morsel.

"I'll have the cake slices." Lisa said, eagerly.

"You'll be lucky if you find slices." Tia handed Lisa the sack.

Lisa wiped her hands on her jeans and had no problems in grabbing a handful of cakes pieces and ate hungrily.

"We can stay here till morning then make our way to Pershee. It can't be too far away, cos you've got red dust all over your trainers," Tia said.

Lisa looked at her trainers and wobbled her feet and watched as some of the dust fell away. "The red hills must be close by - I'm still a little scared."

Tia put her arm around Lisa's shoulders. "We'll be fine. We've done this before, remember?"

"I know. But Rafe was with us."

"Come on. Ray may not be here, but we have all we need. Our tubers for protection, our pendants..."

Lisa fidgeted with her pendant. "Do you think they're still unreliable?"

"Who knows? We got through last time. We'll get through this time," Tia said.

"I'd love one of Arabella's food bars about now. They were so delicious," Lisa said.

Tia cracked a smile. "You'd better finish the mushy cake slices then."

Chapter 10

Boundaries

It was getting dark by the time Alamo and Evan arrived at the stables. Excitement exploded in the previously quiet, hostile stand-off. Their greetings reflected the strong bond they had developed from their time together in Sanguel. Only Mr Peri remained on the far side of the stables, unnecessarily reorganising ceramic pots and boxes filled with all sorts of repair items, he barely acknowledged his sons' presence.

Alamo and Evan were dressed in the all-in-one dark defenders' uniform, trousers tucked into their dark boots.

"It's best if you go with Sam and Alamo. Sam will know what to do if the silent horses have gone wrong. I must go to the Kingdom of Clover early in the morning. I'll meet you later in Pershee, it will be good to see Meela," Evan said.

"Sounds like a plan." Rafe was relieved that they were going to do something about the precarious situation. His evening brightened even more when Izzy happily entered the stables with two bags of goodies, also dressed in her defenders' uniform.

"I'll go too." She smiled. "Arabella told me."

Rafe held back a smile and said, "The more the merrier."

Evan called his father. Mr Peri was hasty in his response and proud to say, "I'll prepare the cart and horses son, you carry on with what you need to do."

"I'll go home and get some refreshments for our night travel," Alamo said.

Izzy held her bags aloft. "No need, I have everything here."

"Arabella knows everything," Ben, happy with this revelation took the bags and had a quick nosy inside, he gave Mr Peri a side glance as he had returned to the stables without the food he had promised earlier.

*

The horse and cart moved quickly through the woods, the track was clear, and the moon was rising slowly in the bright night sky. Sam, Alamo, and Ben sat on the front seat. Rafe and Izzy sat in the back, cushioned on blankets, with the provisions and tools to repair the contraption about them. When they got to the outskirts of the woods Sam slowed the horses.

Sam said, "Silent horses up ahead."

Rafe and Izzy turned to see the shadowy shape of the contraption in the moonlight, a few metres of open ground and woodland up ahead.

"I wonder if the girls are waiting inside," Ben said.

Rafe wasn't so optimistic. "Tia was so resolute to get to Pershee I doubt if she would stay. They've probably made their way to the palace, sleeping soundly in a comfortable bed while we're out here."

Sam stopped the cart off the track. They all wandered over to the contraption, Ben calling out their names, hoping Lisa and Tia might be fast asleep.

"They're not here," Sam said, as he looked inside the contraption, then held up a container.

"That's my dad's," Alamo said.

"That man's got rocks for brains," Rafe whispered to Ben.

"At least he left them with something to drink."

"No use being here," Rafe shot back. Ben shrugged. Alamo took the drinks container and Sam went around to the front of the contraption and noticed that the breast plate was ajar. "This isn't supposed to be open. It's exposing the circuit to the elements. I'd best get to work." Sam went back to the cart to get his tools and a lantern.

Alamo said, "I think it's best for us to camp here until morning. It's not wise to go into those woods now."

“Why?” Ben asked.

“Well, some of the other kingdoms used Evelyn’s technology – his spies and lethal mechagribeas, to protect their territory,” Alamo warned.

Sam shouted over to them, “Wheelots too.”

“I don’t think I want to hear this,” Rafe said.

“Sorry Rafe.” Alamo put a reassuring hand on Rafe’s shoulder. “The wheelots are easily managed but I’ve heard there are creatures called kumelenjahs - a combination of human and something else - messy and aggressive!”

Rafe was quick with his reply. “That’s why we must find the girls.”

Izzy looked at Rafe and calmly said, “Unfortunately, we’re not allowed to intrude on another kingdom at night without permission. Evelyn’s imprisonment has left some kingdoms unhappy and new rules have been put in place. We must comply to keep the peace.”

“How I wish I had talked Tia out of this.” Rafe sighed.

“Like you said, they may be sleeping at the palace now, all snuggled up in a comfy bed.” Ben hoped.

Chapter 11

T-sodon

Tia and Lisa were now sat against the base of the tree wrapped in their sleeping bags on a bed of purple-blue flowers. Heat emanated from the gathered rocks they had rubbed with their tuber to provide much needed heat; the orange glow was enchanting. Tia had made some of the flowers into chains by twisting their soft short stems together around her elastic bracelet; she wondered whether her father would recognise the flowers.

"These sleeping bags are the best," Lisa said, "Arabella certainly knew what she was doing when she gave them to us."

"They are cosy. I hope we get to see her before we head home," Tia said.

"One more game then let's go back into the tree."

"Okay," Tia giggled. "Did you see what I did there? Ha! Ha! Ha!"

Lisa couldn't help but laugh too. "I get it. Kay. How about Patella?"

Tia thought for a brief moment. "Ella, Ella like umbrella."

Lisa joined in, "Umbrella Ella, Ella,"

"Your turn," Tia said.

Lisa looked towards the sky. "Ultraviolet."

"Easy, Violet," Tia said, "Liken."

"Likin?" Lisa thought for a while. "That's hard."

Tia laughed, "Ken silly."

"It's how you said it. Not Liken. You said it like, Likin!"

Tia giggled. "You need to 'lissan' carefully."

"Lisa, I caught that one." Lisa chuckled, then took a more serious tone, "You said you'd tell me why you like those flowers so much."

"It's my mom's favourite. When we visited my Granddad and Nana in Jamaica, she showed me this tree with hundreds of these flowers. Hibiscus…I think that's what my Nana called them. My mom had always loved them and made something like this for me." Tia gently touched the flowers around her bracelet. "Reminds me of her… I think it's supposed to be the national flower for Jamaica too. I think."

"Aw. I'd love one of those chains."

"Let's go up. I'm feeling tired," Tia said.

But Lisa could see Tia looked sad and wished Rafe was there to say something helpful.

They heard a muffled cooing sound as though a bird was calling out to another. They looked at each other wondering if it was real or not. The cooing sound came again, this time with a little chuckle at the end. They slowly stepped out of their sleeping bags, backs against the tree for a shield, their hands disconnecting the tubers from their belts.

A harsh voice said, “Are you friend or foe?”

Tia and Lisa peered in the direction of the hedgerow, which was earlier festooned with red flowers, they were now closed and looked like vicious red spikes.

“Are YOU friend or foe?” Tia replied with firmness.

The voice gave a deep chuckle.

“You’re pretending to be older,” Tia said.

“Bet you’re a kid?” Lisa feigned a laugh.

“Lousy kid.” Tia held her tuber to her side, ready to strike.

“I’m not a kid...” A boy around twelve years old dragged himself from under the bush. He stood up but didn’t dust himself off. Dressed in ruby coloured tunic and trousers, the trousers bound at the ankles by a coarse yarn attached to his flat boot-like footwear. A length of crumpled black fabric hung over one shoulder and across his body. He pulled the green face fabric which covered his nose and mouth below his chin. His cinnamon skin and dark eyes gleamed in the moonlight. His face was stern, “What are you doing out here, at this time?” His tone was like a teacher disciplining errant children.

Tia wasn't interested in answering his questions. "Who are you?" She hid her tuber behind her.

His response was sharp. "Who are you?"

Tia raised her voice. "Stop repeating and answer the question."

"Shush, no need to draw unnecessary attention," he said.

"That's your fault," Lisa said and tucked away her tuber.

On seeing Lisa's actions, he enquired "What's that?"

"Nun-a-ya," Tia said.

"Nose out!" Lisa said.

"Why so serious? I'm T-sodon, call me T-so." He extended his frame with a puffed-out chest, and clenched fists on his hips as though he were regal.

Tia wasn't impressed. "Ok, T-so. Relax."

"I'm Lisa. How old are you?" Lisa stepped forward and extended her hand. He looked towards her hand and said, "What's that thing?"

Lisa, somewhat stumped, looked back to Tia.

"Do you know how to be polite or are you simply rude?" Tia said, eyeing him cautiously.

"You don't look old enough to be out here at this time," Lisa fired, still wanting an answer to her previous question.

"You don't either." He finally cracked a half smile, relaxed, checked the silver rope wrapped in a loose loop hanging from his waist, folded his arms across his chest and looked up, his eyes followed the path of the dark clouds framing the moon. Finally, he said, "You shouldn't be out here so late. It's too dangerous. Is that friendly enough?"

They exchanged amused glances and shrugged.

"You're being watched." He gave a smug nod in the direction of the tree roots beside them.

They looked about them but couldn't see anything unusual.

"It can't see me, but it can see you." T-so slowly released the silver rope from his waist. With a flick of his wrist, the rope flashed out like an elastic band towards a rock at the base of the tree where Tia and Lisa were standing. The rock shattered and debris sprayed the ground, some hitting Tia's ankle. "Watch out!" She yelled and jumped out of the way of the second rope lash. They heard a high pitch whirling sound, and a dark green box twenty centimetres by twenty centimetres whizzed past their feet.

"Missed it," T-so said, calmly and expertly twisting the rope into its small loop and attaching it to his waist.

"What was that?" Lisa asked.

"An ossula." He patted the rope.

"Looks like a lasso," Tia whispered to Lisa.

“That thing was a spy, which means we’ll have a couple of visitors soon.” T-so responded with great urgency. “We need to leave.”

“What type of visitors do you think he means?” Lisa whispered to Tia.

“I’m not sure, but I think we’d better pack up and move on.” Tia slipped her tuber on her belt, and quickly wrapped up her sleeping bag.

Lisa stuffed her sleeping bag into her rucksack, “Ok, we’re doing this on that good-looking, yet strange guy’s say so?”

“No. We’re doing it, ‘cos the sign at the edge of the woods had a warning about night-time.” Tia slipped her sleeping bag into her rucksack and onto her back. “I forgot to tell you, with all the shenanigans of the contraption.”

Lisa didn’t want to hear any more. She put on her rucksack, tucked the food sack opening edge under her belt. Tia and Lisa quickly kicked the loose soil over the fire rocks. A succession of deep grunts, rumblings and snapping branches forced its way through the area.

“Mechagribea!” They both grimaced.

“Follow me,” T-so said, and disappeared under the bush.

Tia and Lisa moved swiftly as they caught sight of the mechagribea rearing onto its thick hind legs. Unlike the mechagribeas they had encountered before, this one had glowing blue metal gears and pulsating grey wiring hideously visible in its jaw and neck where the usual orange fur was missing. This caught the girls off guard, and they struggled under the bush where T-so had escaped. Their rucksacks caught the thicket of the bush. Tia managed to grapple through. Lisa wrestled with the food sack, which, although empty, had snagged against the thicket along with her rucksack. She twisted onto her side, freed the food sack. The pulsating lights were getting closer. She froze, the white snout low to the ground heading towards her. Tia pulled at Lisa's shoulders. Lisa pushed her pendant and disappeared. Now that she was no longer visible, her scent also vanished. The beast didn't give up. It dug wildly at the soil and bush, ripping them apart.

Chapter 12

Fixers

The small group settled around the sleepy crackling fire, having optimistic discussions about Sanguel's future. A warm yellow glow from a lantern aided Sam as he repaired the contraption. The lantern was hung from the neck of one of the metal horses. Ben assisted by using his torch to get to the hard-to-reach areas. He was so intrigued to find out more about the inner workings of the contraption.

"What happened to his owl?" Rafe asked.

"No one knows. It disappeared when Evelyn was captured. We haven't seen it since," Alamo said, as he handed out small, wooden bowls of vegetables and sauce to the group, while Izzy supplied them with warmed flat breads.

"Well, I hope that's the last we hear of it," Ben said, looking over at the fire huggers. "Lisa would hate to know Tulisa got away. She always hated knowing it had part of her name… Don't forget us. My stomach's rumbling."

They all chuckled.

Izzy said, "Arabella's determination and strategy has made Sanguel stronger. She put a new council in place, much to Evelyn's disappointment… I still don't trust him. But

I'm glad Arabella stuck to her plan because she managed to weed out the idiots." Izzy looked embarrassingly over at Alamo.

"It's ok," he said, nonchalantly, placing Ben's and Sam's bowls on a flat stone close to the fire. "My father needed a break from those duties. He still can't believe Evelyn was in the wrong. We later found out that it was he who had agreed with Evelyn that Meela be married to the Lanquint of Pershee. However, we have good word that she is safe and happy there. We've been so busy preventing any retaliation from local villages and kingdoms that we haven't managed to visit her."

Rafe said, "It looks like Tia's visit may not have been necessary but welcomed." He smiled at Izzy and dipped his bread into the bowl. "You've all kept the Defenders' uniforms."

"Yes, we wear them with pride. Even the fledgling Defenders still wear the all-black uniform," Alamo said, folding his arms with pride to show off the gold trim around his hood and cuffs.

"So, I take it that you guys have been promoted -" Rafe started, Izzy happily interrupted him.

"But of course, with all our hard work, this uniform," She kissed the gold trims on her wrist, "is now connected with peace whenever it's seen," Izzy said, "We give this more meaning than the idiots that wore it before."

"Sam and Evan have blue stripes; last I remember, those stripes were for the select few of Evelyn's robotic troop," Ben said.

Alamo was quick to defend their position, "Arabella changed it around, elevating it to those who are on the council and to a select group of wise individuals placed in special positions to keep the peace across our borders."

Ben came over to the fireside, warmed his hands, and then gratefully tucked into his meal, as Sam finished up. "Well Rafe, you seem to be enjoying your time so I don't see why we should be in a hurry to return, perhaps I could don a stripe or two," Ben grinned.

Sam stood beside Ben and threw a small cloth he'd cleaned his hands with on the fire, the fire hissed, rose, and glowed green, before returning to its humble hues.

"Is there any berry tea left?" Sam asked.

Alamo drained the last bit of tea from the pot being kept warm beside the fire, handed the cup to Sam. Sam sat on a nearby tree stump.

"Can it return to the stables?" Alamo asked.

Sam sipped at his tea, "I hope so."

“If you’re not up for eating, I’ll have your bread, if no one else wants….” Ben began.

“Not so quick, Ben,” Sam set down his cup and gathered his meal, “I’ll have mine in a bit,” he chuckled.

Ben looked dismayed.

Izzy offered him the last flatbread.

“What went wrong with the contraption?” Rafe asked, wanting to get back on topic.

“Strangely, one of the rotation pistons kept getting stuck and throws the system into a backward or rocking motion. I had to clean out the debris. I suppose that’s what happened when the breast plate opened. But I still can’t work out why some of the wires were twisted… connected to the wrong channels. It wouldn’t have got to Pershee.”

Rafe felt that somehow Mr Peri had a hand in the contraption’s malfunction.

Chapter 13

Left Behind

Lisa slowed her breath, twisted onto her front, and kept perfectly still. She knew she was invisible by the initial tingle throughout her body. Fragments from the mechagribea's dig lay around her. The bush was now straggly and thin.

Lisa could feel stabbing pains at the back of her leg where the beast had caught her. She was thankful that Tia had used her tuber at the right time and struck the protruding snout with as much force as possible. Its huge body slumped in surrender to the electrical wave that numbed its frame. Its mechanism now whirled with a slow whine; it was temporarily out of action.

"Can you move now?" Tia asked after she zapped the thicket that had caught Lisa's rucksack.

"I'm trying, but it's leaning against my leg."

Tia knelt in front of Lisa, "I'll pull. Try and push."

Lisa screamed out, "No, no, my leg."

"We've got to hurry. I don't know how long that thing is going to stay put."

"I can't move," Lisa whimpered.

"Close your eyes. I'll cut away remaining shrubs. Thankfully, the beast did a good job at removing so much of it." Tia hacked away at the bush with her tuber, it crumbled away like dust. Lisa covered her face to avoid breathing in the debris. She slowly pulled away from the large pulsating paw that held her down; grateful her leg wasn't broken. The mechagribea let out a deep groan.

Lisa froze.

Tia jumped back. "Stinks! Poohdonga!"

Claws began to twitch. Another groan - this sounded like a growl to the girls.

Lisa's eyes widened. "It's waking up!" She managed to scramble up, abandoning the food sack on the ground, her rucksack firmly on her back.

Tia grabbed Lisa. "Hold on to me."

Lisa used Tia to aid her movements and limped away.

"Where is that T-so?" Lisa asked, gritting her teeth at the pain rising in her calf.

"Forget him let's concentrate on getting as far away from that beast before our invisibility wears off."

They moved as quickly as they could.

Chapter 14

Mistrust

As the others slept, Rafe whispered to Ben, "Do you think Mr Peri had something to do with the contraption's failure?"

"Who knows… when I was trapped in it, there were no problems, it carried me to Sanguel. It didn't stop. It didn't pass go. It just went straight to the stables, and it wasn't as comfortable; lumps of straw and darkness, I was thrown around in it." Ben grimaced at the thought of it.

"When Sam mentioned the malfunction, it reminded me of how shifty Mr Peri was behaving."

"To be honest I'm so tired I can't think…. I remember how happy I was when the Peri's found me," Ben yawned. "He may have been embarrassed that it had a problem and didn't want to say."

"Best get some sleep," Rafe said, but he still mulled over Mr Peri's reactions. He heard echoing grunting calls of mechagribeas stalking the woodlands. He hoped the girls were alright.

Chapter 15

Wounded

Lisa hobbled next to Tia, who tried her best to keep Lisa upright.

"Over here."

They were shocked to see T-so waving to them to follow him. They trailed as T-so kept a good distance ahead of them, pointing them to the direction which he was going to take. They eventually arrived in an open area, populated with lofty trees their trunks at least three metres wide. T-so was waiting impatiently at the base of one of the slightly smaller trunks. He pulled at a lever on the ground, low auburn light revealed an opening.

"Quick, Quick." He swung his right hand like a propeller to hasten them into a secret hiding place underground. As they approached the entrance, warm air and a strange smell of clay greeted them. Tia looked over her shoulder and saw a dull blue light and bulky mass charging their way. She was relieved when T-so bolted the door in three places. They descended a slope into a dimly lit passageway. Smooth red soil surrounded them; light dripped down the corridor.

"I thought you were over with," T-so gasped.

"Thanks a lot for waiting for us," Lisa snapped.

T-so ignored her sharp tone, "I just saved your life." He turned to Tia. "Along here." He headed towards the dull light.

Lisa tried her best to stay off her right ankle, every time she placed her foot against the ground a shooting pain ran up her leg. Tia tried her best to help, as she felt Lisa flinch when her heel accidentally hit a lumpy part of the ground.

"That was close," T-so said.

"Close? Look at my leg!"

"Keep your voice down. Everyone's sleeping." He stared at them, his eyes bulging with disdain, "I rescued you." He pointed with his thumb stabbing repeatedly at his chest. He turned to the shelf beside him that was formed from an inset in the wall, opened the shutter, and picked up a small glass box by its ceramic hook, although it was small enough to be carried in the palm of his hand; inside, a clear spore provided extra light. With a hard whisper T-so said, "I rescued you!"

"No, you didn't! Tia did!"

"I didn't see where you went - vanished. When I doubled round, I saw the gribea trapped and you were heading into the woods, the wrong way, may I add, right into the path of another gribea!"

"Thank you," Tia said, not wanting to reveal the source of their invisibility.

"My leg's hurting!" Lisa cried.

T-so seemed indifferent. "Come this way." He led them down a quiet narrow corridor, their feet shuffling along the clay soil. At the end of the short passage was a circular space, with large green cushions scattered around tree roots embedded in the red soil walls and flooring.

"Stay here," he muttered, placed the glass light at the entrance and left them.

Lisa rolled her eyes.

Tia helped Lisa to sit on one of the cushions, away from the opening. She was amazed to find the ground and the cushions were pleasantly warm although mildly lumpy.

"Try not to argue with him, there was another mechagribea on our trail. I saw it as we entered."

Lisa nodded, rubbing her leg.

"I've lost my bearings, he'll have to show us the way to Pershee, or he may even know Meela," Tia thought out aloud.

"I doubt if he knows her," Lisa said, as she winced from the pain.

"But he may know where the palace is. We need to find out what he meant when he said we were being watched, and what that thing was that he smashed to bits," Tia yawned.

T-so came back with blankets, linen cloth, a small metal bucket and small wooden board. He handed the blankets to Tia. "Now, let me take a look at your leg."

Before Lisa could reject this offer, T-so was on his knees, carefully removing her footwear. Lisa grabbed her sock from him and stuffed it in her jeans pocket. T-so carefully looked at the injured area. Tia glanced over at Lisa as she organised their sleeping area where there were fewer roots, she secretly smiled as Lisa relaxed. The intense look she saw on T-so's face made her feel he knew what he was doing. T-so took a handful of dried leaves out of one of his many hidden pockets in his body sash. He crushed the leaves in one hand, sprinkled them in the bucket, swirled them around for a few minutes. Laying the cloth on the board beside him, he scooped the leaves into a pulp which he spread in a line across the cloth. He folded the cloth in half and wrapped it neatly, carefully around Lisa's ankle and calf. He made sure the pulp covered the wound.

"You'll sleep well," he finally smiled, as he helped her up and over to the sleep area which Tia had layered with cushions and blankets.

Chapter 16

New Day

"I'll have to travel back to Sanguel with the contraption," Sam said, after a breakfast of fruits from the nearby trees.

"Can we use it to go to Pershee? Mr Peri said it would get us there in no time at all." Rafe felt better after a good night's sleep.

"Well…." Sam looked at the contraption.

"It would help us out," Ben pleaded with his palms together as if in prayer.

"Alright," Sam said, "but I'm still not sure about its stability."

"I can follow with the horse and cart," Alamo said.

Rafe turned to Izzy. "It's probably best for you to go with Alamo."

Izzy was hesitant. "You sure?" Rafe took her by the hand and led her away from the group.

Ben sniggered, "I don't think Izzy liked that idea."

Alamo looked over at the heated discussion going on between Rafe and Izzy. "She really looks disappointed about having to travel with me."

"I don't think it's you," Ben said.

Sam grinned, “No Alamo, it’s the not being with Rafe.”

Alamo was oblivious. “What?”

Ben rolled around laughing. “You have so much to learn about women.”

*

The contraption sped off so swiftly, the boys were pinned against its seat with a force so hard they couldn’t move for a few minutes until it settled down.

“So,” Ben smiled at Rafe, “you let the love of your life go with Alamo.” He nudged Sam. Sam looked across at Rafe.

Rafe said nothing, staring out of the window.

“Come on Rafe, why?”

Rafe remained silent.

Sam grinned.

Ben pushed a little further with a whiny tone, “Rafe. Rafe… why?”

Rafe finally gave in. “Don’t say anything to Tia, or Lisa and least of all Izzy.” He stared at them for compliance.

Ben nodded enthusiastically.

Sam gave an open nod, “Go ahead. Spill.”

Rafe took a deep breath, “I’m going to give Tia the lecture of her life. And I don’t want Izzy to see me doing it.”

Ben tried his best not to laugh, but it was too strong an urge and it spluttered out in intermittent gushes. “You can’t be… cool all the time…. she has to see the real you sometime."

"I don't know her well enough yet. She may take it the wrong way."

"Izzy isn't stupid. She'd get it," Sam said, covering a smile.

Rafe started to say something in response, paused, looked at Ben and decided to reserve his opinion.

The contraption lurched and stopped, throwing them together on the limited floor space.

They tried to get up.

It whizzed ahead.

Stopped.

Rocked back and forth.

"Oh no," Sam groaned.

Chapter 17

Unreliable

The morning started very early for the girls. T-so woke them up with two cinnamon rolls and grape juice, he had also agreed to take them to the palace.

Lisa was feeling bright. Although her ankle was not swollen it still gave her some discomfort when she started walking.

"I thought you said the palace wasn't far from here," Lisa moaned.

They had travelled back into the woods, into open glades.

"It isn't. But I thought you would like to see something," T-so said.

Tia wasn't impressed either. "Whatever it is, it can wait until after the palace visit."

"This sight is magnificent. MAGNIFICENT. You wait and see."

Lisa wanted to wipe the smug smile from his face. T-so pointed with the fruit he was still eating. They turned past embankments of stones and shrubs onto an incline filled with copper-coloured trees. Their branches bent over, reaching for the ground.

"I can't do hills. My ankle feels like jelly."

“It’ll be fine,” T-so said. “When I take off the linen, it’ll be much better.”

“Promises, promises.” Lisa turned to Tia. “We should have gone back to the track, I’m sure we’d have made it to the palace grounds.”

“Grounds?” T-so furrowed his brow.

“The area around the palace,” Lisa’s tone was sarcastic, emphasising each word.

T-so looked at her with a bewildered gaze. “Now, we’ll go over this little slope.”

“It’s more like a hill,” Tia said, “and it looks quite steep.”

“You’ll see.” T-so trotted on ahead.

“I think he’s gone on because he doesn’t like what we’re saying.”’ Tia observed him throw the carcass of the fruit ahead of him, run up to it, pick it up and hurl it again. He continued this game until he stopped at a collection of rocks which made him look like a dwarf.

“My breakfast has evaporated - he’s cute.”

“Lisa? I got the impression you didn’t like him.”

“That was on meeting him. Seemed a bit too sure of himself, but my ankle is feeling a lot better. I’m not going to let him know that though,” She giggled. “He was very careful wrapping it and….”

"If you're going to get all mushy, I don't want to know. It's just like you, going all crazy over Adrian the one minute and then someone else the next day."

"Exaggeration!"

Tia laughed. "Let's stay focussed. We need to see Meela, make sure she's alright, then get back home before Ray or Ben finds out we've gone. I can explain it all to them afterwards. In the meantime, keep things sweet between you and T-so."

"I know." Lisa fell silent for a moment. "Why are you so worried about Meela?"

"Since we got back from Sanguel I kept feeling that she was missing from her family. Ray said I need to stop feeling concerned about everyone else and not myself. But I know he only said that because, well, I overheard him talking with my aunt and they think because my mom is no longer with us, I've been too concerned about other people."

Tentatively Lisa said, "And are you?"

Tia shrugged.

"I think that is one of your qualities and that's why I'm friends with you."

"Qualities?"

Lisa began to explain, "One of the good things about you."

"I know what qualities are, doofus." Tia gave her a playful nudge.

"Careful, I can easily topple."

"Sorry."

"I'm joking," Lisa laughed, "that's what I mean. Anyway, it's good that you care for others. I wished Ben cared about me. He's probably playing video games now, glad I'm not around."

"T-so's calling us. Let's get this over and done with. It had better be good." Tia helped Lisa hasten her steps.

By the time Tia and Lisa caught up with T-so he was clearly irritated by their tardiness.

"Come on or else we'll miss it." His tone though irritated, his eyes were glowing with excitement.

Lisa was going to fire back a quick disparaging remark but caught Tia's warning stare and refrained.

T-so lowered his voice. "Now when we enter THE area, be… quiet - listen." He gave the instruction like a parent who expected nothing but the best from their children.

The area had many pockets of dense shrubs, and meandering pathways of silver soil. Tall wiry trees stood in the middle of each shrub pocket like giraffes caring for their young. Giant leaves, like awnings sprayed from large yellow and pink flower heads, silvery weeds wrapped about them.

T-so crouched down beside one of the shrubs. He remained silent and closed his eyes. Tia and Lisa crouched down too, but looked at each other quizzically, wondering if T-so had fallen asleep. They listened but didn't close their eyes; a sweet fragrance of lavender and roses surrounded them, silvery leaves dangled above their heads.

Birds chirped away merrily, they heard other sounds that they weren't familiar with, but nothing they thought they should be fearful of. Lisa slumped to the ground, as her ankle started to become uncomfortable in the crouched position. T-so opened his eyes, glanced at her disapprovingly and closed his eyes again. Tia and Lisa couldn't help themselves and stifled giggles that soon became uncontrollable.

"It's no good if you do that!" T-so said and shuffled away from them, still in his crouched stance. Tia mouthed '*grumpy*', which set them off in another fit of giggles. This time T-so was furious.

With a hard whispered tone, he said, "You'll be sorry!"

Tia and Lisa tried their best to stop giggling and followed him. "Sorry," Lisa said raising her voice above his murmurs of disdain. He flapped his hand in the air as though he could stop her words from entering his space.

Lisa rolled her eyes, “Doomed if you do or don’t.” She sat down again, and gently massaged her ankle. Tia sidled up beside T-so who had now stopped and gazed at the scenery below.

“What are we…you, looking for?” Tia whispered.

T-so’s face lit up with excitement. “The Musca.”

“What?”

“The Musca, it’s a sacred creature that is rarely seen. We don’t want to scare it away. It’s amazing to see.”

“What does it look like?”

“You just have to see it,” he said, his focus on the way ahead.

Tia slipped back to Lisa, her foot catching something on the ground. She looked down and saw a golden strip jutting above the soil. She picked it up and was surprised to find it was a brooch. The clip was broken, but the purple-blue flower surrounded by golden vines was intact and looked luxurious, a small crest was embedded in the metal. It felt cool in her palm.

“Look.”

“Pretty,” Lisa said and took it from Tia. “What’s wrong with him?”

They spoke in lowered tones.

“He wanted to show us the Musca,” Tia said.

"What?"

Tia put the brooch in her rucksack, shrugged, "He couldn't explain it; said we needed to see it."

"Well, that's helpful." Lisa's sarcasm made Tia smile.

T-so returned, his face stern not willing to make eye contact with them.

"Can we go now?" Tia asked, in a demanding tone.

T-so knelt, gently took hold of Lisa's bandaged foot, removed her trainer, carefully removed the cloth; the crushed leaves had disappeared. Lisa wiggled her foot as T-so got up and folded the cloth, placed it into a pocket in his sash. Lisa pulled on her sock, surprised the pain had subsided.

"Follow me." He marched away totally uninterested in what they were doing.

"Well!" Lisa stretched and looked at Tia.

"Don't look at me. That's your lover boy."

"Don't call him that. I'm going off him already."

"He's too temperamental," Tia said.

"What does that mean?"

"Unpredictable."

"I think I liked it when you used to make up words, funny not hurtful."

“I wasn’t being hurtful.” Tia was apologetic. “Just saying…”

“I know… but he’s still cute.” Lisa was happy her leg was already feeling better, “we’d better catch up with him or he may take us back to goodness knows where.”

“He had better take us to where we want to go, or I won’t be so easy going,” Tia said.

Before Lisa could respond, a sudden burst of activity came out of the foliage; heavy, quickened footsteps surrounded them with a strange swirling coloured cloth. With no time to comprehend what was happening or identify the intruders, the strange cloth enveloped them. Sacks were dropped over their heads, yanked down to their knees. Before they knew it, they were being carried in complete darkness, struggling and screaming.

Chapter 18

Wheelot

The distant red hills remained in Rafe and Ben's view as they made their way on foot to the town of Pershee. They had left Sam to work out how to get the contraption back to Sanguel. They hoped Izzy and Alamo would catch up with them before they got to the palace.

"Isn't it funny that they say look for the red hills, yet Sam has just said it depends on which way you enter Pershee," Ben pondered.

"The other side of the red hills are pink cliffs, apparently," Rafe said.

"So why didn't he say it as plain as that?" Ben asked.

"He did. You were just looking for some type of riddle."

The view of the red hills was soon blocked by the woodland. Ben looked ahead wondering how long it would take to leave this part of the woods behind. Sam had instructed them to stay on the left dirt track lined with intermittent logs, as other meandering paths would lead them astray. Ben hoped they would come out the other side soon, as foliage narrowly missed his head.

Rafe lowered his voice, "Don't look back - have you noticed that something is following us? It's not far …behind… and, well... it looks like the -" Before Rafe could complete his sentence, Ben began to turn, "Don't look back!"

"Sorry. It's automatic."

"It's small. Close to the ground. I don't think it's an animal."

"Let's see what it is." Ben felt ready for a fight.

They slowly reached for their tubers, the subtle opening in their tunics made it easy to conceal and access the tubers.

Rafe glanced behind them, "It's four steps behind you. Looks like a green box."

"Box?"

Rafe nodded.

Rafe held his left hand across his chest, clenched in a fist so that Ben could see him count, releasing each finger - One. Two. THREE. They turned swiftly. The thing stopped, a moss-like blanket covered its rectangular body and hid its wheels. They crashed their tubers into the top of it. Small zipping sounds could be heard as it clunked to the ground. Visible green electric waves fizzed from its sides, four times and stopped. Rafe and Ben waited for a moment. They took a closer look at the peculiar object. Rafe used a twig to clear the moss, exposing a green object with curved edges, 40cm in length, 27cm wide and 40cm tall. Three silver stripes with tiny holes ran along the sides. Ben poked the object with his tuber. It fell on its side and exposed six small wheels embedded in its base and words partially covered with soil.

Ben picked it up once his tuber was secured back on his belt. He brushed the soil away, “wheelot 2244966 or the last numbers could be 88. It’s like one of those bot things you see on those gadget programs. I wonder what the stripes are for.”

“I’m wondering why you picked it up.”

“Investigation.” Ben turned it around viewing all the sides, “could be a serial number.”

Rafe surveyed the area.

“It feels quite cold. Like metal. Wait a minute…it’s got lids.’

“Lids?”

“Eyelids.” Ben turned it to Rafe then turned it back to himself and peered closely at the lids, holding it just a few inches away from his face. The eyelids looked as though they were painted on with a thick black brush, no eyelashes.

“Careful,” Rafe was getting uncomfortable with how comfortable Ben was dealing with this strange thing.

Pulsating green lights could be seen along the silver strips. The eyes flashed open. A silver ray beamed into Ben's face then eyes. Ben dropped the wheelot and instead of shattering apart, it flipped over, got back on its wheels, and whizzed away with an amplified frequency like a hinge that needed oiling. Ben rubbed his eyes.

"Are you ok?"

"It doesn't hurt… itches."

"Don't rub so hard. You'll damage your eyes. Gently does it."

"It feels like it blew itching powder …" Ben was bent over rubbing even harder.

Rafe grabbed Ben's water bottle from his rucksack, "Lean back."

The best Ben could do was straighten up and kept rubbing. "Feels like a handful of sand in my eyes."

Rafe splashed a hand full of water on Ben's face. "Pour some into your eyes it should help to clear them."

"I can't do that." Ben shuddered.

"Hold still."

Ben managed to tilt his head back so Rafe could pour some of the water across Ben's eyes.

"Blink, Blink… take the water in."

"It's difficult, my eyes don't want to open."

"Hope it's not gluing your eyes together."

"Don't scare me."

"I'm not… Hold still." This time Rafe poured water over Ben's forehead; his fringe clung to his brow.

This time Ben used his fingers to open and close his eyelids to absorb the water. He eventually shook his hair free of the water.

"That's better." Ben rested against a tree, took his water bottle from Rafe, and had a satisfying drink.

"What was that thing?" Ben wiped his mouth with the back of his hand. "I'm sure they sell them at Earl's Electrics."

"But, at Earl's they're tiny with two wheels, battery operated and tame."

"That thing could be the same, just larger. Like a curved brick!" Ben said.

"It was following us. It stopped when we stopped." Rafe was still observing the area, focussing on any quick movements.

"When did you notice it?" Ben asked.

"Not long after we had a bathroom break."

"That's a long time ago… It's a spy! Alamo said there are spies out here. That could be one of them."

“Well, here’s hoping whatever it is, it's not harmful. Let’s get going,” Rafe said, hoping it was a one-off incident, although his gut told him otherwise.

Chapter 19

Languin Elleba

A strong fabric bound their body and arms tightly against a chair, a coarse sack over their heads. Tia and Lisa had been delivered to the palace by a strange type of animal transport; a bumpy, swift ride that left them disorientated and sore. They couldn't identify their kidnappers, or hear them speak, but they knew they wore dark green clothing.

Feet trundled into the room, neither of them was able to see who removed their sacks, but a strong smell of smoke accompanied them. They heard when their captors left the room.

Tia whispered. "Lisa?"

"Thank goodness, I thought you had gone with them."

"Can you see anything?" Tia asked.

"No."

"I can't either."

"Let's squeeze our eyes shut and quickly open them. That works when I'm in a dark room," Lisa hoped.

A slow grinding sound could be heard beneath them, it increased as their chairs rose slowly, the sounds bounced around what felt like an empty room. The chairs jerked to a standstill. Their feet dangled freely, unnerving them at not being able to rest on something solid and not being able to see clearly.

Tia whispered. “I wish I could get to my tuber.”

“You could fall. Who knows how high off the ground we are?” Lisa paused, swallowed hard and eventually said, “I’m so thirsty.”

“I’m thirsty too.”

After a few minutes, fear intensified in Lisa’s mind, she yelled, “How long are you going to keep us here?” Her words echoed through the airy space.

“I wished I could have covered my ears. That was loud but needed.”

“Sorry Tia,” Lisa muttered.

They fell into an unfamiliar silence.

After a few minutes, Lisa said, “I wonder what happened to T-so.”

Tia replied, “He must have got away.”

Silence.

“Are you cold?” Tia asked.

“No. Did they take your jacket?”

“No. I’ve got it on.”

“Why are you cold?”

“I don’t know,” Tia sighed. “Have you got yours on?”

"Yes. I'm feeling a bit warm, with this stiff stuff pinning me to the chair. Are you on a chair?"

"Yes."

Silence.

A thin hazy blue light appeared above them. They looked at the light for a brief moment, averting their gaze as it brightened and expanded. They focussed on what was being revealed two metres in front of them; a balcony with white panelled walls, marked by gold railings which ran around the upper space. The ceiling boasted elaborate, intertwined patterns. They couldn't identify its true colours as the blinding blue light seemed to alter the true nature of what they could see. Tia looked down into the darkened void and just about made out movements which confused her, Box-like shadows, zigzagging across the ground.

A panel at the far right of them silently slipped open. A tall male stepped out onto the balcony followed by two females, their unhurried strides resonating in the vast space a swishing sound accompanied the swirling of two gold triangular time pieces, both worn at the waist of the taller woman, she swirled them alternately as she went. The females stopped under spotlights emitting a warm lemon glare, the taller of the two females wore heavy black boots, her elaborate silvery gown rested on top of silver laces. Her black braids, sprinkled with beads, created a crown effect around the front of her head, the others flowing down her back, her brown skin without blemish or scars. She lifted her right hand and pointed three ringed fingers firstly at Tia and then Lisa.

"What is your name?" Her voice harsh, yet firm.

"Tia."

"Lisa."

The man dressed like the guards at Sanguel, stood back with the plainly dressed female.

"I am Languin Elleba. You WILL address me as your Royal Highest."

Tia and Lisa reluctantly nodded.

"You have only been in my kingdom for a short while, and yet you have managed to release our prized possession…. You are tasked with getting it back."

Tia and Lisa looked at each other stunned that they had been accused of something they had no idea about. Tia wanted to diffuse the situation, and at the same time wanted to ask if they were in Pershee, but instead, with a drying throat she managed to say, "Your Royal Highest, we came to see Meela."

"Meela? What has she got to do with our stolen Musca?" Elleba grimaced, her tone severe.

"We didn't steal anything!" Lisa yelled. She regretted it the moment she released the words. Her throat throbbed. Elleba elevated her voice to a deafening bawl.

"HOW DARE YOU!"

Tia wanted to avoid any more unpleasantness. "Royal Highest, it's... difficult to…speak. Please - water."

"Please." Lisa closed her eyes and nodded several times, she hoped to demonstrate how sorry she was for not addressing the Languin properly. The Languin stepped back and said something to the guard and then to the female stood beside her.

Elleba stepped towards them again, this time the female averted her gaze to the ground.

Elleba's tone was unmoved "Meela has no idea who you are." She studied the time pieces as though they were sending her a message, then tucked them away in her pockets, which offered no indication of their presence.

Tia and Lisa wide-eyed, mouths agape glanced at each other at the revelation that the female stood next to the Languin could possibly be Meela.

"She doesn't know us, but -" Tia wasn't permitted to say anymore, Elleba interrupted her as though Tia wasn't saying anything of relevance.

"Enough!"

The female gently touched Elleba's arm, the Languin listened then said in a yielding tone, "Where have you come from?"

Tia responded hesitantly, "Sanguel,"

"Sanguel - your Royalty," Lisa added.

Elleba pointed, an accusatory tone blasting them, "Just as I thought, impostors! Tricksters!" She slapped the rail. "The ones who ruined Evelyn's system. Now listen to me!" She leant forward, as though they couldn't quite hear her. "You will not ruin me! You have done enough already. You WILL find my Musca and return it to its rightful place. Then you WILL LEAVE this kingdom." She ended with a dramatic strike of her hand to the right.

Tia tried to speak but nothing came out, she noticed a brooch on Elleba's upper arm but couldn't see its detail. Tia hoped that Lisa in her annoying, yet helpful way would say something. But Lisa had lost her ability to say anymore. They sat powerless and dismayed.

The guard spoke to Elleba in muted tones. She composed herself and said, "You will be allowed refreshments and a guide," her voice strong and irritated, she turned with a defiant hand in the air and left the gallery, Meela close behind.

Tia whispered, "There goes someone who lights up the room when she leaves."

Lisa nodded.

The guard pressed a stone button beside him. The girls heard movements below them. He pressed it again and a droning sound accompanied the chairs' descent and lighting in the lower part of the room. As the chairs touched the ground, they rotated to seat them at opposite sides of a metal table with a jug, two glasses and two silver platters.

Tia rolled her eyes in dismay as she struggled to free herself from her bonds. She mouthed, "What's the point of the food - we can't get to it!?"

Lisa nodded in solidarity.

After a few minutes, a tall woman dressed in the same attire as the guard appeared behind Tia; she slipped in so silently that Lisa only noticed her when she reached for her sword. Lisa screamed as she saw the sword come down over Tia's head, the blade slicing into the fabric that bound Tia. Lisa squeezed her eyelids together, waiting for the same thing to happen to her. Tia twisted away as she heard the blade rip through Lisa's fabric.

"Lisa. It's okay," Tia croaked.

Lisa slowly opened her eyes relieved to see they were both alive.

"You will eat and drink," the guard ordered, and took the silver covers off the platters, placing them on the ground. Tia and Lisa watched in amazement as the silver covers zoomed away, along with the fabric that tied them. Tia felt the urge to drink as much as she could, her throat desperate for lubrication. She looked with intent at the meats, bread and what she presumed was salad. She poured herself a glass of juice and enjoyed the soothing orange flavour. Tia noticed that Lisa was having a great time putting together a stack sandwich.

Lisa had another glass of juice, "She must be some sort of samurai," Lisa whispered after glancing over her shoulder at the guard, now watching them from a distance.

"That must have been Meela," Tia whispered, now that her throat felt refreshed. She took a slice of bread and piled on the meat and salad.

"No talking!" The guard bellowed.

They ate their meal in silence.

When they stopped eating, the guard strode over and dropped their rucksacks on the table.

"You will do as her Royal Highest has requested."

Tia appealed to the guard. "We didn't steal anything."

Lisa chimed in, "Wouldn't it be better if she got her intelligent guards to find the thingy? Because you …they, well, would know what it looks like."

"You were the last ones in the vicinity. The order has been declared!" The guard hesitated for a brief moment and hurriedly said, "The Languin will not send out her guards. It would not be fitting for the other kingdoms to know that this court is in turmoil while the Royal Lanquis, his majesty, is away. Therefore, you must return the Musca before HE returns."

"When does the Royal Lanquis return?" Tia asked.

The guard looked on.

"But it's not -" Lisa began to protest.

Tia stopped her by saying. "What will happen if we don't get it back in time?"

"You will be disposed of!"

Lisa gasped, "We're in serious trouble."

"Serious danger," Tia said.

"Your lives for the Musca. It's simple."

"We don't know where to find it," Tia protested. "What is it?"

"You will have the aid of two guards to escort you out of this Palace - You will have a guide to help you to the Shobi people." The guard left the room.

"This is unfair. Who are the Shobis?" Lisa's cries fell on deaf ears.

They remained in a despondent silence.

Shortly after, two guards entered the room, at the same time the chairs and table shook. Tia and Lisa had no other choice but to jump up before the chairs shot upwards and the table collapsed downwards.

The guards shoved them roughly towards the door.

Chapter 20

Unreal Hello

As they continued their journey, a green wheelot, shot towards them. Rafe and Ben jumped out of the way of the wild wheelot; it zipped about their feet as they hopped about to avoid it. They were unaware of the large green beetle hidden in a tree, watching the scene below. It rubbed its hind antennae together. Multiple wheelots shot out of the undergrowth, their high-pitched squeals startling Rafe and Ben who got caught in an unwanted game of dodge with the attacking moss and lichen. A mild shock ran up their legs every time they stomped on the wheelots, their shells were too sturdy and slimy to shatter in one go. To maintain these exhausting antics was confusing and dizzying for the boys. Ben was the first to hit the ground with a groan, covering his ears, then his eyes. Rafe tumbled as a silver wheelot, moss covering its side wheels, slammed into his ankles. It zoomed around him and beamed its grey light into his eyes. Rafe clamped his lids shut, his vision momentarily disturbed by a stream of hazy numbers and white dots.

"Hello," it said, the voice emanating from inside its shell. "You need the quickest way to the palace. Follow me."

Rafe lay squinting at the wheelot. Ben curled up, drained, and temporarily nodded off. The other wheelots retreated into the undergrowth. The green wheelot waited until Rafe attempted to lift himself from the ground, then beamed its ray into his eyes. Rafe slumped, his back against the base of a tree, rubbing his itching eyes uncontrollably.

"No - no." Rafe struggled to take off his rucksack. Eventually he found his water canister and splashed water over his eyes.

"Rafe! Ben! Rafe, Ben." The silver wheelot shrieked.

Rafe thought it was asking who they were, he was irritated by this fake formality, "Who wants to know?" Rafe staggered to his feet, disgusted that he had allowed himself to be caught off guard, his head throbbed, his eyes sore, but no longer itching.

The green wheelot hurled itself against Ben's back until he stirred.

"Does. Not. Matter," The silver wheelot slammed into his companion. "The Palace!"

It zipped to Ben who had dragged himself up, leant against a tree, dazed.

"You go now," the silver wheelot demanded. "Come, come." It whizzed ahead and waited for them.

Although they felt compelled to go, Ben stammered, “Do… you think… we… should go?”

“I’m not comfortable with it, but bossy one over there said ‘palace’. I’m hoping that’s where the girls are. I don’t believe we have an option.” Rafe argued.

“If all else fails, we’ll smash them to bits with our tubers and get out of there!” Ben said, knowing he didn’t have the strength to do this immediately, but later would be a different matter. They staggered behind the wheelots with their plan in mind.

*

They entered the busy town via the market. They had no time to admire the red hills as the wheelots rammed into their feet every time they tried to stop. It was clear that the townspeople were accustomed to these wheeling devices. They moved about the pathways with ease. Occasionally, they could unintentionally be kicked or stepped on, this was seen as a mild disturbance that often went unnoticed unless a wayward child decided to deliberately attack them. The wheelot would release a piercing screech which children found amusing and adults infuriating; those adults would punish the child for the offence.

Rows of timber-framed houses ran along several side roads on the outskirts of the marketplace, red brick walls enclosed specific quadrants of the market where many market traders built small shacks behind their stalls to store their merchandise.

Rising from the marketplace were two arid hillsides. Stone steps led to an elevated palace, which sat neatly above the market stalls' canopies, with its marble frontage and numerous sparkling slit windows. Magnificent white and gold pillars ran up to the elegant main entrance. Grey beast statutes flanked the engraved metal doorway, only opened for celebrations and royal birthdays. Opulent black pillars marked the palace courtyard which no one could enter, unless tending to the fruit trees and flowers grown in designated wooden boxes.

Ridges ran from the top of the hillside to the base. Rafe observed doorways and windows embedded along these ridges. These were special homes for the employees connected with the palace.

Ben nudged Rafe. "Imagine living up there."

They stopped for a moment to take in the magnificent views but the wheelots slammed at their feet, the silver wheelot accompanied this with a piercing squeal, Rafe didn't want any unwanted attention, so he grunted, “Stop that. We’re moving.” Rafe marched on.

The green wheelot took a sharp turn into a passageway leading to the side entrance of the palace. A line of ornamental shrubs welcomed visitors into this wide-open passageway crowded with people carrying parcels, pulling wheelbarrows and trolleys loaded with vegetables, fruits, expensive fabrics, jewels, anything the royal household and their employees required.

At the end of the passageway limestone walls loomed above them, enclosing the corridor, overlooked by slit windows. Guards blocked the main entrance leading to a myriad of hallways. They checked all those entering and leaving the palace. This checkpoint was heavily guarded. A female guard roughly escorted a man with his merchandise back down the passageway. Ben and Rafe avoided the skirmish. Fortunately, they were not stopped, and Rafe wondered how they were waved through without incident.

The wheelots escorted them through a short corridor into a small side room; the door slid shut as they left. Three wooden tables with benches were neatly assembled in this limited space. At the centre of each table sat a jug surrounded by wooden mugs, and a setting of spoons and forks.

“We must be close to the kitchens. I can smell something baking.” Ben smiled.

“What did you zero in on first, the smell or table settings?” Rafe chuckled.

“Come on, you can’t say you’re not hungry, we haven’t eaten since this morning.”

“I’d prefer to find the girls first, then eat.”

“Sometimes we don’t have an option. Besides, I’m tired,” Ben said, and sprawled on a bench. “And hungry.” He glanced inside the jug, saw it was empty, stared in the other jug, “empty!” He sighed.

Rafe looked through each of the three narrow windows, one after the other. “You should see this. You can see parts of the market and hillside.”

“I haven’t got the energy to get up again. I need -”

“Food,” Rafe said with mild humour. “It would be good to eat.”

“Finally! You’re hungry too.”

“Yes. But I’m wondering why they left us here.”

“Think about that later. Let’s hope we’ll get fed first.”

The door slid open. No one entered.

Strangely, there were no sounds of a busy corridor.

A male voice announced, “Stand for – Royal Highest Languin.”

Rafe and Ben, glanced uneasily at each other, stood together facing the door. Elleba entered with two guards, her boots were accompanied with a glistening all-in-one navy trousers suit, the time pieces out of sight. She strode in with a regal air, smiled a wide welcoming smile and instructed them to sit down. She remained standing; the train of her silver cloak filled the space around her.

"Welcome to my kingdom."

The boys didn't know what to say, they hesitated and said, "Thank you."

"Welcome to my home."

"Thank you," Ben said with an awkward, hesitant bow from the waist.

"What can I do for you?" She asked, her palms open, her smile warm.

"I would love some food…" Ben began.

Rafe cut in, "We came to find Tia and Lisa."

One of the guards said sternly, "When addressing thc Royal Languin, you will say 'your Royal Highest Languin'."

Neither Ben nor Rafe knew whether to use the title at the beginning of the sentence or at the end, and neither of them wanted to ask just in case it prompted another unpleasant reaction. In fact, Rafe wondered why she wore heavy boots with such an elegant garment. Ben looked to Rafe. Rafe said, "Your... Royal Highest Languin, we come looking for my cousin Tia and," he displayed one hand towards Ben as though presenting Ben to her, "Ben's sister, Lisa."

"Your names?" The other guard asked, her tone unsympathetic as she glared at Rafe then Ben.

"Your Highest Languin - Rafe." He didn't know why he bowed.

Ben stifled a chuckle. "Ben."

"We don't know of the individuals you speak of," The male guard said.

Ben said, "They - Your Royal – sorry, Your Royal Highest Languin..." He looked to the guard to see if he had got the title right, when she stared back Ben quickly finished his sentence. "They came here to visit Meela."

"Meela has had no such guests." The female guard looked irritated.

Ben whispered to Rafe, "Perhaps they didn't make it."

Rafe didn't respond as he saw the vexation on the faces of the guards.

Elleba wanted the meeting over with; however, her tone was gracious. "You have come a long way. Please have food and drink. There are rooms for you to take a rest. Enjoy our hospitality while we look for your family."

“Thank you,” Ben said far too hastily. “Your Royal Highest Languin,” He added with another awkward half bow.

“Send a message to the outer palace. Make sure our young guests are treated well. We will find out where your family members are,” Elleba reassured them.

“Your Royal Highest Languin, could we meet with Meela?” Rafe asked.

Elleba stiffened, smiled, and said warmly, “Of course.” She turned and left the room.

Rafe squinted. “I don’t know about her. She’s strange.”

“Don’t read anymore into it, Rafe. Perhaps the girls are still on their way, and we made it here before them.” Ben laughed. “I can’t wait to see Lisa’s face when they get here. She’ll be so surprised to see us. So will Tia. After all, they thought they would sneak here and get back before we knew they had gone. How wrong they were.”

“You’re so smug,” Rafe grinned. “At least if we see Meela, this trip may be worthwhile.”

“Your trip has already been made worthwhile; you’ve seen Izzy.” Ben slapped Rafe on the back. “Is that bashfulness Rafe, or joy?” Ben laughed so loud, Rafe raised an eyebrow but couldn’t help himself, and laughed along too. They smelt the food arrive before the door opened.

They were given two full plates of food and drinks in silver goblets.

"Ooooh, the royal treatment," Ben beamed.

They had no problem demolishing the food and enjoying the delicious juice.

"I hope Meela comes soon. I'm tired." Rafe gazed at his goblet. "How did they know we travelled from afar?"

"Why are you slurring your words?" Ben yawned.

Rafe looked at Ben drowsily. "Why are you wobbling?"

"I'm not. The room is going round, and round…"

"Wobble, wobble, wobble…" Ben muttered. His goblet fell to the ground with a clink, rolled under the bench with a trail of blue liquid. Ben's head hit the table, just missing his plate. Rafe tried to lift Ben's head, but his hands wouldn't do as he intended, instead they seemed to move around uncontrollably along with the spinning room. He felt a strong impulse to sleep. He tried to keep his eyes open, but it was no use,

"Sh…e's str..an..ge…" were the last words he uttered before he sunk into a deep, sleep.

Chapter 21

Beside the Sea

It was late in the afternoon. Two guards carried lamps down narrow tunnels. Water trickled along the dark stone walls; a musty damp stench clawed at their nostrils. Their footsteps, against the uneven ground, echoed in the stillness. The guards stopped at a double-bolted iron door. It opened with ease. They felt intermittent blasts of wind and heard what sounded like waves, subtle natural light could be seen ahead of them. The tunnel opened into a cavern overlooking a buoyant, frothing shoreline.

"Wait here. And don't get in the way of the Shobi people!" Was the forceful order.

They heard the booming reverberations of the iron door being slammed shut as the guards returned to the palace.

"I think they were the ones that captured us," Tia said.

Lisa's eyes widened.

"Or they wore the same smoky perfume as those guards."

"What are we supposed to do here?" Lisa looked at the grey sky. "It's cold. I don't like this."

"I'm sorry. I didn't expect our adventure to come to this." Tia looked out at the sea, gentle waves folding over a rocky shoreline. Further out, boats bobbed, the crews looked like matchstick people. Tia zipped her jacket and shoved her hands in her pockets, she stared at pink sand beneath them, which ran around the rocky plains like multiple pathways. "I thought we'd be able to see Meela and go home. She didn't even acknowledge us!"

Lisa leant against the smooth stone wall, her hood over her head.

"I wonder if Ray would have done things differently."

Lisa sighed, "He'd have an idea of what to do now."

Tia shrugged, "I suppose so - Meela wasn't even friendly, not like her brothers."

"Evan and Alamo are lovely." Lisa fastened her jacket, wrapped her arms around her middle, "We didn't steal anything... What's a Musca? How's it missing? How can we find something we didn't know existed!"

Tia gazed, silently, scanning the coastline to the right. She stepped further out of the cavern to see a stone wall between the rocky area and the palace. A waterway ran under a large archway below the palace. A bit further on, small boats were moored against jetties leading to homes on the water's edge, some on stone foundations jutting into the water. Pink cliffs with pockets of bold purple flowers brightened the area. Children were running along the sandy shore with baskets. Tia couldn't see what they were scooping into their baskets.

"Who knew the Palace had an entrance to the sea?" Tia said.

"I don't care. I'm cold," Lisa moaned. She could see what seemed like a line of market stalls in the distance, all bobbing on the water; these stalls could be accessed by boat or a strip of land, which was more visible at low tide. There were people coming and going, wrapped in heavy clothing to fend off the winds.

"Do you think they're selling fishy food down there?"

"Who knows?" Tia muttered.

Tia looked at her flower chain around her wrist, she was glad to see the flowers hadn't wilted, but she had lost a few on the way. "Let's make a fire, keep warm while we wait for whoever is supposed to guide us. Or we could make sure that these are the Shobi people."

"I'd prefer to go back to the underground people," Lisa said, "the Gakinde -"

"How do you know that?"

"T-so told me."

"Someone called my name?" T-so was stood behind them with a big grin.

*

Tia gave him a fierce look, with hands on her hips she shouted, "Where have you been?"

"You've got us into a lot of trouble. Waste of space. Where were you hiding?" Lisa yelled.

T-so put his hands up as if defending himself from the attack of words. "One thing at a time - Let's go." He jumped down from the edge of the cavern onto the pink sand.

Tia and Lisa glared at him.

"I'm your guide, come on!" He ran in the opposite direction of the Shobi people, around the curve of the land. Tia and Lisa jumped down and slowly followed the path T-so had taken. T-so ran inland towards high blue grass and green mounds. Tia and Lisa began to jog as they noticed the distance T-so had advanced ahead. White rocks lay along this part of the coastline, as though they were seating for giants who would enjoy this nautical scene.

"Stop! Stop!" Lisa puffed.

Tia slowed down, but T-so looked over his shoulder and kept running.

"T-SO!" Tia shouted. "STOP. T-SO!"

Lisa was bent low trying to get her breath back. “My leg’s hurting.”

“Stay here. I’ll go after him.” Tia sprinted on seeing T-so disappear behind a cluster of huge rocks.

Lisa lowered herself against a sandy mound not wanting to hurt her ankle as it felt quite sore. “That T-so is so impatient,” she said aloud, annoyed at being unable to keep up with the others. She examined the blue grass to see if there were any strange creatures scuttling around her.

*

Lisa knew that Tia hadn’t forgotten about her even though daylight was fading; layers of purple and grey clouds drifted over the pink cliffs. But she felt that T-so could have distracted Tia from getting back to her. Lisa took out her tuber, hoping they would return before nightfall. She wasn’t willing to face a mechagribea on her own. She slipped down the mound to hide in the long grass. She was surprised to find that it was warmer and hoped her pendant would work if she needed it. The long grass swayed in mild winds which carried their rustles and whispers across the coastline. It was quite soothing to Lisa until she heard snorting grunts. She stared anxiously, hoping to identify what was making the peculiar sounds.

“LISA. LISA.”

Lisa was relieved to hear Tia calling her. She put her tuber away and shuffled to her feet. Tia was riding a large lumbering beast which was slightly smaller than T-so's huge beast. It reminded her of a cuddly elephant without large ears, with curly grey and brown fur. Lisa waved and didn't stop waving until they got to her. The beast's huge steps left indentations in the grass. Its short tubular nose hanging just over its obscured mouth, and gentle eyes, made Lisa develop an instant liking for the creature.

"We saw you. There was no need to keep waving," T-so said.

Lisa ignored him, "Tia. Tia," Lisa sang, "so good, they named you twice."

Tia giggled. "Your comfy chariot awaits."

"How do I get up there?"

"Over here. Tia's chukkan won't carry two people," T-so said, with an arrogance that said I know about these things. "You're with me." He pointed at himself as though Lisa wouldn't have guessed who he meant.

Lisa wished with all her heart she could say something to take T-so down a peg or two, but she saw Tia's face say let him have his moment. Lisa stepped over to the chukkan. Its eyes looked down at her, its nose extended to the top of her head, studying this new traveller. T-so tugged on the looped section of a reed harness that ran around the chukkan's neck and shoulders, it extended its thick front right leg. Lisa tentatively walked towards the leg, sprigs of long fur dangling from it.

"Grab hold of the fur and use it to walk up the leg," Tia said.

"It's a 'stretch', not a leg," T-so corrected.

"No need for that tone," Lisa said

Tia could see Lisa was hesitant with the chukkan's fur, "It won't hurt."

"I'm scared it's going to kick me," Lisa said

T-so chuckled, "I can let Kee-kee do that - if you wish."

"No thanks."

"It took me a couple of times. Don't worry, Lisa, grab hold tightly it won't hurt her, it will just make it easier for you to climb."

"Here goes." Lisa took hold of the long fur on either side of the hefty limb. She placed her foot on the lower part of the limb. It felt soft yet solid.

"Don't think. Run up it," T-so encouraged, with a hint of amusement.

The chukkan lowered its head to Lisa's level, its friendly eyes gazed at her, its nostrils sniffed and gently nudged her, which Lisa didn't mind but when its nostril flared and released a stream of warm air, like she was under a massive hair dryer, Lisa covered her face, expecting a blast of snot. When none was forthcoming, Lisa exhaled in relief, clutched the long fur, tugged down firmly, and ran up the leg, stopped and almost toppled backward. T-so grabbed the fur and pulled Lisa forward causing her to land on top of the chukkan's broad shoulder. T-so laughed hysterically at Lisa laying face down beside him.

Tia rolled her eyes at him. "It's not that funny!"

Tia addressed Lisa, "Pull yourself up to the seat, you'll be fine."

Lisa rose upon her elbows, saw an orange and red seat tied into the fur behind T-so. She pushed herself forward onto her stomach until she got to the curved woven material seating; she found it to be softer than she had expected. Lisa managed to get herself in seating position, ignoring T-so's fading hilarity.

"Thanks a lot," Lisa said to T-so.

"You're welcome." He whistled low into the tucked away ears of the chukkan and gave his loop a right tug. Tia followed suit and felt the gentle power through the reins as the animal turned and headed in the direction of T-so's home. Tia kept calm as instructed by T-so, she didn't want the animal to quicken its pace to a trot, which meant it would have been an uncomfortable bumpy ride. They travelled harmoniously side-by-side.

It took Lisa no time to get used to the rocking motion of the animal's steady strides, the seating made her feel as though she was snuggled in a warm, soft cloud.

"Tia, have you told T-so what's happened?"

"No. I was concerned about getting back to you and how to manage Chug-chug, my temporary chukkan." Tia smiled, proudly, and stroked the animal's head. "This is Kee-kee's son."

Lisa felt pleased her friend hadn't forgotten about her. "What's this thing called?"

"It's not a thing! It's a chukkan. They are friendly creatures, very sensitive, good for travelling and gentle with humans. They can see and smell over great distances. When they get to this size, they can carry quite a few passengers and produce. Chug-chug is still young, but very obedient. Kee-kee is an expert. Anyway, what happened to you?" T-so asked.

"I didn't ask for a history lesson!" Lisa scoffed.

"More importantly, what happened to you - when we were kidnapped?" Tia asked.

"I don't know what you mean."

"You must have seen who or what grabbed us!" Lisa accused.

"I heard my uncle calling me. I saw nothing. Heard nothing."

Lisa glanced over at Tia. "So, how did you find us?"

"I was looking for my sister, but she wasn't there. I saw you as I was going home."

"You said you were our guide," Tia said.

"You're strangers. Strangers do strange things," he said, and turned his head into the air as though he heard something.

"Because of your trip to the Musca, the Languin thinks we stole it," Tia said.

Lisa added, "Your trip, not ours!" She pushed him in the back with her foot and quickly grabbed the curved seating to steady her.

T-so rocked along with the motion of his chukkan.

"Your silence isn't helping." Tia's tone was much sharper than before.

T-so mustered a fake cough.

"Have you been listening?" Tia glared over at him, holding her loop steady so as not to jerk the chukkan in the wrong path. "The Languin, Elleba, said it was our fault that the Musca is missing, and we need to get it back."

After a troubled pause T-so said, "The Languin will not be put to shame while her family are away."

"You think?!" Lisa yelled. The chukkan shuddered and almost shook Lisa out of her seat.

"What's that smell?" Lisa covered her nose. "Smells like onions and garlic," she gasped between her fingers.

"I carry food for the market. And you mustn't do that. Kee-kee hates screamers," T-so smirked.

"It's not funny," Tia said, making sure she didn't raise her voice.

"You should do as you're told," T-so said.

"Are you going to help us? Mr Guide…." Tia's sentence was interrupted by T-so's loud sneeze. He wiped his nose on his sleeve.

"Get a tissue," Lisa scoffed.

"I don't think he knows what that is," Tia said, genuinely.

"The Languin said the guide should take us to…, I can't remember what they're called," Lisa said.

"I think the guard said it was the Showboat people," Tia said trying to remember the name.

T-so mocked their lack of knowledge. "The Shobi people are of the sea - live by the sea - for the sea. Don't you know anything?!"

Tia was the first to react. "Know-it-all!"

Lisa added, “So we’re going the wrong way!?” Lisa folded her arms in anger.

“It’s getting dark. You can stay the night. In the morning you must go,” T-so said, and encouraged his chukkan to go faster, moving ahead of Tia’s to lead the way. He remained silent for the rest of the journey.

Chapter 22

Meela

Rafe woke up feeling groggy. He lay fully clothed in a comfortable bed. His eyes took a while to focus on white walls and vertical timber bars at the far end of the room. Evening light strained through a pane of frosted glass, providing a tranquil feel; the pane of glass was situated in a short corridor on the other side of the bars. Rafe's arms and legs felt sore, he rubbed at them hoping the blood flow would ease the throbbing. He slipped his feet to the ground, holding his head he closed his eyes and took deep breaths. He remembered someone pulling his rucksack, and being carried somewhere, he felt the pain of several injections. In a panic his eyes sprung open, he quickly checked for his rucksack and tuber; neither of them was beside him. He stood up, waited for a moment for his brain to orientate itself. He spotted his trainers beside a small cupboard, the only other piece of furniture in this limited space.

Rafe pushed at the wooden bars, to his amazement they swung open with ease. There was only one way to go - he turned left into the corridor; shadows of greenery revealed itself on the other side of the frosted pane. He followed the frosted glass wall into a brightly lit communal room. A metal door at the far end of the room was open, with a corridor leading off it. A line of stools sat under a long table with a clear jug filled with water and glass tumblers in the middle.

"You're awake." The voice was relieved.

Rafe turned to see a young woman enter the room from the other corridor. She reminded him of Alamo. She was slightly shorter than Rafe. Her black hair, held in two cornrows, rested on her shoulders; she wore blue trousers and a matching long tunic with gold stars around the neckline and hem. She exhibited an air of calm and grace. She stood and extended her hand towards Rafe, "I'm Meela."

Rafe was amazed at meeting Meela but showed no obvious signs of his elation. He glanced around the room then calmly said, "It's very minimalist."

"These quarters are the comfortable ones. We are fortunate to have them," Meela said.

"We?"

"I believe your comrade is still sleeping," Meela said, "his room is along the same corridor as mine." She pointed to the corridor she had appeared from.

Rafe was surprised that he hadn't heard Ben's snores come from wherever he was sleeping.

"It's really good to meet you." Rafe pulled out a stool.

Meela sat opposite him.

"I know your brothers, met your parents too."

Meela brightened, "How are they?"

"Very well."

Meela looked pleased.

"Have you met Tia and Lisa?" Rafe didn't want to waste any time in small talk.

"Who?" She seemed puzzled.

Rafe slowed down, "Tia and Lisa."

"I don't know who you mean. Perhaps you should rest a bit more. Your memory will return."

"Tia…, my cousin. She's eleven, so high." He used his hand to indicate Tia's height in comparison to Meela. "Yes, this tall, her hair is in long, thin plaits… ponytail… I think. Lisa, same age, has brown wavy hair and talks a lot, white, so high." He raised his hand slightly.

"Have a drink, it will help."

"There's nothing wrong with my memory," Rafe said, a bit sharper than he had intended. Meela didn't seem alarmed. She poured him a glass of water. "Here, this will refresh you."

"I'm not sure if I should drink it. I remember drinking something which made me feel strange."

"So, you've met Elleba." Meela still extended the glass to Rafe. He took it but did not drink. "The Languin - this water is good, the goblet juices not so good," Meela sighed.

For some reason Rafe wanted to trust her, he didn't know if it was because he had such a loyalty to her brothers and mother or that she seemed genuine. He drank rapidly, astonished that he was so thirsty.

"You needed that." She smiled, took his glass, and filled it again. Rafe didn't refuse this time and gulped it down as quickly as the first. Meela went around the table and sat next to Rafe. She looked around as though there were others in the room who shouldn't be privy to their conversation - her voice lowered. "The others won't be back they've gone to the rejuvenating facility. It's where you get exchanged -"

"What do you mean 'exchanged'?" Rafe whispered back, not sure why he was whispering but feeling a sense of foreboding.

"I would show you, but we're locked in. We normally have the gardens open to us. Today, it's off limits."

"How do we get into the gardens?"

"Through there." She pointed to the wall of frosted glass. "It's locked."

Rafe strolled over to the glass but couldn't see a door.

"Further down," Meela said,

Rafe spied a section with an outline of a keyhole and the shadow of a handle on the other side of the pane. "No use," Rafe muttered.

"Your friend is awake," Meela said excitedly. Rafe moved quickly down the short corridor past three doors and found Ben in a room exactly like his.

Ben was sat on the side of the bed rubbing his head, his voice croaky, "Did someone hit me over the head? And punch my arms into numbness?"

"I think we were given some type of sleeping potion," Rafe said.

"It certainly worked, that's probably why my arms are floppy."

"Take your time, it'll all come back."

Meela came in with a glass of water.

"Ben, this is Meela, and she hasn't seen Tia or Lisa."

Meela offered the water to Ben. He waved it away.

"It's fine Ben, I had some."

Ben stared at Rafe, "What's your cousin's name?"

Rafe chuckled, "It's really me Ben, I had the water ages ago and I don't feel strange, not like that drink earlier."

"Ok. Thanks." Ben held his hand out, Meela cradled the glass into Ben's hand. "I'm so thirsty." He swallowed hard. "Where's my rucksack and…?" Ben and Rafe exchanged a look of acknowledgement that their precious belongings were missing - this was worrying for both of them.

Ben said, “I need some air.”

“Here.” Rafe threw Ben his trainers.

Rafe rushed back to his room, pulled on his trainers. As he was about to leave the room, he returned to the cupboard, anticipating that his belongings might be inside. Unfortunately, the cupboard was empty, except for a white card with black inscription ‘R37i’. Rafe flung the card back in the cupboard and slammed the door, giving it no further thought.

Meela assisted Ben into the communal room. Rafe was shocked to see one of the panes was open, releasing a cool breeze into the white space.

“How…?” Rafe began.

“I found a key,” Meela said, as she helped Ben to sit down. She poured him another glass of water. Ben guzzled it down, it seemed to give him more clarity. “Another, please.”

“Steady,” Rafe said, “you’ll need the loo soon.”

Ben smiled and drank the last glass more slowly. “That hit the spot.”

“Ready to see what’s out there?” Rafe asked.

“I’m ready.”

They made their way into the grounds. The garden was well maintained with flowers and plants the boys didn't recognise. Rafe looked back at the building before they set off along a parting in the foliage. Creepers flowed over the building and along the pane of glass. He could just about make out the faded and partial lettering over the entrance – 'Installation block.'

Rafe didn't like the sound of that. "What is this place?"

"Not here," Meela said and grabbed their arms. "We'll speak over there, it's safer." She took them to an inner quadrangle surrounded by trees and large shrubs.

"Can you remember anything before you got here?" Meela asked.

Rafe and Ben both stared blankly.

"Well, my memory comes and goes," Meela said, "but I now know what happened. It's too long to explain so it's best if I show you. We may just have enough time before Elleba or her Ellebanites return."

"Ellebanites?"

"Some of the guards are her comrades," Meela said to Ben.

As they hurried along with Meela, Rafe said, "I can remember searching for the girls."

"I remember the delicious food."

"Talking with the Royal whatsit," Rafe tutted.

Ben said, "The drink was sweet then bitter. After that nothing, not even a dream. And I have great dreams about defeating dragons and all sorts - this time, nothing!"

Rafe raised an eyebrow. "Slaying dragons - Really?"

Ben shrugged with amusement. "Yes, I know. Whatever you do, don't tell Lisa, she'll laugh at me for weeks."

"Your secret is safe with me."

Meela said, "If we get caught, act like you've lost your memory and don't know how you left the installation rooms. I'll take all the blame."

"We can't let you do that," Rafe said.

"They won't destroy me, but they may destroy you. Many people don't get their memories back and remain confused."

"Ok," Ben said. "I think my brain is still fuzzy anyway."

"When we get into the rejuvenation building, don't talk, just look. We can talk later."

Meela hurried through the foliage, away from the designated paths. Rafe made a mental note as best he could, of any key features, just in case they needed a route of escape; he didn't like the idea of a rejuvenation building where people lost their memories.

Chapter 23

Awkward

Blue moonlight illuminated the well-worn pathway up the hilly terrain. The chukkans climbed the hillside with ease.

A blanket of vines greeted them at the end of the path which veiled an enclosed space for the chukkans to shelter. They stopped without prompting. T-so expertly ran down the stretch without using the creature's long fur to assist him. Lisa and Tia watched as he pushed at the wall of vines. The vines parted to reveal a dark cavern entrance. T-so stepped aside and Chug-chug and Kee-kee wandered in at a steady pace.

"Let go of your loop," T-so said, "Chug-chug will do the rest."

Tia relaxed the loop, she felt like this was what being on autopilot felt like. "It smells."

"Ben's old socks." Lisa fanned in front of her nose. "Millions of them! Yuk."

The warm pungent smell engulfed them. Tia felt a drip of dampness against the top of her head, she leant forwards, hoping she wasn't going to bump her head on any ridges in the ceiling. "A little light wouldn't go amiss," she said, "keep low, Lisa,"

"I am, I felt something brush my hair, yuk."

T-so finally lit a lantern. They eventually saw him stood next to a row of lanterns. He hooked his lantern on a pole and raised it high in the air. The girls were able to see the area more clearly. "Hurry and get down! I need to sleep."

The height was considerable for someone who hadn't ridden such a large animal before, Tia and Lisa feared falling.

"How do I get down?" Tia asked.

"Slide down," T-so said, uninterested as he moved off to a corner of the cavern where more of these animals were lying fast asleep, muffled, slow snorts perforating the stillness.

Tia looked over at Lisa. "He's probably upset."

"He doesn't even wear socks. I think he's just rude." She glanced over at T-so who was spreading long grass in a section of the cave for the chukkans to sleep on.

"He told me that the chukkan will lengthen its leg… stretch, to allow a rider to slide down. He was showing off when he got down. Anyway, here goes." Tia swung both her legs over to the right side of the animal and sat at the top of its wide shoulder. The animal slowly relaxed its leg, which created a dip in its shoulder, enabling Tia to slide down to the ground. "Not too bad," She smiled. "Good boy." She patted the leg of her chukkan. Lisa pushed herself off the seating to the shoulder of the animal, it extended its leg, and she flew down at great speed, falling to the side as she hit the ground. Tia rushed to her aid. "Are you ok?"

"Ha-ha, ha-ha." T-so howled.

"It wasn't that funny," Tia said, although she really wanted to shout at him, but not disturb the animals.

"Ignore him. I'm fine." Lisa dusted herself off. "Good fun." She gave T-so a side glare.

T-so continued his outburst, "I've got chores to get on with, but this will make it more enjoyable."

"Just show us where to sleep and we'll be out of your hair tomorrow," Tia said firmly.

"Did you loosen the seat cradles?" T-so asked cunningly.

"Do you mean the things we were sitting on?" Lisa asked.

T-so was clearly irritated. "Yes, you're supposed to loosen them before you dismount!"

"Well, you should have told us!" Tia shot back.

"You should have known!"

"How? Einstein."

T-so screwed up his face with confusion, "Who?"

Lisa looked as though she was going to explain, in the way only Lisa would when someone was frustrating her, but Tia jumped in. "You didn't say, so we didn't know. OK."

T-so started to sulk. "I guess I'll add that to my already long list of things to do. You'll have to help me in the morning." With that he trundled off, Tia and Lisa followed his light which was the only thing that was now illuminating the way to their sleeping quarters.

Lisa's heart sank as T-so led them down a steep gradient, he spoke without turning around, "hold on to the sides, we don't want any accidents." They heard the sarcastic nature of his tone, which Lisa would take as her cue to do the opposite to what he had said, but she knew that it was in her best interest to do as he said until they saw the back of him the next day. He opened a locked door, on one side of a fork in the passageway, a familiar glass light in an alcove. T-so took the corridor to the left which led them back to the room they had slept in previously.

"You know your way out," T-so said.

Lisa was happy to say, "Yes we do."

"Goodnight and good riddance." T-so stomped away before they could reply, leaving them in the dark. Tia quickly found her torch. It brightened the area far more than T-so's lantern.

"He's so rude. I'm not helping him in the morning."

"I know."

"Just dumped us!"

"I'm glad we're sleeping here and not with Chug-chug," Tia said.

"He would have left us there if he could!" Lisa said this as if T-so had left them with the chukkans.

"Let's get some sleep." Tia fashioned the cushions together for her and Lisa then unfolded her sleeping bag.

"I was think…" Lisa began.

"That's dangerous Miss Rosen," Tia giggled.

Lisa smiled knowing Tia was trying to help her relax. "I was thinking that perhaps we can't go home, because we may have put Meela in danger. I mean…" she took off her trainers and struggled into her sleeping bag, Tia was already snuggled in hers, trainers beside her head. "If the Languin is willing to get rid of us, we could disappear. But she sounds like a woman who holds a grudge, and I would hate to know that Meela would get the brunt of it, she's probably in danger now."

Tia yawned, "I'm with you, Supergirl. We're not going home. Not yet. Meela may be in danger."

"Just as I thought."

Chapter 24

Rejuvenation

By nightfall they had entered the rejuvenation facility through a deep archway, decorated by an abundance of blue ivy. Shadows from the dense foliage obscured the doorway set in a red brick wall.

Meela felt around for the lock, "It's here somewhere," she muttered.

Rafe and Ben heard her turning a clumsy latch; it clicked and churned several times before the creaky door opened.

On first entry, it looked as though there was nothing interesting in this space due to the gloomy coloured vestibule, but closer inspection highlighted floor to ceiling brown curtains, matching the walls. A red door and a white door sat at opposite ends of the rectangular space.

"So boring," Ben groaned.

Rafe peeped behind one of the curtains, revealing a stream of light which flowed through a wall of glass into the vestibule. "It's a viewing gallery!"

Ben pulled the curtains wider. "It's like something out of a Sci-Fi movie."

Meela looked puzzled so Rafe said, "It's something you watch, you know – out of this world," Meela still looked confused. Rafe tried again, "We've never seen anything like this, in real life… I mean…."

"Not many people have," Meela said.

Rafe's attention was drawn back to taking in every detail of the clinical room. Fluorescent strips lit the room. The section to the left of where Rafe stood was dominated by wires and machinery.

Meela pointed to the oblong windows that ran around the room. "They normally occupy those rooms - you can't see the machines from here," she whispered.

Ben whispered back, "Who's they?"

Meela didn't reply as though scared someone would hear her.

To the right of the gallery was an open exit which led to a small, railed platform with a metal staircase giving access to the lower floor. Under the staircase were grey double doors next to a cupboard and a row of silver cylinders with neighbouring glass cylinders, each half-filled with green liquid. A system of measurement ran down the body of each cylinder. Rubber tubes connected these cylinders together with a small wheel and tap in the middle of the tubes. Adjacent to the cylinders were a line of metal framed beds all precisely made up with grey linen, except two with grey striped mattresses. Rafe read the labels at the bottom of each bed - L35i, T34i, B33i, C36i, R37i, he stopped at R37i, but couldn't recollect where he first saw it. He wanted to ask Meela what the labels meant but remembered her warning to be silent, and now that she was only pointing at things but not saying anything, he thought he'd raise his questions later.

Ben had wandered off to the red door in the vestibule, "This door's open," Ben whispered excitedly, glad to enter what he believed to be a side room. Instead, his boredom turned to intrigue as he stepped into a vast storage area. A large panel of glass in the roof space funnelled moonlight down a central region, illuminating three levels in this airy space.

As they entered, floorboards creaked under their weight. A staircase to their right led to the upper and lower levels. They remained on the entry level, Ben had already darted through the central aisle to the opposite side of the floor, peering into the open crates. He ran from crate to crate, picking out bits of metal or plastic and throwing them back in the crates, sounding like a large rat scurrying around to find something to eat. Rafe strolled over to a group of seven unmade beds, with large syringes secured on metal, rectangular panels to the side of each bed. He looked across at a glass partition and noticed piles of spare panels laid out on a large silver table. Several boxes, overflowing with syringes, stood beside the panels. Rafe assumed this was a workstation and that the grey machinery beside the table made the holes to insert the syringes into the panels. Meela stood at the door observing them.

The items clinked and clanked as Ben rummaged in one of the containers. "Looks like those things that attacked us! They're broken." Ben waved a dismantled wheelot at Rafe. Rafe wished Ben would calm his excitement, so he moved closer to where Ben was standing and gestured with his hands, palms pumping downwards, for Ben to keep it down. Ben got the message and put his index finger against his lips and raised both eyebrows to say sorry, carefully placing the green box back in the container.

Rafe read the brief information on the side of the crates silently, 'Series DF 300. Series DF 400.'

Meela tugged their tunics and hurried quietly back to the staircase, their descent accompanied by grumbling steps and partial moonlight. The ground floor was set out in quadrants; one section had more modern computers set up in workstations - another section had beds, wires dangled from the metal headboards down into the ground, Rafe noticed that several beds had wires trailing to the computers in the workstation section.

Ben jumped down from the bottom steps, a solo strip light provided a dull beam that turned on and off lazily. Ben tracked chains looped along the ceiling like metal snakes. They disappeared behind a partition, and appeared on the other side of the partition, attached to what resembled large glass coffins. The chains eventually came to an end where they dangled freely. Ben didn't fancy staying too long in this area.

Rafe caught sight of what he could only describe as a primitive screen, buttons and glass tubes on shelves surrounding it. The energy powering the unit throbbed through this space, producing a low hum which caused the small glass tubes to vibrate like chattering teeth. A few flickers of a horizontal white light on the screen looked as though it was getting ready to burst into life, it never did. Meela wondered over to a set of glass tanks.

Ben disappeared into a section filled with metal shelving, stacked with boxes. He began exploring anything that was open. He popped his head out of one of the rows and whistled. Rafe jogged over to him, Ben looked like the cat that got the cream, he happily flung Rafe's rucksack to him.

Rafe was elated and wasted no time in grabbing his tuber and concealed it under his tunic, glad that Meela was preoccupied with the floating red and green liquid in the large tanks that looked like enormous larva lamps. He handed the rucksack back to Ben. Ben looked perplexed and pushed it back to Rafe. Rafe shook his head, pushed it back, Ben's eyes widened as he mouthed *why?*

Rafe eventually gave in and whispered, "Whoever brought them here may look for them."

"They were on a pile of rubbish!" Ben shot back, determined to keep his bag, paused, then dropped Rafe's bag and opened his rucksack, snatched the tuber out including four coins. On seeing Rafe's raised eyebrow, Ben whispered, "Alamo gave me these coins - they're called Zuz," with a smile he continued, "just in case I get hungry." He grabbed Rafe's bag and ran off to throw them back where he had found them, his footsteps reverberating as he went.

Rafe made his way back to Meela who was studying the flow of green and red glistening liquid in two 1000 litre glass tanks, moonlight gave them a hazy glow as the gel liquids floated slowly up and down in blobs and spirals. Meela leant forward on the ledge where the tanks were stationed, her nose almost touching the glass. Rafe wondered if she was being hypnotised.

A loud grinding sound broke through the fragile stillness. The floor burst into brightness; lights beamed in their direction. Ben appeared, red-faced and out of breath. "Go, go, go!"

Rafe knew better than to start asking questions, the fear on Ben's face was enough for Rafe to know trouble had arrived. They ducked between the crates. Meela led them swiftly along the shady side of the steps to the next level. But those who had entered the area had outwitted them; they were already ahead of them. A door opened from the top level, shooting an unwelcomed yellow glow into the shadowy space.

Meela halted abruptly at the top of the stairs, her hands at her side, firmly whispered, "You know nothing."

They responded to what she had told them earlier. Ben closed his eyes and swayed, this helped him to get his breath back, but he hoped he seemed confused. Rafe stared upwards and looked from side to side, yawning repeatedly.

"Well now, my visitors are far away from their comfortable residence." Elleba emerged, dressed in elegant dark clothing, her boots gleaming as though they had just been polished, two guards flanking her. Rafe was disgusted to see what he could only describe as a wheelot with thin metal arms that crackled as they spun, bulbous legs, oozing an orange fluid. The squelching sound made him feel queasy, so he concentrated on appearing dazed. Three guards ran up behind them swords drawn, they shoved them up the stairs towards the Languin.

"Rafe, Ben. How are you?" Elleba said, her voice was searching, but considerably crafty. She took out a time piece from a concealed pocket angled it to catch the light, then replaced it. They didn't look at her, Ben gave a lazy smile, Rafe produced a weak smile and lowered his eyelids as though he wanted to sleep, glanced at Meela who waited patiently.

Elleba gave Meela a hard malicious stare. "Meela, why have you bought them back here?"

"Sorry your Royal Highest Elleba." Meela took hold of Ben's arm. "Let's go." Ben tugged at his tunic to hide his tuber.

"And so, you should be…you're trespassing."

Meela bowed, stood behind Rafe, and pulled Ben beside her. "I'm so sorry I forgot."

"I'm… I'm…." Rafe stammered, hoping he was acting vague and confused enough to be convincing.

Elleba moved gracefully towards him, gently cupped his face with both hands and stared. Rafe lowered his eyes, her stare was quite powerful, intimidating.

"Such a good structure." She tossed these words to the guards beside her. Then she spoke to Rafe, her tone relaxed. "Don't worry. You'll be reunited with your friends, R37 will complete my plans, a simple switch and it will all work out perfectly." She grabbed Ben's chin, tilted it towards her and studied his eyes. He clamped his eyes shut; she tried to prise them open with her long nails, so he slumped to the ground. Unfortunately, he landed on her boots, his stomach now sore, he didn't fancy being kicked by her, so he remained still. The Languin gently pulled her feet away, adjusted her flowing hem and directed her response to Meela.

Her voice was low and firm. "You see Missy! Look what you've done! You have confused the candidates. This will make it harder for them to recover. I need them to survive. Evelyn was right about them. Very strong." With a fleeting look she said, "They can be used to help us, and if you don't do as you're told," she stepped in front of Meela, her tone now light but condescending, "You may be done away with as your imprint is doing a wonderful job," she laughed, coarsely and snapped back to her firm tone, "You must return to your quarters. You will all be safe there, for the time being."

Ben slowly got to his feet making it look more difficult than he was finding it. Rafe and Ben waited for Meela to lead the way.

"Not that way down." Elleba shooed them away, her elegant fingers flicked for dramatic effect. Meela took them both by the arm and steered them in the direction Elleba had demanded, back down the stairs to the ground floor exit.

"Get them back safely or it will be worse for you. After all, you want your wedding to take place for the benefit it will bestow on your family."

The female guard taunted, "Put the key back, Missy Meela!"

Elleba watched them leave, her posture one of victory. The three guards followed with Elleba's wheelots, which flipped and jumped around them. Rafe resisted the urge to kick them out of the way.

Ben glimpsed down the aisle where the rucksacks were; they were still there. They passed through the door at the end of the room. Laughter met them as they entered the corridor. Opposite, a guard room door was open, the guards ignored them and continued their breaktime relief. This seemed to make the guiding guards more aggressive as they unnecessarily pushed and shoved the trio down the myriad of corridors until they arrived at the installation room, where they were promptly deposited, the door slammed and locked to secure their miserable fate.

Chapter 25

Gakinde Homestead

Tia awoke to shuffling noises. Their underground location made It difficult for her to work out the time of day. She pulled herself out of her sleeping bag and slipped her trainers on without tying her laces. A dim lantern light framed the archway where a person stood silently watching. When Tia got up and turned around, she was surprised to see a teenaged girl.

"So, this is the big secret," the girl said without smiling.

Tia composed herself. The girl looked about fourteen; two long braids with gold coloured thread binding the end of each braid. Tia hoped she was friendly. "Hello. I'm Tia."

"Zee." This time she smiled. She wore a ruby top and leggings with a sash and an ossula hanging from her waist, like T-so.

"T-sodon is my brother."

"Lucky you." Tia hoped she wouldn't take offence. "He said he was called T-so."

Zee laughed. "I knew he was up to something. Coming in late, dashing out early without doing his chores. But this morning he's out because he had no choice, my uncle made sure of that."

"Good," Lisa said and stretched. "I'm Lisa."

Zee smiled and said, "Did you sleep well?"

"Yes," Tia and Lisa said in unison, they swapped glances and giggled.

"That's surprising, we rarely use this area, because of the smell from the animal enclosure above."

"Hadn't noticed, slept like a log," Tia smiled.

"You're lucky the enclosures are not wet, or the chukkans either, it's awful when they're wet." Zee looked as though she had just swallowed something bitter, she fanned under her nose.

"I'd have still slept through," Lisa beamed. "My ankle's feels much better."

"Where's your bedding?"

"Here," Tia said, folding her sleeping bag.

"He didn't provide you with any?" Zee said, shaking her head.

Lisa began to put on her trainers. "He did the last time. I think he got fed up with us…"

"The last time? So, you've been here before?"

Tia and Lisa glanced nervously at each other.

"You won't be in trouble," Zee said, kindly.

"We're in enough trouble," Lisa said and began folding up her sleeping bag. Tia scowled at her.

"Why are you in trouble?"

Lisa said nothing. Tia placed her sleeping bag in her rucksack. An uncomfortable silence remained between them until Zee spoke, "You might as well get something to eat before it all goes. T-sodon should have at least made sure of that. We always treat visitors well; he's made us look bad." She gave a disappointed sigh then said with an uplifted tone, "Where have you come from?"

Tia hurriedly replied, "Sanguel."

"It's lovely there, especially with Evelyn gone."

"If it's not too much trouble, I'd love breakfast," Lisa said, glad that Zee disliked Evelyn too.

"Lisa is always really hungry." Tia gave a light-hearted laugh. Lisa looked slightly embarrassed but didn't say anything because she knew this to be true.

"Well at least you can have a meal before you go."

*

They sat on colourful floor mats with low mounds of red clay, tables spread around the circular communal space. There were a few people left in the room. Light filtered through from funnel openings in the ceiling, wall tapestry adorned the space, as it did in the corridors. Inbuilt clay ovens kept them warm as the workers delivered a hearty breakfast of eggs and sliced meats that they couldn't identify but it was delicious. They finished off with fresh juice, bread, and a wooden dish of sweet sticky berries.

"We are known as the Gakinde people because we live under ground and love the deep valleys and hills that provide us with all we need, I bet T-sodon didn't tell you that." Zee didn't wait for an answer. "We only go to town to sell our goods. Everyone, from the oldest to the youngest, has tasks to complement our living, health, and education."

"Sorry to interrupt…, but could you take us to the edge of Sanguel?" Tia asked. "You see, T-so was supposed -"

"Say no more, I'll do it, but it has to be after I finish my tasks."

"We'll help," Tia said. Lisa looked alarmed. Tia laughed. "I'll help. It'll make it quicker."

Lisa was relieved when Zee told her she could help hang the new cloth that had been woven the previous day. Tia would help with feeding the animals.

Tia and Lisa left their belongings where they had slept except their tubers, which were secured out of sight, and followed Zee along a corridor and up a series of stone steps.

Zee opened a metal trap door revealing a clear blue sky, not a cloud in sight. Passers-by greeted them as they went about their daily chores. The girls realised that this open space was like a vast front garden for the Gakinde people. They could see the chukkans grazing on the surrounding hillside. At the base of the hills were various enclosures which ran around the open space, encircling the homestead and extending just inside the woods.

"I've already dealt with the chickens, now I need to get the iggogos out and feed them. I'm a little late, so the quicker we do this the better, as they'll be getting restless." Zee didn't wait to answer any questions. Tia and Lisa had to follow her swift charge up a short incline between clusters of huge grey rocks, hiding a crevice with a metal grate across the entrance. Zee unlocked the grate and vanished through the gap. Outside light filtered into the chambers. Tia and Lisa made out three chambers and heard Zee gently talking in one. Light seeped between cracks and crevices. An unusual smell hit them as they neared the central space between the chambers, it wasn't unpleasant, but it wasn't pleasant either, tolerable at best. They stepped on trodden long reeds. Lisa looked down to make sure she wasn't stepping in animal pooh.

"Try not to look down, I don't want you to bump into anything." Zee unhooked two ropes from the wall, she was surrounded by long-necked furry animals called iggogos.

"We're trying to avoid stepping in anything unpleasant," Tia said.

Zee laughed, "That's normally over the grainy end, just behind Lisa."

Lisa jumped forward.

Zee placed the ropes around the long necks of two of the larger animals. "I'll lead them to the exit. Give them a push on their rumps to make sure the others go in the right direction. Normally I'd have to come down a couple of times to get the errant ones out. They'll go to the grazing field by themselves, but there are a few troublesome warriors, as I like to call them. They won't hurt you."

Lisa and Tia waited until Zee passed. "Up we go," Zee said, cheerily, moving and whistled a little tune. The iggogos trotted obediently beside her, the others followed in a disorderly fashion. A few lagged behind, so Tia and Lisa tentatively, at first, tapped their rumps for them to move up the slope instead of turning back into their sleeping quarters. As they got into the swing of things, they pushed the little troublesome ones to the slope. Both Lisa and Tia narrowly missed falling flat on their faces dealing with the real rascals of the pack. Zee led them all out into the open, across the main area where people were coming and going. They finally herded them to the bushy feeding area where the girls were able to admire their long thick necks, their faces, which reminded them of camels, with large ears and long wiry tufts of fur under their chins. The iggogos had sturdy bodies and gangly, but strong, legs. The tallest stood six feet tall, their fleece grey and orange, thick and soft. They were friendly animals, although, at times, troublesome.

"We use their fleece for our warm clothing," Zee said, as they leant against the fence watching the animals drink greedily at the hollowed-out tree trunks, where their drinking water was kept. Special treats of brambles and berries would be spread in a circular-fenced area for them to graze throughout the day. The iggogos' fleece glimmered in the morning light.

"Let's get their treat for the day," Zee said.

"Can I hang the woven cloth?" This was more of a plea from Lisa than a question.

"Come this way," Zee said and called a little boy over, "This is Lisa, take her to Aunt Oti or nana Bilal." Then to Lisa she said, "They will show you what to do, just let them know Zee sent you. Come on Tia."

Tia looked back to see the little boy grab hold of Lisa's hand and run off towards a circle of trees where a group of young people were wringing out lengths of coloured cloth between them.

"What's that?" Tia asked, amused by a flock of green and white feathered birds, their glossy plumage gave them a sleek appearance. Some were using their red bills to dig away at the soil, while others stood motionless.

"They look frozen because they're showing off. Whatever you do, don't get pecked by that beak, it hurts so much. They're called dippers."

"Dippers?" Tia remembered the big dipper at an amusement park.

Zee explained, "They use their beak to disrupt the soil to find food. They don't really belong up here, they are marshland birds, they can dip so far into the ground it's interesting what they dig up, and their eggs are delicious."

*

Once all the chores were completed and a small snack enjoyed, Zee led Tia and Lisa out of the Gakinde homestead, the open red land behind them. As they were about to enter the woods, T-so leapt out of the trees with a big grin.

"Where have you been?" Zee yelled.

"None of your business, but I do have a surprise for Tia and Lisa." T-so immediately turned away from them and shouted between cupped hands towards the woods. "Come on out!" He watched the girls' reaction as R37 and B33 jumped out from behind the trees. Lisa and Tia were excited, they sped towards them.

"Ray." Tia leapt at R37 almost knocking him over. "So glad you've come."

R37's response was quite restrained. He smiled but did not meet Tia with the same enthusiasm. B33 and Lisa's exchange was a similar affair. Lisa ran to Ben and gave him a friendly punch on the arm. "Sooo. You made it."

"So I did." He punched her back, rather hard.

"No need for that." Lisa rubbed her arm.

B33 looked on.

"This is Rafe and Ben, Tia's cousin and Lisa's brother." T-so was pleased with himself.

"Nice to meet you." Zee smiled uncomfortably and whispered to T-so. "They don't seem very happy to see them."

T-so batted her off. "Course they are."

"T-sodon, Uncle is going to give you more chores if he finds out you ran off again!"

T-so shrugged, “Don’t call me that!” He shuffled over to the siblings.

The woods behind them started to murmur. Zee stared and shuddered as the trees began to slowly wobble. Faint shafts of luminous reds hues moved through the woods, the colours deepened and hung in the air as though a giant had belched out a putrid gas that slowly engulfed anything it came into contact with. Green foliage was quickly turning into red foliage.

“I don’t want to break up the reunion, but we need to get back,” Zee stated. “We need to get back NOW.” She started running back to the homestead.

T-so glanced over his shoulder, he ran screaming, “ZANTACCA! ZANTACCA!” The others didn’t like the sound of the word or the fear in their friend’s voices, they charged after them, hoping whatever it was wouldn’t catch them.

Chapter 26

Imprints

The breakfast remnants were cleared away by two guards who wheeled the food trolley into the corridor. The accompanying wheelot left via the glass door. They could see its shadow as it patrolled the sunny area.

Rafe knew that he and Ben had exhausted Meela last night with all the questions about the rejuvenation facility and the two curious gold triangular objects which Elleba wore on her waist. The information Meela imparted preyed on their minds; they were still in a state of shock knowing that Elleba had misused the kingdom's capability to mutate creatures in her quest to clone individuals.

"I get an awful feeling that R37 has something to do with me." Rafe looked at Meela for an answer. He couldn't relax until his suspicions were confirmed.

Meela slowly nodded and looked as though she were searching for the right words. Ben had wandered over to the table, rubbed his stomach, and got a drink of water, he sat back watching Rafe and Meela.

After a minute of Rafe's agonising wait, Meela said, "R37 is you." She turned to Ben. "And B33 is you, Ben."

*

Ben found himself whispering, “Meela can you explain it again…, imprints?”

Meela stretched then sat on the bench next to Rafe, opposite Ben. She reached out over the table, gently taking hold of Ben’s hands to reassure him.

“When I first arrived here, I had no idea. Just like you.” She looked at Rafe, his attention focussed, taking in every word. “It takes a while to remember everything. It comes in flashes. I had to keep reminding myself…I am Meela. There is another Meela. Meela number two, I mean M555i, lives in the palace. She is doing everything Elleba wants me to do, but I won’t. She expects everyone to do as she says. Obey no matter what the cost.”

“Say that again,” Ben said.

“Obey no matter ...”

“No, about another me - you.”

“Meela two is what I call her. She lives in the castle, carries out my duties…they call her M555i out of ear shot.”

“So, you’re saying...” Rafe was measured, not wanting to really hear the answer again. “There is another me? R37?”

Meela nodded slowly.

"No wonder there was injection central in that facility."

"And me? Another Ben?" Ben pointed at himself, "B33."

"Yes. Dressed like you."

Rafe sighed in grief. "How?"

"Duplication imprint," Meela said.

Rafe got up. Ben watched as Rafe paced the room. Ben didn't have the energy, even after a large breakfast.

"How can she do that?" Rafe's frustration was building. "Why would she?"

"Because she can," Meela said.

"No wonder my arm was sore. They took our DNA!"

Ben sighed and slouched, removing his hands from Meela's soothing grasp.

"My imprint is out there playing me. Like yours will be playing you." Ben half laughed and moaned.

Rafe didn't like this one bit. "Fakes! Total fakes!

"Remember, they don't always get things right and she'll need you at some point, because they can't last."

Rafe stopped pacing. "How long do they last?"

"What do they get wrong?" Ben asked.

Meela looked at one, then the other, her head moving like a ping pong ball. Rafe nodded in Ben's direction, prompting Meela to answer Ben's questions first, as Rafe paced around the table, pondering the situation.

"Ok. Because the imprints are not perfect, a lot can go wrong, and they have to bring them back for an upgrade. There is no time limit, it all depends on the program. There is always a weakness. I'm called back into the rejuvenation room when they need to reset the imprint." Her tone became more intense. "They use that green liquid as a type of cleanser and the other liquid does other things, I'm not sure what. Be clear on this, they can fool anyone!"

Ben was bewildered.

Rafe said, "We are out there." He shivered. "There's an imprint out there." He pointed to the large pane of glass, "pretending to be me!"

Chapter 27

Zantacca

They hurried back to the homestead followed by a billowing dust cloud, sluggish but purposeful. A terrifying howl ran through the trees freeing itself in the open plains with a tepid breeze. The villagers heard Zantacca's harrowing cry. They rushed about, scooped up children, equipment, and livestock to shelter from the putrid smell already reaching their nostrils. Many wrapped their head and face with lengths of fabric, dashed to the hillside to make safe the chukkans and protect as much of their crops as possible.

Zee and R37 were the first to get to the homestead, followed by Tia and B33. Lisa did her best to keep up, T-so at her side. Zee grabbed a hand full of fabric and quickly handed them out.

"Wrap it around like this." Zee wrapped her head and face, overlapping the fabric to leave a gap for her eyes. T-so and Zee helped the others to get it right.

"The iggogos need to be safe," Zee gasped, T-so started herding them out of their enclosure. The others helped as best they could; they found it difficult to stay on their feet as the soil began to lap like waves, taking with it the debris and anything that could be easily sucked in the direction of Zantacca. Zee led the iggogos to the safety of their cave and remained around the entrance shoving any stray iggogo in.

T-so darted after the dippers, flapping his arms, they ran around in a blind panic, their thin necks wobbling out of control. They were unable to fly but flapped their wings with elegant strides, only getting a few inches off the ground. The others watched as Zee pushed T-so a couple of times to attend to these creatures. He swiftly removed his ossula and lassoed the dippers together, saving them from being thrown into bushes or being sucked into Zantacca.

Once the iggogos were safely inside the cave, Zee also released her ossula and lassoed as many of the dippers as possible. The others helped to pull them into the cave; although these strange creatures wanted to be saved, they loved the air ruffling through their feathers. When they were untethered, they tried to escape. R37 and B33 calmly kept them in line by standing at the mouth of the cave to prevent them from escaping.

Tia and Lisa were horrified to see the red sludge-like mist, heading their way, a strong, sewage-like stench swirled in the air. Anything that was not safely secured was being sucked towards this ever-growing fog. Zee and T-so eventually gave up on saving any more creatures; the wind was gaining pace and the stench was too strong to remain outside. Zee and T-so blocked the iggogos' cave entrance with several metal grids set against the entrance wall. A final sheet of heavy tapestry was released by a rope above their heads. It rolled over the grids and was held down at either side by metal bolts. Zantacca roared through the homestead, smothering any light source emitted through crevices and light wells.

"You idiot! You should have dealt with the dippers. Many will be lost because you didn't tend to them this morning."

"I did." T-so lied.

"No, you didn't." Zee unwrapped her face cloth, allowing it to drop around her shoulders. "They wouldn't have been caught out like that. Uncle Asa will stop you from looking after his livestock you foolish boy. Now we have to stay here instead of being safe with the rest of our folks in the higher caves."

The others felt embarrassed for T-so, but Lisa shuffled over to Tia nudged her and whispered, "He's always up to something."

The stomps and squeals of the animals, even the rapid winds outside of the cave could not dull the telling off that T-so received from his sister. Zee turned to the others as T-so took a lamp with him, he shuffled away without unveiling its light, to herd the dippers into another section of the cave before they got trampled by the iggogos.

Zee opened the tiny shutters on the lamps that hung in the entrance of the cave, revealing a gold and green orb, emitting enough light for them to see clearly, “You can lower your face guards. You’ll need them when we leave.”

Tia noticed that the boys hadn’t made any attempt to remove their face guards, they were watching the animals. Zee roped the remaining stray iggogos together and led them into their part of the chamber with the rest of the herd. They clustered together and started to settle down.

“What’s that thing out there?” Tia asked, they could hear the wind rattling the metal grids.

T-so re-entered the space and spoke up boldly. “It’s a violent storm that takes what it wants.”

“Can you feel it?” Lisa quizzed.

“Of course you can. It will strip the flesh from your bones.” T-so seemed to take great pleasure in recounting a story of someone who was sucked into Zantacca and was found barely alive. Lisa felt scared and didn’t want to hear any more of his ghoulish stories.

Something large slammed into the grids, the sound exploded throughout the chambers. The iggogos grunted and shunted backwards and forwards. Another bang, and another and another. They held their ears and prayed for it to stop.

Chapter 28

Double Trouble

"This means that Tia and Lisa may have been here. They may have imprints too." Rafe was baffled. "How are we going to tell who's who?"

Rafe and Ben had been sat around the table in the communal area for the past few hours, talking about what they had witnessed in the palace, who was making the imprints, and why.

"It's kind of cool that there's another me out there," Ben beamed. "Can't wait to meet him. We could get up to all sorts of tricks, like being a twin. I wonder if he'll fool Lisa, the jokes I could play on her -"

Rafe held his hand up for Ben to stop. "I think you're missing the point."

Ben was still dreaming of the pranks he could play. "It's hilarious Rafe. Me - You. You - me." Ben laughed as he continually pointed to himself then Rafe with both hands like a swapping game.

Rafe nervously tapped the table then stood and flexed his arms and legs. "It's not funny. Those clowns, imprints… whatever they call themselves could be up to no good."

"Or they could be funny."

"Or idiots, getting us in to trouble."

"But we're here."

Rafe slowly nodded and began to pace around the table. "Yes…. and they could be creating havoc."

Ben's countenance changed with the realisation that the imprints could be dangerous. "Here's hoping my fun thoughts are true and perhaps…"

"Don't say it. I've a bad feeling about this, and you know from previous experiences we shouldn't take anything for granted…. What if they hurt Lisa or Tia?"

"They'd better not. I'll -"

"We can't do anything in here. We need to get out."

Meela entered the room.

"Do you know how we can get out of here?" Ben asked.

"I thought you'd never ask." Her smile was one of relief.

Rafe raised an eyebrow, pulled up a stool and said, "Seriously, how can we get out of here?"

"They keep me here because they need me. I'm to marry K-dee, the Lanquint, when he returns from the royal family's peace keeping voyage. Since Evelyn's capture, negotiations between kingdoms have been unsettled. Elleba is K-dee's grand-mother. Although she holds the Lanquin title like her daughter…, she doesn't have the same powers or authority.

Therefore, she needs a puppet to control." Meela sighed, "They are similar in look, but Ziba is kind. Elleba perceives her daughter as being too weak and her son-in-law too strong. She hopes that once K-dee and I get married, he'll be given the region of the land where the Musca resides, she is obsessed -."

"But what's that got to do with you?" Ben asked.

At first Meela wasn't sure how to explain it, then said, "I'm to help her."

Ben still couldn't understand it. "Why not use her daughter?"

Rafe said, "You mentioned earlier that Ziba hasn't been well and doesn't listen to Elleba - and the Lanquis makes sure his wife has a lot of help with special people around her."

"Yes, I think you may have found a reason, she can't get close to Ziba like she used to." Meela pondered.

Rafe continued, "Elleba wouldn't imprint her own daughter, just in case something went wrong with her daughter during the procedure. This would leave the Lanquis open to marry someone else and Elleba would be..."

"Kicked out!" Ben cheered.

Rafe grinned at Ben's stance, pretending to kick a football into the air then said, "She's a complicated woman, hungry for control."

"I think you're right. When I was presented to the inner court, there were many suitors for K-dee, we had to go through a strict system of understanding what the kingdom rules were. During this time, the Lanquin became very ill after losing a child and Elleba had to step in to conduct our training. By the time I got to know K-dee, I found him to be a loyal, good person, and although I thought I wouldn't… I did fall in love with him." Meela turned her face away from them, feeling a little embarrassed. "Elleba's husband was exiled not long afterwards, when his dealings with Evelyn came to light."

"All this time we were fighting Evelyn's forces," Ben said, with a victorious tone.

Rafe nodded in agreement.

"I was told by Ziba that I was the chosen one, and that Elleba would help me with all the necessary arrangements and understanding of my role in the palace, which she did. At first, she was pleasant, but gradually I found that she disagreed with whatever I did. It didn't matter what it was, and she wouldn't allow me to speak to Ziba. She was the only one that reported to the heads of the court about my progress."

"Why didn't you tell someone?" Rafe asked.

"Or escape from the palace," Ben said, "I would have busted out and -"

Rafe wasn't impressed with Ben's comments, seeing Meela cringe at his suggestion, he hoped Ben would just listen.

Meela clasped her hands and rubbed them together. "It's not so easy. If you are given a title or position, you must operate in that position. Not everyone is willing to listen or believe you because they want to safeguard their own position. As long as they are not in harm's way, they're happy."

Rafe said, "You were going to explain why you think they still want you around."

Meela thought for a moment. "If anything goes wrong with the imprint, they call on me. It's happened a few times."

Ben was aghast. "What?"

Rafe said, "A default?"

"Yes. My right hand…, I mean M555i's right hand kept twitching and rising at inappropriate times." Meela released a little laugh. "And its head kept flopping to the left and then to the right, it kept saying 'trees' to every question. I couldn't imagine what the court thought of those blips. I know it was frightening for Elleba, she was so distraught."

"So, what happened?" Ben asked

"I went back to the palace while they did repairs."

"Why didn't you escape?" Ben asked.

"I tried, but they caught me." Meela's tone took on a nervous edge. "I tried again, but… well, I didn't know they had given me a click."

"Click?" Rafe and Ben both quizzed.

"I received an electric pulse if I did anything out of the ordinary."

The boys were aghast. They glanced at each other, open-mouthed, both wondering if Meela was losing her mind.

"In my arm at first, then my head. It was horrible."

"An electric shock!" Ben cringed.

"Barbaric," Rafe said.

Meela sighed.

"Is the click a thing or just a pulse, I mean only a pulse, you know what I mean," Rafe said, trying not to sound glib.

"Where is it?" Ben asked.

"I don't know where they put it, but I heard one of the workers in the facility say she puts something in the liquid. I can't remember what it's called, but it's really tiny and settles in your body - it hurts. It starts like this." Meela snapped her fingers three times. "No one else can hear it. It sent me into shivers, and it hurts, terribly."

"That's torture!" Ben yelled, "I hope I haven't got one of them!"

Rafe said, "In other words they give you an electric shock to stop you from talking?"

Meela nodded.

Ben shuddered.

"How do they do it? How often? How do they know you are talking?" Rafe asked

Before Meela could explain, the door was thrust open. "Her Royal Highest Languin invites you to meet her."

Meela didn't reply or show any disrespect; she strolled out obediently with the guard.

Chapter 29

Barriers

The atmosphere in the chambers was fractious as Zantacca intermittently clattered the metal grids with force. The animals responded with snorts and squeals. Tia felt anxious and played with her flower bracelet to summon some calm. Lisa wasn't faring any better. A loud bang accompanied Lisa's involuntary cry. "WHEN WILL THIS STOP?!"

"It won't break in," T-so said, seeing the horror on the faces of Tia and Lisa. "The wooden barriers had no chance and many of our animals were killed and hurt."

Zee interrupted, "Wooden barriers were what we had before. We were lucky to get away with our lives until Uncle Asa and council leader Vik built the barriers we have now."

"Alright Zee, I know." T-so's tone had a disrespectful edge.

Tia whispered to Lisa, "It's taking him too long to apologise. Zee looks as though she could take him out."

Zee said, "Make yourself useful and feed the animals before they get too restless. I'll sort out our guests." T-so quickly did as he was told. Zee addressed the others, "Anybody hungry?"

"Yes," Lisa said.

R37 and B33 were sat in the furthest part of the small third chamber watching the dippers huddled on the other side. They said nothing. Zee went over to them and had a conversation. Tia and Lisa observed their exchange.

Tia's voice was sad. "Ray isn't speaking to me. I think he's far more upset than I had expected."

Lisa put her arm around Tia's shoulders. "Not to worry, he won't stay mad for long. Ben's been quiet too, which is good for me. Perhaps we should tell them what's happened so far. Perhaps they can help us find the Musca."

Tia wasn't so sure; she didn't like falling out with her cousin. He always defended her and took care of her since her mother had died, so this silence made her feel very uncomfortable. When Zee left the chamber Lisa sat next to R37, while Tia leant against the warm earth wall, next to Lisa.

Lisa smiled hoping to start off on a good footing. "You guys took your time getting here."

"What do you mean?" B33 asked, in a serious manner.

"Nothing just thought you'd have got here sooner, that's all." There was a short prickly silence before Lisa started again, her tone much lighter. "Did you go to Sanguel?"

"Why?" R37 asked.

"Because…" Lisa was finding this more difficult than she had thought. "Ermm, Tia has something to say." She looked up at Tia, who didn't want to say anything having witnessed the reception that Lisa was getting. Lisa's quirky eye movements and mouthing 'apologize' indicated that Lisa thought an apology would break the ice.

"Sorry Ray. Sorry Ben for not saying anything." They both looked up at her with little concern. Tia looked away, but continued, "We seem to be in more trouble than I had expected." She shrugged and played with her bracelet again.

Lisa said, "Now that we're all friends again, could you help us find a Musca?"

"That's what we're here for," R37 said. Lisa was relieved and gave R37 an awkward side hug; she didn't notice he didn't hug her back. "Thank you so much." She lowered her voice. "That T-so was supposed to help us but I'm not sure he'll be any good. Zee may be more useful."

"As soon as we leave here, we can start looking," B33 said.

"You want to be the first one to spot it. I'll beat you to it," Lisa laughed, surprised that B33 didn't have a witty comeback. Before she could respond, Zee returned with a wooden tray laid out with a bowl of dried leaves and wooden cups.

"What do we do with this?" Lisa asked as she picked up a leaf and found that although it looked dry, it was a little spongy when she squeezed it between her fingers.

"Chew it, it adds sweetness to the water, it will keep your energy up," Zee said confidently.

Tia took a leaf too, but the boys only took the water, gulped it down in seconds and handed the cups back to Zee. Tia couldn't work out whether B33 was copying R37 or R37 was copying B33. Lisa found their actions highly amusing and teased them about it. R37 said very little, which was what they expected, but when B33 didn't react in his normally argumentative fashion, Lisa got fired up.

"Nothing to say for yourself Ben?" Lisa laughed.

B33 gawped at Lisa and gave a weak smile of amusement. "You need your rest."

"That's fighting talk. I don't need any rest. I'll spot the Musca before you do," Lisa said.

B33 and R37 exchanged knowing glances. R37 closed his eyes, his voice deepened. "You WILL find the Musca."

Chapter 30

Evolving Discoveries

Ben didn't wait for the footsteps to fade before he said, "They'll torture us!"

"Lower your voice," Rafe hushed as he watched the shadows of the guard and Meela fade.

Ben whispered, "We need to get out of here, fast!"

"Of course. But we need to find out what the click thing is and get our rucksacks or all will be futile."

"What?"

"All our efforts will be wasted."

They both thought for a moment. Ben in sheer panic and Rafe in escape and battle mode.

"What if they placed something on us or in us to provide the shock?" Rafe said.

"The click, click."

Rafe continued. "Yes. Like a little bug, button…. something under our skin."

"You mean like an undetectable spy thing?... A microchip thingy?" Ben said

"Now you're thinking."

Without prompting they both started looking at their hands, legs, feeling through their hair and face for any lumps or bumps.

"Check my back." Ben began to yank his top off. "Avoid my crack."

"Too much information." Rafe raised his eyebrow. "Don't take it off, just lift it up. If they come back, we don't want to alert them to anything."

Ben pulled up his top as far up as possible, turned his back so Rafe could examine it.

"You've got a lot of scars."

Ben's response was muffled but enough to be understood. "Yeah. Accidents from camping, you name it I've done it and lived to tell the tale. I call them battle scars." Ben was quite pleased with them, pulled his top down. "Remember when we woke up, I complained about my arm. You too?"

Rafe quickly rolled his right sleeve as far as it could go and found nothing. But as he moved his right hand along his left shoulder, he felt something he'd never felt before. A small oblong shape. "I can't see it, but I can feel it."

Ben could see what Rafe was concerned about.

"It's like an oblong pimple. Just under the skin. I thought Meela said it was something in the fluid."

Ben had a similar shaped pimple, glowing red under his skin, and Rafe had a darkened area where the oblong shape appeared.

“I wonder if we can get it out. We’re fortunate it’s not like that nano technology thing my science teacher keeps banging on about. Controlling us by injecting us with chips you can’t even see with the naked eye.”

Rafe chuckled, “Steady Mr Hyde. Let’s focus on getting these things out.”

“Wait till lights out and use the tuber to remove it, like burn it out,” Ben said.

“Could be painful.”

“I’m not sure if anything else would be any better. Like a knife, or…Let’s leave it at the tuber. It may be kinder to our skin.”

“Says the one with battle scars,” Rafe laughed although he too was concerned about the damage it may cause. “That would be a great Ad.”

Ben saw the funny side of it too and deepened the tone of his voice, “Use Tuber, it’s gentle on the skin and removes all blemishes… scars - leaves skin looking radiant and soft.”

“Remember how we got out of the explosion site in Sanguel?” Rafe asked.

“Yeah.”

“We could do a similar thing.”

Rafe and Ben’s hopes were high. “Use the tubers to burn our way through the rock, like we did in Sanguel.” Ben’s excitement showed promise.

“It’s like Shawshank Redemption.”

“What’s that?”

“A film starring Morgan Freeman.” Rafe didn’t want to explain the film. “It’s about a.... jail break, a concealed means of escape. Anyway, I’m not sure if your parents would want you to watch it, you’re too young.” Rafe scanned the room then ran into his bedroom with Ben close behind. “Like...” He pulled the bed away from the wall, “We could dig our way out and use the bed to hide our escape route. We can see the guards hovering about outside the window, but they never check our rooms, so it would be an easy job.”

“Tidy. Tidy,” Ben grinned, “We could put together makeshift bodies in the bed. Anyone looking in may think we’re still asleep.”

“We can take it in turns to cut away the wall.”

Then Ben looked doubtful. “Where will we hide the rubble?”

They surveyed their limited space.

“The cupboard? The garden?” Rafe suggested.

“The toilet, under the bed?”

Rafe felt dismayed. "I'm not sure this plan will hold together."

"But we've got to try," Ben said.

*

Later that evening, after thinking through their plan, Rafe remembered the attachment Arabella had given them for the tuber.

"Ben, the tuber. Let's see what the attachment does."

"It may help to get us out of here. Arabella does have a way of giving us things without really giving away what they're used for."

They hurried into Ben's room just in case anyone entered the communal area, so they would have enough time to hide the tubers.

"Right," Ben said, as he connected the attachment to the bottom end of his tuber. It wasn't difficult as the metals seemed to gravitate together with a confident click. He held the extended tuber at arm's length, as though ready to strike something in battle mode. He swayed slowly from side to side - nothing happened. Rafe watched Ben but couldn't see any difference in the tuber.

“It’s a dud, just like the way our pendants had a mind of their own,” Ben moaned.

Rafe raised an eyebrow, “Let’s not go back to that sorry tale, ‘cos you did rip the book, which affected the way the pendant worked.”

Ben ignored the comment, turned away from Rafe and hit his bed with a hard smack that left a dark mark on the bed linen.

“Steady, you don’t want to damage anything.”

Ben grunted as he hit out at the bed linen, headboard, side table - nothing.

Rafe held his tuber in front of him, both hands at the top, it extended as usual, the attachment section pointing downwards, just above the floor. He gave it a gentle kick.

“Come on, do your thing!”

“It’s changing colour!” Ben gasped.

Rafe grinned with satisfaction as the tuber turned from grey to bronze. He gave the attachment section another swift kick, prompting the metal strip to flip out and expand into a black platform - 30cms wide by 60cms in length. Before they had time to marvel at this new addition the tuber rose steadily hauling Rafe with it.

“Jump on, jump on!” Ben cheered and began kicking his attachment.

Rafe managed to get one leg on the platform, the other leg trailing. The tuber flipped over, Rafe landed on his back, the tuber on the floor, retracting to its normal state.

"It's like a hover thingy," Ben said, as he kicked his tuber out of his hands, it flew over his head like a twirling baton and banged into the wall, a crumbling dent appeared.

Rafe started again, this time once the platform appeared, he gripped the tuber tightly so that it hovered just above the floor. He placed one foot on the metal plate, to see if it would take his weight. His other leg gave balance, enabling him to rise with the tuber. He glanced up to make sure he wasn't going to crash into the ceiling, but fortunately he had enough room.

"You're flying! You're flying!" Ben shouted as he watched Rafe try to balance on the metal plate and move along with the tuber, but he toppled off onto Ben's bed. The tuber fell to the ground and the metal plate flipped back into place.

"Did you see that? Did you see that, Ben, did you see that?" Rafe was wide-eyed with enthusiasm as he jumped off the bed and grabbed his tuber. Ben was so excited he hadn't noticed that he was holding his tuber upside down. When the attachment didn't open, he was disappointed. "Typical. It's not working."

"At least hold it by the handle," Rafe laughed. Still eager to try again, he held his tuber in front of him with both hands as though pulling a sword out of a stone. The plate flipped out against the ground and stayed there for a moment, which gave Rafe enough time to position both his feet on the plate, one in front of the other. The tuber lifted off the ground but didn't move forwards, simply hovered.

"This is brilliant. Who needs those pendants when this is available?" Ben said, "I just need it to stay still." Ben had fallen off the plate once it started to lift from the ground.

Rafe was busy trying to work out how high they could go. He moved the tuber towards him, as it twisted around, he fell off.

"I'm moving ...Yeah!" Ben laughed and yanked the tuber to the left and promptly fell off, just missing his bed.

They spent some time working out how to use the flight mode. They sat on the floor amazed and excited after exhausting themselves with their trial, error, and moments of success.

"The girls will love this," Rafe said.

"I can't wait to show it off," Ben gleamed.

"Ben, this will identify us..."

"What?"

"Those imprint things haven't got our tubers, an oversight on their part. So, the girls will know that we're not the imprints."

"They may think we've been absent minded and left our tubers at home." He stroked the tuber lovingly.

Rafe said, "I think Tia would know I wouldn't do that."

"I'm not so sure Lisa will though."

"About me?"

"No, me. She knows I'm always forgetting stuff. By-the-way, we didn't bring our pendants."

Rafe nodded deep in thought.

"More importantly we can escape, regardless of the click thing, ride away, easy-peasy."

Rafe said, "Why did Meela tell us about The Click?"

"Because she's on our side." Ben got up and secured the tuber to his belt.

"She said something about the fluid, and we found something in our arm - anyone who talks gets clicked… she didn't look like she was in pain."

"Made of stronger stuff than me." Ben raised his hands as if in surrender to that amount of pain.

Rafe got up and pondered the situation, "How do we know she's the real Meela?"

"She told us an awful lot. And Evan or Alamo will be able to identify her."

"The click thing could be a way of slowing us down. If we feel any discomfort, we should just take the pain and get rid of it." Rafe made his way to the communal area.

Ben hurried after him, "Aren't we going to wait until Meela comes back, she can show us the way out?"

"Or the way for us to be captured." Rafe moved swiftly to the door.

"We should go that way." Ben pointed to the glass exit.

"They went that way; so, we go this way."

"Those corridors are too complicated." Ben scratched his head.

"Not if you know your way back to the rejuvenation facility. Grab all our bags, cos the girls will need their attachments and their tops from Sam."

"Rafe when you get that look in your eyes I have to listen." Ben joined Rafe at the door. "But when you do that thing with your eyebrow, I feel like I've done something wrong."

Rafe chuckled. "You may have done something questionable, but you wouldn't be Ben without your quirks, like I have mine." Rafe studied the lock.

"Perhaps we should wait."

"Being quiet would be helpful."

"Soz."

Rafe placed his tuber gently against the lock.

Ben lowered his voice as Rafe pushed the door. "I wish I had my pendant, being invisible would be great now."

As they edged out of the room, they heard footsteps marching their way.

Chapter 31

All is Well

The warm, crowded environment had become a snug cocoon, and both humans and animals had been drawn into a lull of drowsiness against the backdrop of the devastation taking place outside. They were all fast asleep by the time Zantacca had subsided.

Tia was the last to stir. She remembered being nestled between Lisa and Zee. Zee had left, she glanced over her shoulder and Lisa had gone too. Tia sat up and looked over to where the boys had been sleeping, they were gone, and from the absence of noise in the chambers, the animals had gone too. Tia propped herself up against the wall, she felt comfortable as she gazed at her flower bracelet. Shards of light radiated once again through the crevices. She yawned and stretched; the sleep had been far more restful than the night before. Tia was relieved that Rafe was now around and that he could help sort out the mess they had found themselves in.

Lisa entered the chamber, “Hello, sleepy head.”

“Thanks Lisa. I had a lovely sleep.” Tia smiled, happily. “Where’s everyone?”

"We've been clearing up. I also know where Zee got the water from. It was so tasty with the leaves. Come with me."

Tia followed Lisa down a tunnel into the deeper workings of the hillside. "I can't believe you came down here alone with all these insects and roots sticking through the walls."

"I know." Lisa felt proud of herself because normally she would have wanted someone to be her guide and she wouldn't have wanted to get her clothes dirty. Lisa expertly navigated Tia down two short tunnels, her torch beam lighting the way.

"Here it is." Lisa spread her arms open as though she had created the well that they were now viewing. The well sat in an oddly shaped area; a semicircle of stone masonry created the above ground structure of the well, on the top was a wooden ledge fixed into either side of the red clay walls. Above their heads, a triangular pulley system with connecting gears and metal runners anchored two wooden buckets dangling from metal ropes. Two cranks fixed to the wall served to lift and lower the buckets in turn at an operator's activation.

Lisa rotated the first crank slowly, a half-filled bucket appeared. She took a jug from one of the many shelves laden with cups, jugs, wooden bowls and spoons. She served half a cup to Tia.

"Mmmm, and a refreshing smell too," Tia said, smacking her lips.

"I helped Zee to fill the jugs earlier and water the animals and ourselves. Over there," Lisa pointed to a narrow passageway across the room "That's where a sweet plant grows through the ceiling and all the insects feed off it, a little creepy but interesting."

"All this was going on and I was sleeping?" Tia was surprised. She was normally the one to be alerted by the faintest of sounds.

"We all agreed to let you sleep, although T-so wanted to wake you."

"I bet Ray told him to back off."

"No, he didn't. I did."

"Thanks Lisa."

On seeing Tia's disappointment, Lisa quickly said, "I think I beat him to it."

"It's ok. I appreciate that you stood up for me. Guess Ray's still not too happy with me."

"Everything's quite strange at the moment. He felt quite cold when I hugged him. Perhaps he's coming down with something..." Lisa tried to make light of it. "He'll be okay soon. I told them about finding the Musca, and they're still happy to help. Apparently, T-so is going to take us to find the place where we first, well, should have seen it."

"I thought he had enough to do."

"Zee gave him a good roasting," Lisa chuckled.

"Another one?"

"She ordered him to take the dippers to the marshlands, which he should have done a couple of days ago. He kept adjusting that lasso thingy and Zee told him he was too carefree and should be careful not to lose it, then he just ran off. I think he's getting help from some of the children. And… now he's supposed to help us. I think he's happier to go with us, more than he was letting on."

"Really?"

"Perhaps. I think it's his good deed for the day. Rafe and Ben are coming too, they know everything and…."

"Slow down."

"I'm too excited. It's all coming together," Lisa beamed, satisfied with the situation. "Come on, we're going to eat and get ready to go."

Tia gulped the last bit of water. She felt relieved that Lisa had explained their situation to the boys. She wasn't sure if they would have taken it so well coming from her. Lisa had an effective way of being able to convince Ben, although he could sometimes pretend to be uninterested. But to convince Rafe as well, Tia was impressed.

Chapter 32

Caution

Rafe and Ben's attempt to leave had been thwarted by the unexpected return of Meela with two guards. They had just enough time to scoot back inside the communal area and pretend that they were having a deep conversation around the table. This disturbing occurrence made them decide to leave in the morning.

So, that morning, Rafe and Ben feigned sleep for as long as they could. As expected, guards came regularly to check on them. They heard their heavy footsteps before they saw them. Rafe pretended to be having a bad dream and thrashed about. He glimpsed the guard's satisfying look on her face, as though happy he was in pain. Ben snored as hard as he could to get the guard out of his room. The guard covered his ears and elevated his voice, "Sounds like this one is having a real deep sleep. Elleba must have given them an extra sleeping potion."

"The other one seems to be struggling with it," The other guard said, her tone full of glee.

When they had gone, Rafe and Ben met in the communal area, then went to see Meela.

*

Meela opened her teary eyes, sat up when she saw them at the bars of her room. They couldn't enter as she was locked in.

"What did they do?" Ben asked.

"Questions after questions, after questions. I'm so tired." Her voice was shaky.

"Sorry to hear that," Rafe said, gently, "Meela, we must go. We couldn't tell you last night because you were so distressed."

Ben stared wide-eyed at Rafe, not letting Meela catch his gaze. But Rafe pushed on. "We realise that we have created a real problem for you. So, we're going back home."

"Sanguel?" She looked at them her eyes searching their faces for help.

"Yes," Ben said

Rafe added, "Far away from here as possible."

Meela rubbed her eyes and sat with her head low, hands listlessly in her lap.

"We need your help," Rafe said.

Meela nodded but didn't look at them.

"Where are the guards?"

"They have centres around the palace."

"Where should we go, escape...?" Ben asked.

Rafe added, "The best place to exit… leave."

"There's a key by the door, go to the rejuvenation room, through the gardens. The door at the end of the room on the lower-level leads to the underground exit." Meela ran to the bars. "Be careful."

"Thank you." Rafe touched her hand affirming his goodbye. "We'll tell your father to come and see you."

"We promise," Ben said.

They left Meela holding onto the bars, watching as they departed. Once they were back in the communal area Ben said, "I feel a bit cold-hearted."

"I know. But we can't drag her into this." Rafe pushed the point of his tuber against the lock, he looked over his shoulder at the frosted glass, then back at the lock, a yellow tint ran through the area of the metal door.

"Why are you opening this door, when the key for the glass lock is over there and…," Ben's sentence was interrupted by the shadow of a wheelot zipping past the frosted pane. The image reflected along the floor. Three more shadows followed. Rafe stopped, held his breath, and watched as the shadows faded.

Rafe whispered, "I think you have your answer." He gently opened the door, peeped out to view an empty corridor.

"She was sending us into a trap!" Ben gasped. "That's her imprint."

"All I know is, her hands were cold." Rafe stepped out into the corridor, waited for Ben to close the door with a soft snap.

Ben whispered. "I don't feel so bad if it's the fake one."

They edged along the wall, tuber in hand. Rafe had secretly rubbed marks along the walls with his tuber, but now that the light was so dim in the corridor, he couldn't see the markings. He paused for a moment as they approached an intersection of corridors. He remembered it was all left turns from that point. They shuffled along trying to make as little noise as possible; glancing up and down the corridors as they ventured forward. They heard laughter coming from the last corridor, light pouring out of the open door. Rafe could see the door for the rejuvenation room.

Another cacophony of laughter.

"Guard centre," Ben said, readying his tuber.

Rafe nodded.

They edged their way down the corridor, there was no way they could enter the rejuvenation facility without being seen.

A guard marched out of the room and went up the corridor without looking back. Ben took a quick look into the room. The guards were minding their own business, having a drink with their feet up. Ben signalled to Rafe that there were three guards inside. Rafe put his fist to his chest and counted to three by unfurling a finger at a time. On three, he and Ben sprang into the room and stunned the guards with their tubers - on their head, torso, and neck, sinking them to their knees. One of the guards had a set of keys attached to a rope on his belt. Rafe burned through the rope to release the keys and quickly found the key which locked the door. Ben ran across to the rejuvenation door and opened the lock with his tuber.

They entered the dim hangar. A slow dripping sound could be heard above them. Ahead of them, shafts of moonlight crept to the middle of the stairway. They moved swiftly across the room using the shadows as their cover. Rafe noticed that the glow of the fluid Meela was enchanted with was no longer present. Once they were near the top of the stairs, they could see the floor of the second level.

"The reject pile was over there," Ben said.

"You go first, I'll deal with anyone that enters."

"There are doors behind that unit," Ben whispered back.

Rafe nodded.

Ben hesitated.

Rafe glanced at Ben. Ben took a deep breath and sprinted noiselessly to his goal.

Rafe scanned the area. The dripping sound increased. Rafe could see the green fluid flowing into a network of tubes. One of the tubes was leaking. Rafe heard a sharp whistle. He jerked around to the right to see Ben beckoning him. Rafe headed towards him as he vanished behind the series of shelving. Rafe eventually caught up with Ben who was standing in front of three doors.

Rafe was dismayed. "I can remember five doors."

Ben handed Rafe the rucksacks. "I remember opening the middle one," Ben gulped. "… accidentally I think, that's why Elleba showed up."

Rafe handed Lisa's rucksack to Ben and squeezed Tia's into his rucksack.

"I'd prefer to take Tia's. Lisa's too fussy."

Rafe raised an eyebrow. "Make sure you keep it neat, that's all."

Ben reluctantly took it.

"Now, which door?"

"That one," Ben said.

"This one." Rafe nodded to the door closest to him.

"Why not my choice?"

"That's the door that alerted them to us."

Ben shrugged with acknowledgement.

Rafe stepped to his chosen door, Ben close behind. They heard an echo of thumping, both guessing that the guards must have recovered from their stunned state. They now wished they had tied them up.

Rafe tried the handle. The door sprung open. They both rushed into the small, stone stairwell towards a spiral staircase. They peered up as they heard the metal spindles humming, stirred by a breeze coming from somewhere above them. Moonlight beamed down from an unknown area. They silently motioned to each other to descend as quietly as possible.

There were no exit points on their descent until they came to a small landing. A sign over a grey door stating – **BEWARE** – grabbed their attention.

"There's one more flight of stairs…" Rafe began.

"Let's check if there's another door," Ben whispered back.

They nudged down the last few steps but could see there was no exit point.

"It's just that one," Ben said, a little disappointed that they didn't have a choice.

They headed back to the door. Rafe tried the handle, it was open.

*

Rafe cautiously peeked into the room. It was dark, windowless, it reeked of stale food. Looming shadowy covers hung over, what Rafe described to Ben as, huge domes.

They entered.

Ben closed the door quietly. Rafe was the first to turn on his torch, aiming it at the red flagstone floor.

"I don't like this smell," Ben said, wrinkling his nose. He returned his torch to his rucksack so he could hold his nose and have his tuber ready. They made their way through the central aisle of the large room, aisle after aisle of large, covered items with straw and grain splattered around them.

"What are these things?" Ben asked.

Rafe had no interest, he wanted to find out if this room had an exit point. "Whatever they are, they smell really bad!" Rafe changed aisle; his light caught a scurrying creature.

"Yikes. What's that?" Ben gasped.

"Rat," Rafe said, without flinching.

Two more creatures shot past their feet, the tail of one curled around Ben's ankle, so quickly, effectively pulling his feet from beneath him. Rafe was next to spin off balance against one of the covered items. The object jolted, the cloth slipped a little, revealing the bottom of a dislodged caged container on a short plinth. Its occupant's squawk could be heard like a distant echo. The boys jumped. The container wobbled. A flurry of feathers and screeching came from behind the cloth. Rafe didn't wait for it to reveal itself. He darted back in the direction they had come. Ben gathered himself, but as he glanced behind, he saw six, red, fierce eyes staring at him from beneath the displaced cage. Ben dashed after Rafe, "Rafe, Rafe, my tuber. I've lost my tuber."

*

Rafe darted back to Ben. "Where?"

"Back there." Ben pointed over his shoulder not wanting to see the piercing eyes that haunted him.

"Stay here." Rafe jogged back cautiously, his torch held low, beam searching the ground, tuber ready. He saw the glint from Ben's tuber resting under the dislodged cage. The occupant silent, piercing eyes closed.

Without getting too close to the cage, Rafe slowly extended his leg hoping to kick the tuber towards him. He gave the tuber a quick kick, but it bounced under the cage like a firecracker, white and blue sparks accompanied a sharp snap. The plinth split and toppled the cage. In an instant Rafe was being attacked by claws and multiple sharp, fly-away feathers. His arm shot up to fend off the creature, the beam of the torch caught the creature directly in its beady eyes. This momentarily halted its assault, allowing Rafe to see it properly. He was repulsed by its distorted pink human-like body; scraggy feathers partially covering its spindly legs and pulsating stomach, bird wings and clawed feet. A distinct stench emanated with each flap of its wings. Ben, although horrified by what he was seeing, ran and snatched his tuber from between the broken plinth and began his retaliation. Its shrill cry was deafening as they battled with it.

Rafe shone his torch again into its eyes. It slammed into another cage, knocking it off its pedestal. Another creature, which looked like a human with a bird's head, jumped down, charged at them, grunting. Its teeth and nails like jagged swords, luminous green veins pulsated down its body into grey box-like trousers. Without hesitation, Rafe launched a volley of jabs and strikes.

Rafe and Ben fought valiantly, weaving between the other covered structures in this darkened space hoping not to knock anything else over. Without noticing, they had lost sight of the entrance and had backed themselves into a corner. Strike after strike, these creatures weren't giving up, their ferocity drove them forward. Rafe and Ben were pinned to the panelled wall, striking out as best they could. Ben cut the claws away from the second attacker, it backed away with a harrowing scream then returned with greater intensity. Rafe pressed hard against the wall to escape the sharp wings slicing at his face. He managed a swift strike through the wings of his attacker, and they crumpled to the ground. A putrid aroma arose as the creature squealed.

Rafe fell backward through a panel.

Ben dashed towards the panel.

The panel snapped shut.

They ended in a heap on the floor, the creatures banging violently against the wall.

Rafe lay on the ground groaning.

Ben staggered to his feet, breathing deeply, he said, "I guess that's… what… Meela meant … imprints gone wrong."

Chapter 33

Zantacca Aftermath

Tia was surprised to see how calm everything was after such a violent storm. The animals were all in their grazing areas, groups of children were sat on stools listening to their teachers, while teenagers and adults carried on with their chores as well as clearing the debris left behind by Zantacca. It was clear to see that the dippers were missing. Tia was saddened to see a few dead dippers lodged in the bushes; Lisa hurried her along.

"Things don't look too bad," Tia said, hiding her sadness. "Although, the grass looks like it's still exhausted from the storm."

"Yeah, like it's gone off to sleep," Lisa said.

"Lisa, Tia," Zee called. Lisa and Tia jogged over to Zee who was at the entrance to her home. "There's a meal ready for you and T-sodon is already back, he's sorting out iggogos for both of you, fortunately we didn't lose any of them. Come and eat."

They followed her down the ramp into the cosy underground surroundings.

"Where's Ray and Ben?"

“Looking around.” Zee was nonchalant she showed them to their seats. “There’s so much to do. Zantacca has uprooted and damaged our crops, they’re scattered across the rocky plains. Some of the dippers have been killed and trees felled, and some of our woven materials blown away.” She stopped and took a breath, then handed them each a wooden bowl. “I’m sorry for going on about it.”

“It’ll be ok. No problems if everyone comes together,” Lisa said.

Tia nudged Lisa to say nothing more, she saw how Zee’s demeanour changed, her response was lit with a harsh tone. “Have you carried reeds on your back, have you smelt the stink Zantacca leaves behind? Have you had to put ointment on seeping wounds after clearing the dead bodies, have you…?”

Lisa quickly interrupted, “We’re very sorry, we didn’t know.” Lisa lowered her eyes as she sat down. Zee served them stew and bread and left them to eat.

“Wish I’d kept my big mouth shut.” Lisa’s mouth was full of stew.

“You didn’t know, but you can close your mouth now, you’ll lose all your food…,” Tia said. She tasted a small amount of the stew to see if she would like it. “I hope they don't believe we set off the storm thing. I get the feeling they really don't want us around now."

"I wouldn't want us around." Lisa swallowed her bread, cleared her throat with a deep cough. "I feel like a free-loader because we really haven't done enough to help them."

Tia said, "Perhaps we should offer to help before we leave, as a good will gesture."

Lisa thought for a moment, chomped into the vegetables, and wondered why school meals couldn't be as tasty as this meal. "Well, we could wash these things up when we're finished. And possibly, even, clean the iggogos' sleeping area."

"You'd clear it? I can't believe you'd be willing to clear muck," Tia said.

"Well desperate times call for desperate measures. And if we are to use their iggogos then it'll look like we can take care of them."

Tia took a spoon full of stew. "I can't believe you want to clear the mess."

"I can't believe we're talking about muck when eating." Lisa cleaned her bowl with her last bit of bread. "Honestly, I don't want to make an enemy of Zee."

Chapter 34

A way to escape

Rafe sat resting against the smooth panel. “That smell got to me!”

“Well, they’ve gone, hopefully never to return. I really don’t need to see those mutants again.” Ben shone his torch around the quiet nook.

“There’s wrong and there’s plain WRONG! They must be the kumelenjahs,” Rafe shivered.

“Looks like a secret passage.” Ben’s torch light exposed the thick spider webs above them.

“I was talking about those creatures.”

“Don’t remind me, Alamo was right,” Ben shuddered. “Anyway, I’d like to forget I ever saw them. And thanks to you we got out of that sticky situation.”

Rafe dusted himself off, placed his tuber on his belt, covered his mouth and nose to take a deep breath. “There’s only one way to go.”

Ben led the way.

Rafe stretched his back and arms as they walked. The fall into the nook was painful but he hadn’t broken anything.

"Slow down, I need the rest of my body to catch up with my legs, or the other way round."

"I can see a door at the end," Ben said, "you take your time old man, and I'll go ahead and see if all's clear."

Rafe watched as Ben jogged the rest of the way, his light faded from view, his silhouette and the rising dust from his footfall gave Rafe an indication of Ben's position. When Rafe finally caught up with Ben, he was kneeling with his ear pinned to a crusty wooden door half the height of a normal door.

"It seems quiet," Ben whispered, looked up at Rafe. "I can't find a handle or anything to open it."

"Could be like the one we just came through. We may need to lean on it for it to open. If not, we burn it through with the tuber."

"Let's lean. This old thing looks like it'll easily give way, besides seems like it would attract far too much attention if it started to burn." Ben leant against the door with his palms, Rafe stood back as Ben leant on various parts of the door hoping for an automatic release.

"Let me try. It might respond to my weight."

Ben stood aside. "Try not to fall through this time." Ben smirked.

"Don't remind me." Rafe shuffled into place, his body against the middle of the door. They heard a significant click. The door gave way, only a few inches, a slither of dull light entered the passage. Ben peered through the crack. "It could be a room or a corridor. Can't see anyone but I can hear something, not sure …Let's push it a bit more."

"Tubers at the ready." Rafe held his tuber in both hands and settled his right shoulder against the rough surface. Ben did the same, both alert to any intrusion.

"One, two…" Rafe counted, they pushed on three.

The door gave way slowly, a lazy creak onto a tiled floor. There were several crates stacked around the narrow rectangular gallery. A humdrum din of busy people rose into the space although they couldn't see anyone. Slit windows lined the space. They were dulled by dirt and cobwebs but the noise they could hear emanated from whatever was going on beneath them. They both shuffled into the narrow space. Rafe carefully climbed on top of the crates and saw a floating ribbon of colour. He rubbed away at a section of window with his elbow. He managed to make out a sea of people, busily occupied with their daily activities.

"It looks like the area around the kitchen. It looks like people are carrying stuff - like boxes… pushing carts." Rafe stepped off the crates.

“Look at this, I think it’s a trap door,” Ben said, excitedly.

They examined the area of discoloured tile. “It must be an exit. I mean, it’s not exactly the same as the rest of the floor,” Rafe said, standing over it.

Ben blew dust off the section which held an arched lever. He pulled it, but the lever didn’t budge; he twisted the lever and pulled upwards. The section, held by hinges, slowly folded back to reveal a wooden spiral staircase. The noise rose below them. Rafe’s torch explored the area, dust covered the dull, enclosed walls.

“Lisa would hate this,” Ben chuckled.

They descended the creaky steps. “It feels like it’ll give way,” Ben said.

“Let’s just go as quickly as poss.” Rafe gained speed behind Ben, “I don’t trust it.”

As they hit the lower level, the din grew louder. The bottom of the stairwell was stacked with crocus sacks and crates around the stairs. Rafe led the way as they climbed over the sacks to get to the door.

“Smells like vegetables,” Ben commented.

“Feels like small vegetables.” Rafe stood on the sacks waiting for Ben to catch up. “Walk out with confidence as though you’ve just delivered something,” Rafe said.

"Just a minute," Rafe grabbed a half empty sack, "carry this."
Ben flung the sack over his shoulder hitting Rafe in the process. "Watch out!"

"Sorry... Which way?"
Rafe rebalanced and said, "Left. Keep going, I'll catch up with you."

Ben opened the door and joined the surge of the crowd. Rafe, carrying an empty crate entered the corridor shortly after Ben, encouraged by the fresh breeze he inhaled deeply. He could see the guard station to the right; they were preoccupied, searching a man and his sacks of fabrics. Rafe immediately turned left hoping they hadn't caught sight of him. He just missed walking into a trolley filled with fruit as he hurried towards the market to catch up with Ben. Rafe weaved through the crowd relieved to be intermingling with the marketplace crowd. There wasn't a wheelot in sight.

Ben slowed his pace and Rafe quickened his until they were side by side, heading to the main street of the market. They just wanted to get as far away from the palace as possible.

*

The late afternoon sunlight bathed the market goers as they busily bartered for their last-minute items.

“I must say,” Ben said, rubbing his stomach, “I’m really hungry and thirsty.”

“Use your canister.”

“I forgot about that.” Ben dropped the sack, took the canister from his rucksack, and gulped the water with satisfaction. “Still doesn’t get rid of the hunger.” He handed the canister to Rafe.

“We need to get back to Sanguel, speak to Arabella.” Rafe was hoping to get back to Sanguel without delay.

“Good idea, but I hope we get food first.” Ben thought for a moment, searched through his pockets. Rafe refrained from raising his eyebrows, knowing that when it came to Ben and his stomach, he’d find a way to eat. Ben beamed when he pulled out the money Alamo had given him, kissed the coin and shot off to a food stall. Rafe sat drinking on the crate and watched in wonder as Ben returned with two woven leaves shaped as bowls, filled with a mixture of meat, vegetables, and flatbreads.

Rafe put away his canister, held the delicious smelling meal to his nose and said, “Ben, please correct me if I, or anyone says you have no initiative.” Ben handed him a small wooden spoon.

Ben was already halfway through his portion and enjoying every bite. Some of the stew ran down his chin. It wasn't wasted as Ben skilfully brushed the flat bread against his chin to mop it up and popped it into his mouth with great satisfaction.

"So, here you are, happily filling your faces, while I'm frantically search for you."

"Sam!" Rafe held the spoon in his mouth as he greeted him with a fist bump, Ben too.

Sam said, "Where have you been? We searched everywhere for you until Izzy and Alamo had to return to Sanguel. I couldn't get into the palace."

Ben and Rafe gave a knowing stare at each other.

Sam continued, "I was told that they didn't have any visitors, the Languin wasn't taking guests. That's when I knew something was up and sent out my spies." Sam closed with a satisfied look.

Rafe swallowed the last bit of his meal, wiped his mouth. "Is there some place where we can talk?"

"Don't waste it, eat it," Sam said, pointing to Rafe's empty bowl. Ben didn't need to be told twice, he was trying to work out how to get the rest of the juices from the bowl without licking it; and not betray the good manners his parents had taught him. He crunched into the bowl and encouraged Rafe, who didn't seem so keen.

Sam said, “Along here. My cousin has a stall with dwellings behind. We can avoid any nosy moochers, you know, the wheelots. Although…” he quickly looked about him, “they’re out of the way for a while.”

Rafe grabbed his crate and Ben asked Sam to carry the sack so he could finish his bowl feast. They weaved between stalls at pace, following Sam to a stall that sold an array of goods, from clothing for all ages, horse reins and saddles to wall hangings. Sam greeted a man much taller than himself; Rafe thought the family resemblance was striking. The tall man exchanged a friendly nod with Rafe and Ben, then went back to overseeing the staff and customers. Sam guided them to the side of the stall under a tapestry canopy which displayed a picture of the palace. It led them away from the hustle and bustle of the marketplace to a row of stone buildings where marketers took their breaks, stored their products, and some produced their goods in these much-needed buildings. Sam swung open the door into a hallway, narrowed by piles of crates filled with patches of leathery material. Rafe found a home for his crate atop a pile of empty crates, deciding to have a go at eating the bowl.

“Smells like polished shoes,” Ben said.

Rafe swallowed the last bit of food. "Reminds me of my dad's jackets - loads of them."

They passed through an official storeroom set up with weaving stations in the workshop area, with sewing machines, tables and fabrics, half cut, half sewn. They entered a rear room which was clear of clutter, a living area with a large table against a wall, a couple of wooden chairs, a clay oven with tiled shelving where pots and cups were kept. Sam motioned for them to sit on a set of comfortable chairs facing a small, unlit fireplace.

"What's been going on?" Sam asked.

Ben caught sight of the covered jug on the table. "Before we start Sam, is there something to drink? I mean, after that meal it needs to be washed down -"

Rafe was annoyed that Ben was so distracted.

"It's okay," Sam said, with a chuckle. "What would you like me to do with this?" He held the sack in one hand.

"I forgot about that. It's not mine I took it from the palace."

Sam opened it. "Wooow, it's silk threads, finest quality!"

"Just the finest threads," Ben said, as if it were a natural everyday occurrence.

Sam carefully placed the sack on the table and handed Ben the jug and a cup. "Enjoy."

"Thanks, I hope it tastes like that juice from Sanguel. You know the one at the celebrations," Ben said, with a quick, apologetic glance at Rafe.

Rafe couldn't wait to explain to Sam what had happened. "There's so much to say. We escaped from Elleba. She's up to no good. In trying to duplicate people, she's created some gross looking things," He winced.

Ben jumped in. "Meela's there, but we don't know if she's really her. And Elleba made two of us too." Ben gulped his juice.

Sam stared at them. "What do you mean Meela's not really herself, and there's two of you? And you've seen kumelenjahs?!"

Rafe slowed the conversation down, "They are worse than you can even imagine. I know it's hard to believe, but Elleba makes copies of people."

"What?"

"She has machines that can duplicate -" Rafe began

"She calls them imprints," Ben said, finishing his juice with a burp.

"Imprints?"

"I think it's best if we explain what happened to us," Rafe said, "you start Ben."

Ben turned his attention to telling Sam the whole story. When he finished Sam was dumbfounded.

"It's crazy but plausible. Evelyn used to supply this kingdom with all sorts of things, and we used to hear some wild stories about strange noises and sightings in the woods at night. We didn't believe them because we had enough to deal with in the mines."

"Cousin Vizam lives in the stone cabins close to the palace, he and his family hear all sorts of things. By the way, Tia and Lisa are at the Gakinde homestead."

"How did you know?" Ben asked.

"Like I said, Vizam hears a lot of things, and I have spies."

"Are they safe?" Rafe was relieved although he still had concerns about their safety.

"As far as I know, those people are known for their hospitality. They supply most of the towns with warm clothing and, well…, all sorts of items. Their fruit crops are the best and for some reason their animals provide the finest and warmest yarn. Apparently, they have a yarn that when weaved with special metal thread, provides a defence against different types of attack, that bit is top secret." Sam smiled with his prized nugget of information while Rafe and Ben looked very impressed.

Rafe was ready to take action. "If you direct us to the Gakinde homestead, we'll find Tia and Lisa. You can head back to Sanguel, get Alamo or Evan to come back with you to confirm the real Meela; she's in serious trouble."

Rafe continued. "Mrs Peri should know but don't tell Mr Peri. He's only going to make things worse. He told us Meela was in the kingdom of Clover when he knew full well, she was in Pershee. Idiot! He did it deliberately because he trusted Evelyn, bet he trusts Elleba too. Pathetic!"

"That's right Rafe let it out. Tell us exactly how you feel about him." Ben pretended to rub Rafe's back, amused at the strength of Rafe's dislike for Mr Peri, although Ben understood why and was in full support.

Sam said, "I get the picture. I know the family have his measure. He is so proud of them that he often gets misguided about what his family should do to elevate his status in the kingdom. The silent horses contraption has got serious problems, so I had to leave it behind. I can take you as close to the settlement as possible. We have one problem though."

"I don't know if I want to hear this," Rafe said.

Ben sighed, "No transport."

"Zantacca has been through the area, which means we have to take the safe route which is longer…"

Rafe and Ben groaned in unison.

"What is Zantacca?" Ben asked.

"It's an extremely violent storm that visits this area and takes from us. On the plus side it means that there are few wheelots in that area due to the damage caused by Zantacca."

"Happy days!" Ben yelled.

"Rest here and I'll sort out transport."

*

Sam had done a good job at navigating the single horse and cart through the upturned area near the Gakinde people. Rafe and Ben were amazed at how dishevelled and ravaged the region was.

They were happy to show off their new tuber attachment to Sam who thought they might have made better progress on the tubers than using the horse and cart. However, when Sam could go no further with the horse and cart, due to the upturned terrain of broken, uprooted trees and battered foliage. They travelled carefully on their hover tubers in the direction that Sam had directed. They slipped off the standing plates a couple of times, but quickly got the hang of it, manoeuvring through the devastated terrain. They were grateful that the hover tubers only made a low swishing sound as they sped ahead. The moment they heard the chants and laughter of children they slowed down, dropping closer to the ground, hopped off the tubers, connected them back to their belts and walked the rest of the way.

A group of children ran towards them as they left the woods behind them.

"Rafe, Rafe. Ben, Ben," The children sang as they ran towards them, grabbing hold of their hands and continuing their chants.

"How do they know our names?" Ben quizzed.

Rafe shrugged. As the children pulled him ahead, it suddenly dawned on him; looking over his shoulder at Ben, he mouthed, '*The imprints*.'

Ben stopped wide-eyed. The children pushed him on, to stay at pace with those striding with Rafe.

A teenaged girl ran towards them and shooed the children away. "Hi, back again already."

"It's our first time here," Ben said, uneasily.

She ignored this statement in a laugh and said, "Where's T-sodon?"

"T-so Who?" Ben looked to Rafe to see if he knew what she was talking about.

"Typical, he's hiding, to avoid bringing the cattle in for the night."

Rafe asked, “Where’s Tia and Lisa?”

This time the girl stopped in her tracks. Rafe could see she didn’t believe what he had just said, but he waited for her to respond.

“Wherever you left them.” She paused and then stopped them in their tracks by standing in front of them, her arms folded. “Did T-sodon set you up to tell this joke?”

Rafe didn’t want the situation to become confrontational, so he said, “I’m…, we’re really sorry. But the Rafe and Ben you saw before wasn’t us.” He pointed at Ben and himself as though she didn’t know he was talking about them. She starred at them, from tip to toe, rubbed her cheek. “Are you twins, multiples?”

Ben jumped to respond first, hoping he would clear up the confusion. “Not me or him. The other two… kind of…. but there’s a difference.”

Rafe closed his eyes wishing they could start again. A stray chukkan strode towards the woods.

“Wait here!” Zee ran off to catch it and direct it to its resting place. A young boy joined her and helped to move the chukkan by the belts hanging loosely across its body. Rafe and Ben looked around, noticing the ribbon-like plumes of air rising from various pockets of the ground, weaving around the children as they played; the children instinctively avoided the gusts of warm air coming from the underground cooking stations. Adults gathered at the entrance of their underground dwellings exchanging information about the clear up.

As the sun dimmed, turning the sky to a warm hazy caramel delight, the steady meander of the chukkans heading to their den for the night brought a feeling of calm.

Rafe pulled Ben by the arm and whispered, “The girls must be with those imprints, and whoever that T-sodon is.” He then watched Zee by the outskirts of the woods, giving direction to a group of children. “She’s taking her time to come back to us. We’d best get going.”

“We can do that or,” Ben swallowed hard, “It’s getting dark. We may need to stay here and set off early. Sam said they were welcoming people.”

Rafe was frustrated with the situation. “Why wouldn’t Tia and Lisa stay here after that storm thing Sam told us about? Why not go back to Sanguel?”

Ben hadn’t seen Rafe so frustrated; it was making him nervous, but he knew he had to get rid of his nerves and step up to the plate. “Ok, I think I’ll wait for warrior girl to finish and find out what she knows. You could find out from one of the adults, I don’t know, but get some more info.”

Rafe finally breathed out loudly through his mouth in surrender to help him relax, Ben's suggestion seemed to make sense. "Ok. Go for it," Rafe said. "Warrior girl? You'd best find out what her name is. I think she'd kick your butt if you called her that."

*

Rafe and Ben managed to grab a few minutes to catch up before entering the raucous conversations and laughter in the communal dining space.

"It's a bit confusing, so I made out like those imprint brats were our twins and our parents weren't intelligent to calls us by different names."

Rafe held down his laughter listening to Ben's explanation of how his conversation went with Zee. "My mom would do her nut if she heard me say she was unintelligent."

Ben continued; flush faced. "Anyway, it seemed to get through, I didn't want to say they were evil or anything just in case she thought we were the crazy ones. And besides, she really does look like she could rough someone up real bad." Rafe nodded.

"Anyway," Ben said, after clearing his throat, as though he had something caught in it, "her name's Zee and T-sodon is her brother. I wouldn't like to be in his shoes when he gets back. Apparently, they've gone looking for a Musca thingy. And listen to this …" Ben leaned in, "the Languin ordered it."

"What's she up to? And why would Tia and Lisa follow such a ludicrous demand?"

Ben shrugged. "She didn't say anymore. But she did offer us food and a place for the night. How did you get on?"

"Did you ask?"

Ben flung his hands up exasperated. "Honestly. She offered! I didn't ask to stay."

Rafe found this amusing as Ben genuinely looked as if Zee had told him he had to sleep in the cattle shelter, he would have agreed, just so he wouldn't get on the wrong side of her. He decided not to tease him. "I helped a group of the elders bring in the vegetables for the meal tonight."

"No wonder you took so long."

"Nice group of people. They told me how helpful Tia and Lisa were, including those desperado imprints! Get this - they called them helpful, very strong young men. I felt like being sick. They also knew that they had gone in search of the Musca."

"What is the Musca?'

"It's quite a big deal around here, It's a flying creature that..."

Ben was horrified and said, "Please, don't say it's a mutant!"

"Keep your hair on! It pollinates the marshlands and surrounding areas along with its colonies. No one seems to know when it does this as it keeps a low profile, only a few individuals have spotted it, normally in the early hours of the morning. They didn't like the idea that it seems to have gone missing. So were glad that someone would go looking for it, instead of taking them away from their own work."

"They said 'low profile'?"

"No, that was my interpretation of what they said."

"What does it look like?"

"That, I don't know." Rafe had tried his best to get a description of the Musca out of the group. "What I don't get is, if they've hardly seen it, how are Tia and Lisa going to find it?"

Ben said, "This T-sodon kid is supposed to have seen it, that's why he's taking them to the most likely places. I assume."

"The elders also offered us food and a place to sleep for the night, because even though the storm has been through here, they said that didn't mean that the mechagribeas would take a night off."

Ben shivered with fear. "I hate those things."

"Well, they assured me that T-sodon would make sure they were all safe in a cavern or other safe areas along the route that the Gakindes use, especially when they have to be out late looking for stray animals."

"So, we stay tonight. Leave early?" Ben wanted to make sure.

"Suppose so," Rafe said, "but didn't you say that Zee had a few issues with her brother doing the right thing?"

"Could just be a sibling thing."

"Where do we stay tonight?"

"We'll toss for it. Heads my lead, tails yours," Ben said, searching for a coin.

Rafe handed him a coin.

"Where did you get this from?"

"It's no good here."

Ben looked closely at the pound coin hoping it was a zuz. "We should see how much this is worth here," Ben smiled, "It may be worth more than we expect."

"Toss the coin."

Chapter 35

Moan a Minute

They travelled steadily through the woods. Zee had to intervene and select two of the calmer iggogos when she saw that T-so was selecting the skittish ones for the girls to ride. After a few instructions on how to treat the iggogos, R37 and B33 had no problems with adjusting to the ride. However, Tia and Lisa were having difficulties which T-so had ignored. So, once again, Zee stepped in, and with her gentle guidance, they got the hang of it. T-so allowed R37 and B33 to ride ahead while he rode alongside the girls to give further guidance as Zee had instructed; one such instruction was to keep the iggogo at a moderate speed. But once they were out of Zee's sight, T-so increased the pace. This made the ride uncomfortable for the girls.

"If it wasn't for you two, I'd be home. Nice and snug. You've got me into so much trouble with Zee, my uncle, the elders. I wish I could lock you up in the marshlands."

"Don't blame us. From what Zee said, you seem to get in trouble without any help from anyone else," Tia shot back, finally ending her silence to T-so's continual complaints. His stony glare aimed at Lisa and Tia was ignored by Tia and met with an eye roll of discontent from Lisa. T-so made his iggogo trot ahead to catch up with the imprints.

"What's wrong with those two?" Lisa flicked her head in the direction of the imprints. "Rafe's normally quiet, but this is super quiet."

"I haven't seen him raise his eyebrows once," Tia said, straight-faced.

"He must be coming down with something."

"He could be." Tia pondered.

"And let's be real, there's been a lot of eyebrow raising moments with T-so." Lisa looked sad.

"Sorry Lisa, lover boy's not who you thought he was."

"I suppose," Lisa sighed.

"Don't do that thing."

"What thing?"

Tia changed her tone to mimic Lisa, "I only like bad boys."

Lisa giggled.

"I think I could be an actor," Tia said.

"Pray tell," Lisa mused.

"Because…" Tia started with a theatrical edge. "I've acted so well, like I don't care what Ray thinks, that I'm beginning to believe it." Tia's sad eyes told Lisa her friend was in emotional pain, but Lisa didn't know what to do about it except give Rafe a good telling off, which she knew wasn't going to happen; how could she lambast the one person who normally has the best ideas and looks out for everyone, even when Ben was being selfish.

"It'll all come good. Just wait and see." Lisa tried to give Tia a friendly pat on her back but the sudden change in weight made her iggogo lurch forward, Lisa tugged hard at the reins as it galloped off down a side path. T-so caught a glimpse of what was happening but ignored it.

Tia managed to stop her iggogo. "T-SO, T-SO HELP!" Tia shouted, pointing in Lisa's direction, trying not to unnerve her animal. T-so wearily edged his iggogo to give chase. Tia followed at a slower pace. She couldn't understand why the boys hadn't given chase too. T-so caught up with Lisa who was leaning forward against the galloping iggogo; her arms wrapped around its neck, reins dangling beside her.

"Calm down, get the reins - the reins," T-so shouted, "Pull the reins together."

Lisa was annoyed at T-so's sarcastic tone but knew she had to listen. She grabbed hold of the reins, one hand still around the animal's long neck. She hesitated then sat up, snatching the reins in both hands, and holding them far apart across the back of the animal, bouncing along.

"Put the reins together, together, not so far apart. You idiot. Try it again!"

"Be helpful," Tia shouted at T-so.

Lisa gently pulled the reins together. "Slow, sloooow, it's ok."

"Lisa, do as Zee said. Lean back a bit, balance your weight, slowly. Good, good." Tia encouraged.

Lisa leant backwards, the iggogo began to slow its pace and eventually came to a halt when T-so managed to grab hold of the long fur under its chin.

"Ok you two. Fun and games are over. I think it's best if you travel together."

"Why?" Lisa asked.

"Your iggogo is limping. You may have injured her so ride with Tia."

Lisa gave him a cold stare.

"It's getting dark, and we need to get back to the ridge, to the hide out before the gribeas make us their meal." His tone filled with sarcasm and cheek. "Come on, make it snappy."

Lisa didn't want him to see her fear, so she eased off the iggogo. Tia positioned her animal against a large stone which Lisa was able to use to step up onto the back of Tia's iggogo. T-so took hold of the reins of Lisa's iggogo and guided the animal alongside his own.

Tia and Lisa said nothing at first, they were afraid that T-so would ride off and leave them to face any lurking predators. Tia caught sight of his smug look as he turned his iggogo to head back up the path and felt compelled to say something. "Less of the - you two! We didn't do this deliberately."

He rode on and waved his hand in the air to say come on. Lisa's iggogo trailed obediently.

"I could slap him right off that thing!"

"Tia, calm down," Lisa said.

"Silly snuckhead!"

Lisa giggled as her ordeal was over. "Now that's the Tia I know. Make up a name for him."

"I'd like to add something else to it, but Ray wouldn't be too pleased, and my mom would turn in her grave!"

"Well best not do that then." Lisa softened her tone, gave Tia a hug knowing how much Tia missed her mother.

*

When they got back on track, R37 and B33 were waiting.

"Everything ok?" B33 asked.

"Yes," Lisa said.

Tia nodded. “Ray, we may be in danger of the mechagribeas, do you think it would be ok if we used our tubers in front of T-so?”

R37 looked blankly at Tia. Tia waited for a response. B33 looked uninterested. Lisa didn’t know what was going on. T-so interrupted the peculiar silence between them, shouting back at them. “We have a little way to go. Get a move on.” His voice was harsh and unforgiving - he cantered off the track through the trees.

The imprints’ iggogos hurried after T-so.

“Have we got the slowest animal?” Lisa asked.

“Don’t say that too loudly, I think these things understand what we’re saying. Besides T-so isn’t a very good guide, I can’t see him anywhere. We’ve got to follow Ray and Ben. And talking about Ray he looked as if he didn’t know what I was talking about.”

“I know, how strange,” Lisa said, “and Ben looked as gormless as ever - no surprise there.”

“Ben’s not that bad,” Tia replied.

“Did you hear that?”

“What?”

Lisa clung to Tia.

They listened to the breath of the iggogo, a heavy long snort, quick inhale, long snort. But another sound resonated from the bushes behind them. The iggogo quickened its pace without the girls giving it any instructions. Its hind legs kicking out as it went, jolting the girls around, they held firm hoping not to fall off. They clearly heard the tell-tale deep growl then grunt and the rustling of undergrowth.

"Go, go," Tia said, urgently, to the iggogo; it surprisingly increased its pace.

"Pendant, pendant," Lisa cried.

"Even if we disappear, the iggogo won't," Tia said, willing the animal to move quicker.

They both thumped their pendant.

"Jump!" Tia cried as she caught sight of the first mechagribea launching out of the bushes beside her, its large metal claws dug into the soil behind the hoofs of the iggogo. Its jaws wide like a chasm, ready to devour its prey.

Lisa jumped and rolled out of the path of the second mechagribea. It made after the iggogo which had sped out of sight without the girls' weight.

Tia ran to Lisa, "Press your pendant again."

Lisa panicked "I'm not invisible." She couldn't reach her pendant; the fall had twisted it around to the nape of her neck. The second mechagribea lost interest in the chase of the iggogo, turning its interest towards Lisa as it heard her twisting on the ground. Its gears churning in its chest, pulsating blue light.

"Run!" Tia cried and dragged Lisa up.

The beast smelt the air, felt the movements, and charged towards them. Tia and Lisa sprinted into the woods through the undergrowth, the mechagribea gaining with each powerful stride. Lisa was tiring, she could hear its heavy breath getting closer. She knew she wasn't the strongest runner, so she was ready to stand and fight if she had to, as frightened as she was. Tia could see Lisa slip out of her side view. Tia grabbed her tuber and turned back, horrified to see that Lisa had stopped, tuber in hand, waiting for the beast to arrive. Tia charged back into its path, swung her tuber upwards as the beast launched itself at Lisa, who was poised, intending to strike as it came towards her, but its intimidating large mass rendered her motionless. Tia smacked into the underbelly of the beast. Its leap was short-changed as it landed with its jaw yawning wide in front of Lisa's paralysed feet. Lisa swung down and smashed the metal teeth from its gaping jaw. She sprung backwards and stunned it into further submission. It slumped and let out an injured breath. Lisa slowly stepped backwards from the mass, its orange fur seemed gentle and smooth, but the moon had it firmly in its gaze, revealing the metal claws and teeth shed on the ground, the gears emitting a dull flicker.

"Its eyes are still open," Tia breathed out as she stood beside Lisa looking down on the mass. "It's huge." Tia scanned the area.

Lisa was lost for words. She swallowed hard then whispered, "It's as if the eyes are staring."

"RUN!" Tia was off. Lisa saw the other mechagribea heading their way. She tore after Tia with new life in her legs, adrenaline surging.

Chapter 36

Arrival

Rafe and Ben had had a lovely meal, prepared by the youngsters of the Gakinde people. The meal was shared amongst the different families, and they all went into their own quarters to prepare for the next day. Rafe and Ben had ended up with the older men and women who were reminiscing about the old days and the rulers of their land. Rafe and Ben were interested in the history and were getting a better understanding of how Elleba was left in charge. There was a general mistrust of her, but the Lanquis and his family were greatly admired and revered.

“I hope I get enough sleep. Because these lot look as though they are snorers,” Ben whispered.

“Well, you’ll be right at home then,” Rafe chuckled.

Ben gave him a friendly shove. “I can’t keep my eyes open.”

“I think I’m going to listen to some more of this, every little helps. Anyway, I’ll still be up before you wake up.”

“A good-looking lad like me needs all the sleep he can get.” Ben stroked his non-existent beard.

“I won’t wake you.”

"Ha, ha, funny, see you in the morning. And, seriously, don't leave without me. We need to catch up with those impostors."

"Don't worry, we'll get them. I wouldn't be surprised if the girls are giving them a good run for their money. Good night, sleeping beauty." Rafe grinned.

Chapter 37

Running

Moonlight disappeared behind darkened clouds. Tia felt the mechagribea gaining on her, the shaking of the ground as it got closer made her heart pound loudly in her chest. She couldn't turn and fight, she had to get away. She prayed for her invisibility to last but knew that her movements were only giving the beast instructions on where she and Lisa were heading. She thought of running in another direction to save Lisa, how she wished they had worked out a strategy for moments like this. As purple clouds gave way to shards of moonlight, Tia heard Lisa cry out as she vanished from her eye-line. It was in that split second that Tia's shock turned to horror, as she too lost the ground beneath her feet. She was falling, foliage closing in behind her.

Chapter 38

Goodbye

"Come on sleeping beauty, breakfast awaits." Rafe shook the plant he was holding, the bell-shaped petals released droplets of cold water over Ben's face.

"Really?" Ben muttered as he swiped the irritating drops away from him.

"As you know, after trying the gentle treatment, you need something to awaken the senses," Rafe chortled. "Anyway, I've eaten, and I've got you a mini sack bowl to go." Rafe dangled a brown cotton sack over Ben's head. The aroma made him jump.

"Great. You're a real pal." Ben snatched at the sack.

Rafe pulled it out of his reach. "Get washed, and let's get going."

"You're no fun."

Rafe pointed in the direction of the door.

*

They waved at the crowd of children who were happy to be told to walk them to the edge of the woods and show them the track.

"Bye Rafe, Bye Ben," rang the chorus repeatedly until the boys entered the woods. An older boy, Gopal, pointed to a short gradient that would lead them to the track T-so's small group had taken.

"Thanks Gopal." Rafe and Ben were grateful for the helpful tips Gopal gave them about the terrain and where the marshland territory met with the Gakinde territory. Their farewell group waved a final goodbye and returned to their homes.

"Those kids are funny," Ben said, with his mouth full of the last bit of his breakfast. Rafe jogged to the wide grassy track. "Think it's time to catch up with the girls. Let's see how fast these hover tubers can really go."

Ben tucked his empty breakfast bag into his rucksack and hopped on his tuber to join Rafe. "If I can keep my balance, I think I could pick up more speed."

"Well let's see." Rafe was eager to test out the tuber's new capabilities, he zoomed off.

"Hold on," Ben said, not realising Rafe was going to take off at such a speed. He was soon in hot pursuit, both overtaking each other, making a good game of it as they enjoyed the smooth ride. The sun high in the cornflower sky, open plains lay around them as they headed towards the hilly area in the distance. They enjoyed the open space and freedom.

Chapter 39

Marshlands

The morning sun revealed a veil of mist, under which hid a deep valley populated with enormous flowers and plants, moss and lemon leafy vines crawled as far as they could up the hillside, weaving through the clusters of large flowers, masking protruding roots, creating relief beds for unsuspecting visitors who had no idea of the cliff edge above.

Tia was cuddled in a cluster bed, its large purple petals laid out under her and curled over her torso. Warm sunrays woke her up. A gentle breeze quietly whistled though the foliage. Tia finally focused on the green stalks bowed over her, the flower heads devoid of petals from her fall last night. Tia stretched out and inhaled the sweet fragrance. She sat up, surveying the area, trying to recollect what had happened. She noticed that the area was sprinkled with her mother's favourite flower. She looked past the leaves above her and to her delight she saw trees over hanging the valley, their flowers drifting in the warm breeze. Tia scooped up the ones around her into a pile and tried to remember what happened the night before, but her head felt groggy. She looked about for her rucksack and saw it a few paces away. She noticed there was a gentle slope below her. Tia crawled out of her bed along the flower trail and pulled her rucksack to her, located her canister, and guzzled the water. She couldn't understand why she was so thirsty until she remembered being chased by the mechagribea.

"Lisa!" Tia called out, scanning the area for Lisa and her tuber. She proceeded on her hands and knees, searching the area. She looked like a tiny baby dragging a bag along in a land of gigantic plants. Tia finally settled her rucksack over her shoulders and staggered to her feet. She could hear a low moan in front of her and, followed the sound to a circle of orange sunflowers. As she approached, she could see Lisa's feet poking out of the foliage.

"Thank goodness you're ok."

Lisa groaned, "I feel ill, like I've been spun in a tumble dryer."

"I felt strange too. I can't find my tuber." Tia continued to inspect the area as she spoke to Lisa's feet.

"Give me a minute the flowers are spinning; I can't take them all in." Lisa curled up on the moss bed.

"Rest, the flowers are humungous. You're not seeing things."

"I don't know if I slept. I kept seeing that mechagribea." Fear entered her voice. "Please tell me it's not anywhere near us."

"Nope… No sign of it." Tia shielded her eyes to look up the cliff side. "I can see why we're still feeling the effects of the fall. Boy, that's high. If I'd seen it coming -"

"We'd have had to fight the mechagribea and one of them for a night was enough for me!"

"My tuber!"

"Where are you going?"

"Getting my tuber silly."

Lisa poked her head out of the circle. "Where are you?"

Tia walked around to where Lisa was peering.

"Like I said rest, and I'll be back in a minute…. It's up there on that bush."

Lisa looked up but couldn't focus. "Ok, you go. I'll wait for you here." She slumped on her bed and closed her eyes, a sweet minty smell wafting around her. Lisa inhaled deeply enjoying the freshness.

With the gradient being so steep and not wanting to fall backwards, Tia decided to crawl to the bush. She was grateful her tuber wasn't damaged. She clipped it to her belt, warily looking around, she had no intentions of being caught by any type of fierce animal in this wilderness of giant plants.

Tia carefully made her way back to Lisa. She entered Lisa's circle. Lisa was sat admiring the petals and drinking from her canister, her rucksack beside her.

"How did you manage to hold onto your rucksack?" Tia asked

"No idea, I remember sliding with it, but how it got beside me when I awoke – no idea. These petals are gigantic!" Lisa picked up some of the small purple-blue flowers scattered beside her. "Makes these look like doll's flowers, sorry Tia."

"No offence taken. I still love them." She smiled at her bracelet and sat beside Lisa. "All the flowers in this area are quite large, these…" She tapped her bracelet lovingly, "These come from the trees above the ridge. It's like my mom protected us."

"She must have 'cos I can't remember seeing our invisibility at work."

"Everything was happening all at once."

"It seems useless, I mean the pendants. They're behaving like when we first went to Sanguel. I don't know why we're still wearing them - What do we do now?" Lisa said, with a tone of desperation.

"To get back to the track is difficult, I only climbed part of the way to get my tuber and that was hard. Perhaps, if we go down and keep the cliff in sight, we may find another way up."

"Hopefully, Rafe and Ben will be looking for us," Lisa said, "I doubt if T-so is going to care."

"Ray and Ben will."

They fell silent, thinking about last night's horrific experience.

"Do you think they killed the iggogo?" Tia asked, frightened at the possible answer.

"Or ate it?" Lisa trembled

Tia paused then said, "I hope not, it could've just injured it and then come after us."

Lisa put her canister in her rucksack. "I don't think there's any point using the pendants because they're so unreliable. Even if we tried to stay still, whilst being invisible, I think those things would have caught us."

"We panicked."

"I know. But it's hard to stay still when the invisibility isn't working."

"We did alright though." Tia touched her bracelet.

"You sliced it through the middle," Lisa gasped.

"It didn't split open."

"Stopped it from landing on me."

"You crushed its teeth; it's now toothless," Tia cheered.

"I know," Lisa chuckled. "Do you think it still has a terrifying cry now that the teeth are gone?"

"Well, if we come across it again, you can find out." Tia really didn't want to see another mechagribea.

"Anyway, I need to eat something."

"Ok, there were apples and some other fruits on the track, remember T-so pointed them out between all his moaning. Perhaps there're some around here too."

"We may not be able to carry them, if they are anything like the flowers!" Lisa said.

Tia laughed.

"Help me up. I need to teach my legs to walk again," Lisa smiled.

*

Tia and Lisa sauntered along the lower ground, the cliff edge in view. The sun took its toll on them, so they wandered into the basin of the giant plants. It was a blur of colour but much cooler under the giant canopy. Leaves and flowers panned out like large awnings, it was difficult to see the sky, although the sunlight trickled through gaps and penetrated though lightly coloured leaves.

They heard a gradual build-up of indistinct noise. They stopped and tried to work out where the noise was coming from.

"I hope the insects aren't the same size as the flowers." Lisa anxiously scanned around her. "Sounds like insects…no like a blue bottle trapped in a box or something weird." Lisa kept looking behind her.

Tia was drawn to the way her feet was squelching against the ground. "The ground is getting wet – but it doesn't look soggy."

Lisa looked down not sure what Tia meant.

Tia studied the ground. "Didn't they say that the Musca lives in the marshlands?"

"I think it pollinates certain areas including the marshlands," Lisa said, cautiously, trying to recollect what Zee had told them. "Wouldn't it be fun if we found it…" Lisa laughed and clapped her hands then did a little skip and dance. "This would really put T-so in his place."

Tia was still concerned about the ground. "I hope this doesn't turn into quicksand."

"Quicksand?! It's not that soft." Lisa looked down, lifted her feet to see if the soil was sticking to her trainers. "Let's slow down. Make sure of our footing." Lisa carefully put one foot in front of the other, as though she was on a tight rope.

"Oh no… I can't move my feet. I mean my left foot," Tia cried.

"Lean towards me." Lisa stopped to brace Tia's weight, but Tia was having difficulty trying to move.

Tia was alarmed. "I'm stuck. Truly stuck."

"I'll find something for you to…. pull on," Lisa said, stepping to the side until she reached the foot of the gradient where a grove of trees grew. She could see Tia trying to move forward, which only made her look as if she were rocking back and forth. Lisa became scared and looked frantically for something to act like a rope to pull Tia out. She shouted back to Tia "Are you ok?"

"I don't know."

"Are you sinking?"

"No."

"Are you okay?" Lisa pulled at a clump of vines, they lifted easily, but their runners rose from the ground and turned over a stone. Brown and grey creepy crawlies scurried away; Lisa jumped out of the way. "Yuk." The vines wouldn't break away no matter how hard Lisa tried to pull them out of the soil.

Tia looked above her to see if she could grab hold of one of the thick leaves above her head. She extended her arms but couldn't quite get hold of any of them.

"Try this." Lisa held what looked like a piece of a branch.

"I don't think it's strong enough."

"Try it."

Lisa levered a part of the branch under her arm and gripped the section in front of her to angle it in Tia's direction. It was still out of reach. She stepped closer, mindful to avoid the area that surrounded Tia, Tia touched the tip, a handful of drying leaves and twigs.

"Closer?" Lisa asked.

"Yes Sherlock."

"No need for sarcasm." Lisa shuffled forward.

"Come on," Tia muttered, willing it to get to her.

"Hold on. This thing weighs a ton… I know it's a slight exaggeration, but it's heavy, doesn't look it…" Lisa dragged the branch and then pushed it to the edge of the soggy soil. She managed to heave it under her arm again. Tia got hold of it. It felt more like rubber than wood to her. Lisa tried her best to manage the weight of the branch, she was unbalanced and toppled sideward against a giant stem, which snapped, its leaves covering Lisa like a blanket, the sudden movement taking the branch out of Tia's reach. The fall of the leaves allowed a shaft of light into their immediate dense surroundings. Tia fell forwards, clamping her eyes shut as her body and chin hit the cold soil, momentarily dazing her. Tia slowly got on her hands and knees. She felt the earth shifting beneath her, sucking at her hands, knees and feet.

Tia stopped moving.

Lisa struggled to get the leaves off her; it was like being lost under a collapsed parachute; finally, she found her way out. “Sorry Tia. Let’s try again.” Lisa was on her feet again breathing heavily.

Tia muttered. “I can’t move… yet.” She hoped the lack of movement would stop the suction beneath her.

Lisa crouched and pushed the branch toward Tia again. It landed just in front of her fingers. “When you’re ready.”

A cluster of flying insects floated out of the trees and drifted towards Lisa. “Not now clouds.”

The insects loomed over her threatening to strike with a whistling hum. Lisa whacked away a few strays, but they became more of a nuisance as their whistle elevated; Lisa looked up anxiously and said, “Tia, I don’t know what to make of these things but they’re actually looking at me.”

Tia didn’t reply. She had managed to manoeuvre a few inches to the branch but felt that if she spoke, she would sink even deeper. She looked at her hands, which were now submerged in the ground, tiny bubbles outlined wherever her body was slowly being sucked into the sticky bog.

Lisa rose to her feet, the cluster dispersed for a brief moment making way for her to stand, then re-grouped a little distance away from her head. On closer inspection, Lisa could see their bodies were hairy, indigo coloured. She couldn't believe that she could make out faces on these tiny flying insects.

"They look mean!" Lisa puffed, she grabbed her tuber, took a stance as though she was holding a bat, ready to swing and knock the insects for six. Another swarm burst out of the vegetation adding to the noise, Lisa had to cover her ears. The swarm of flying insects gathered under the leaves of the flowers covering Tia. Lisa watched helplessly as they descended on Tia.

Tia heard the hum of the cluster like a lullaby. Their fine hairs dangled and attached themselves to her with small suction pads on the ends of each tentacle. The ones on her hands tickled and she tried not to giggle. A swooping popping sound accompanied her body being gently released from the soil. She watched as their little wings fluttered rapidly, as though pulsating with electricity. Tia remained on all fours as they lifted her above the awning leaves and past Lisa.

"Don't take her away," Lisa shouted, "Wait for me." Lisa ran after them, calling out to Tia. "Tia, say something - Are you alright?"

Tia was enjoying the feeling of flying above the flowers. She caught glimpses of Lisa running alongside, weaving between the foliage, saying something she couldn't quite hear. The other swarm followed Lisa.

They lowered Tia onto a large green toadstool, a metre off the ground, and flew over to a tightly packed set of stalks opposite them. Lisa eventually caught up with Tia, glad that her friend was safe. Tia jumped off the toadstool.

"That was fantastic," Tia laughed. "I flew. In the air. It was like being a feather."

They sat under the shade of the toadstool arch, catching their breath. "Amazing!"

Tia watched as the insects spread themselves across the stalks.

Lisa continued, patting her brow with her sleeve, "I'd have loved it."

"Perhaps it was better it was me. You know how you hate insects and may have tried to zap them."

"Maybe not," Lisa said, as she hastily returned her tuber to its rightful place. "Flying must be the best thing ever."

"Look, there's an opening," Tia said, as she observed the gap that the insects had created, parting the stalks.

A voice, soft yet audible, came from somewhere deep in the giant flower land, "I'm the one you seek."

Chapter 40

Led Astray

"I'm not too sure if we're still heading in the right direction. I mean, we should have caught up with them by now," Ben said.

"We may be close. I need to walk; my legs are getting stiff," Rafe said. They both hopped off their tubers and stretched their legs after travelling for an hour.

"Takes a while to get used to it, but it's great," Ben said.

"Look at this." Rafe looked down on a section of the track. "That looks like blood."

Ben took a closer look. "It can't be."

"I think it is. Look at the flies."

"Flies? I thought they were pebbles or something."

"Perhaps something got injured or killed by a mechagribea last night."

"Natural life, a cat, perhaps, caught a bird or a mouse."

Rafe screwed his face up. "When did you see a cat in these parts?"

Ben shrugged.

"Ben, Rafe, good to see yah."

Rafe and Ben saw a young boy sauntering to them looking quite pleased.

"And you are?" Rafe said.

"I'm T-so." He beamed, his iggogo out of sight.

"You're the one that took my sister and Tia to find the Musca," Ben said, far too eagerly for Rafe's liking.

"Where are they?" Rafe asked.

"Who?" T-so stopped in front of them, with a friendly expression.

"Tia and Lisa." Rafe glared down at him; hands folded across his chest.

"They found the Musca and are taking her to the palace, I think."

"You think?" Rafe narrowed his brow. "Why don't you know?"

"Hold on," T-so said, feeling a little intimidated by Rafe but trying his best not to show it. "They're fine. No danger. Everything is going well. You can see for yourself." He pointed to a hilly area covered by a grove of mushroom trees.

"Past that rise, they're just over there. I'm going home, my job is done here." He grinned and backed away from Rafe, giving Ben a friendly nod.

Rafe read his grin as being sly, he attempted to grab hold of T-so, but Ben stepped between them and said, "Its best if you go now. Thanks for your help."

T-so dashed off in the direction he had come. They watched as he ducked behind thick hedges followed by the sound of ruffling, but they didn't catch another sight of him, just heard his voice commanding something to move.

"Why so hostile?" Ben asked.

"You're too trusting. There's something not right about Mr Smug. How did he know who we were?"

"Perhaps, he was trying to help...." Ben started to defend T-so's actions, then fell silent.

Rafe continued. "We've never met him before. Or have you met him? Come on Ben, say something."

Ben looked on sensing that Rafe was right.

Rafe pushed harder. "Has he met you? So, who has he met that's called Rafe and Ben?"

"The fakers!" Ben now wished he hadn't intervened.

"Yes."

"But he could have been fooled by them too." Ben pondered.

"He came across as too arrogant, like he's not saying something."

"Well, let's find Tia and Lisa and then all will be revealed," Ben said, as though he had just performed an impressive magic trick. "We'll soon know if he told us the truth, so let's just see if they're over that ridge somewhere, if not we go on our way," Ben said.

"Your call - I'd prefer to head on the way we were going," Rafe said, resigned to Ben's thoughts on the matter.

"Just to the top, we don't have to search any further. It's just there." Ben had a hint of pleading in his voice, so Rafe gave him the benefit of the doubt.

*

Rafe and Ben arrived at the top of the rise, out of breath, yet elated. The challenge was to see who would get there first, and of course Rafe won, even though Ben had a head start, which he had given himself when trying to talk Rafe out of running to the ridge instead of using the hover tuber. They surveyed the scene; the land was full of rocky patches for miles, the sea in the distance, some vegetation but nothing too dense. Rocks stood in clumps about them, the larger rocks obscured the open views.

Rafe thought they would see the girls, walking side by side, accompanied by the Musca.

"Is that a bird or a statue?" Ben shielded his eyes as he pointed at the motionless birds in the distance, their glossy green feathers fluttering in the mild breeze.

"Don't know." Rafe was more concerned with finding the girls. He called out. "Tia. Lisa. Where are you?" His voice echoed and drifted back. A few of the dippers flapped a little way past the others.

"They're real!" Ben exclaimed.

"Weird," Rafe said, "I can't see why they would have come this far into nothing ness."

"It's probably their habitat," Ben said, holding his side and breathing deeply to avoid the nagging ache telling him that he had a stitch coming on.

"What are you talking about?"

"Those birds."

"Yeah, interesting - I didn't trust that kid any way. Let's head back." Rafe was about to turn back.

"Just a minute - water." Ben sat on a rock and took two long gulps from his canister. "I can't believe how much water I drink when I'm in this state. At home I'd need a fizzy drink. I'm not missing it one bit though 'cos the water's so satisfying, I'd like to bottle it and sell it." He chuckled. "What do you reckon? I could bottle it and sell it as special water - pure and fresh from the most natural springs you would ever have tasted."

"I think you'll need to work on your strapline." Rafe smiled and settled on the rock too, fascinated as he watched some of the green birds dip their heads to drill the soil and others stalked along in groups. Rafe jerked his head around as a strange sound caught his attention. "Did you hear that?" Rafe sprung up. "I think we've got company."

Ben listened.

Beyond the calmness of the scene, he could hear a repeated clunk-click sound, like toys failing to work properly, but they knew full well that the clucking sounds came from wheelots. Ben stuffed his canister away, unclipped his tuber and secured it in his hand as they both turned to see two lines of mutants and wheelots approaching them as though they were a welcoming committee. This time they were not all wheeling along the ground, they were marching towards them on stubby legs, some fleshy, others made of metal. Their robotic arms stretched out, red metal clippers snapping rapidly. A charred smell filled the air around them.

"Just when you think you've seen everything…" Rafe began. Something struck him at the back of his heel, he twisted out of the way and looked down where he saw a large black beetle, thirty centimetres long, a thick red stripe along its back, forked over its head down its jaw onto its mouth pincers.

"What on earth is that?!" Rafe yelled.

Chapter 41

Musca

"I'm so glad my little ones were gentle with you." The voice was soft, with a magical quality to it. Tia and Lisa tried to find out where the voice was coming from, a wall of large green and brown stalks encased the body of the voice. A two metre sunflower head on a platform of short yellow stalks lay before them. Tia and Lisa glanced at each other with glee and mouthed '*The Musca!*'

Lisa whispered, "Surely, it can't be a talking sunflower?"

"Who knows?" Tia looked to see if she could locate a mouth on the flower head.

The Musca floated above the walled encasement into the darkened region of the shelter. Her transparent wings pulsed with light, her rounded purple and blue stripes ran from tip to tail with two rows of feathers glowing. She made her descent with light gradual flutters, six blue legs landed on the sunflower. She took a little while to settle, her two rows of tail feathers fanned out behind her, the smaller feathers first then the larger ones.

The girls were amazed that they were unexpectantly in the presence of the Musca. It certainly felt like a special experience as they watched a small swarm gather themselves on the yellow petals beside her. Her small eyes gazed at Tia and Lisa. She was as large as the sunflower.

Tia whispered. "I thought we'd be able to pop her in our pockets."

"Who knew she would be this big and so delicate," Lisa whispered back hoping the Musca was as kind as she sounded.

"What can I do for you?"

Tia cleared her throat. "The Languin said that you were missing, and we were sent to find you."

"The Languin? Why would she want me? I do my duties every year, year after year, month after month." Her voice was melodic and soothing, "There's been so much disturbance this year that I don't have much time."

Tia hoped the Musca wouldn't get angry with her request. "Would you come back to the palace with us, to show her we didn't steal you?"

"We won't take much of your time," Lisa added quickly.

Tia stepped forward, ready to make another plea, but the Musca interrupted her with a loud warning. "Don't come any closer, you will sink." She fell silent for a moment, her wings fluttered, producing a gentle humming sound. Tia was going to break the silence then thought better of it, she moved back and watched as the Musca closed her eyes and faded into the background.

Lisa stared wide eyed at what was happening and whispered to Tia, "That's why she's so hard to find."

Tia nodded as the Musca reappeared and faded again.

Lisa began to panic. "What if she vanishes and we never see her again."

The Musca reappeared; her eyes now open. "I cannot be far away from this land for too long. My work would not be done. The Languin knows where to find me. The question is whether I go willingly." Her tone was determined.

Lisa couldn't imagine how they could possibly take the Musca against her will.

The sudden frantic buzzing of the swarm alerted them that something was wrong. Tia and Lisa's hands shot to their ears as a repetition of piercing hacking resounded about them. They dodged and ducked as the canopy of leaves collapsed around them. The buzzing grew, as the Musca's army swarmed the offending mechagribea that had entered the area, but their stings had no effect. The mechagribea avoided the swampy soil and swiftly cast its silver mesh over the Musca as she attempted to fly away. The swarm darted to the mesh to remove it, but it was too late, the mesh had already rendered the Musca powerless; her colour dulled, humming ceased, she couldn't create a camouflage to hide her position. Tia and Lisa were still dodging the tumbling foliage as the Musca was being hauled over the path of crushed vegetation.

Everything was so chaotic that Tia and Lisa unintentionally dashed into the area the Musca had warned them about. They tried their best to scramble out, but the ground was sucking them in. Petals and leaves fell over them. They managed to push them away. The ground dragged them in, slowly making them too exhausted to fight. Just when they thought they would lose the battle, R37 ambled into the ravaged site.

"Ray, Ray over here. Come quickly."

B33 entered, ran straight to them, and pulled them up. R37 stood and looked around.

"A mechagribea has the Musca!" Lisa yelled.

The girls tried to chase after the imprisoned Musca but R37 blocked their way.

"Ray, out the way, we need to rescue the Musca." Tia tried to get past R37, but he grabbed her firmly by the waist, she couldn't get away. Lisa stopped and didn't tackle B33 who had his arms spread to obstruct her path with a grim expression. Lisa saw what R37 had done and thought they were trying to protect them from whoever had captured the Musca.

"She's in good hands," R37 said, "I'll show you." He pulled Tia aggressively to the edge of the collapsed entrance. They watched as T-so, sporting a cheesy grin, waved regally to them from the back of the mechagribea. The silver mesh firmly encased the Musca; multiple silver ropes leading from the caged mesh, twined together into a central rope which was attached around the middle of the mechagribea. Tia was confused. She looked up at R37 then across at B33 and saw their stony gaze.

Tia pulled her arm away from R37's grasp. "Why?"

R37 said nothing.

She turned to B33, "Can you tell me what's going on with your friend?"

B33 looked at Tia, then Lisa and burst out laughing.

"You idiot." Lisa shouted. "You've cost us the Musca. We're in big trouble!"

B33 continued to laugh. This mocking laugh would normally irritate Lisa, but this one held a sinister quality that Lisa couldn't believe. "Stop it, Ben! Stop. Stop it!"

B33 paused, in fake surrender, then started laughing again, even louder. Lisa charged at him and pushed him over. He rolled around laughing. Lisa was about to kick at him when Tia pulled her away.

"It's not worth it. I don't know what's got into them."

Lisa was still furious, she grabbed a stone and flung it at B33, it just missed his head, he stopped laughing and sprung to his feet. "I wouldn't do that again," he said.

"Or what? Because I'll tell mom you've been a right pain, or I'll knock some sense into you." She grabbed at a pile of stones.

Tia glanced at R37, he would normally calm Ben and Lisa down in situations like this, instead he watched on, he had an unconscious twitch. His head would flick to the right side, every few seconds as though there was an annoying fly at his ear, and the flick would see it away, only for it to quickly return. Tia was about to say something to him, but R37 caught her gaze and returned it with a harsh stare, the twitch abruptly disappeared. Tia's unsettled focus returned to Ben and Lisa.

Tia jumped in. "That's enough. We need to follow where they've taken the Musca, not stay here and fight against each other." Tia shook the stones from Lisa's reluctant hands and looked at R37 for support. He was leaning against a woody stalk watching the heated exchange.

R37 yawned and said, “We needed to go that way to a hiding place. T-so knows what to do, the Languin will be informed.”

“Why a hiding place?” Tia asked.

“Because.”

“Because isn’t an answer,” Tia said, annoyed by R37 demeanour.

“Let me show you what I mean. Follow me.” R37 marched out of the giant garden, scooped up a sack lying under a cluster of trees, flung it over his shoulder without stopping. B33 ran ahead to where their iggogos were waiting for them. B33 untied his iggogo and called for Tia to ride with him. Tia didn’t get a chance to protest as R37 helped Lisa onto his iggogo and sped off. They followed him over a hilly terrain, large rocks and long grass in the distance. The iggogos had no problems navigating the hilly terrain in their almost clumsy pattern. They finally passed under an archway created by a gnarly set of trees. A trail of bushes ended at the mouth of a cave. R37 jumped off his animal and took the sack with him into the cave.

The cave overlooked a cramped bushy terrain. The entrance to the cave had been skilfully carved out with a wide arch. Patterned white and grey stonework ran inside the mouth of the cave, which was mirrored on the walls and dusty ground. Pockets of leaves and twigs from the bushes decorated the inner cave floor. The ceiling was a dark void in the domed upper space.

Once inside, daylight revealed three worse-for-wear camp beds in the far corner.

Two shelves housed wooden crockery and metal cups. The fireplace looked like it had been used recently. A set of organised stones had a metal pot on top of them and pieces of wood stacked at its side. R37 dumped the sack on the table and kicked one of the chairs to an open position, “Make yourselves at home,” he said, and walked away.

The girls hadn’t noticed that B33 didn’t enter the cave. R37 stepped out from the cave and B33 pulled a lever. A jarring clatter dropped a copper-coloured grate; a framework of cross bars slammed down just inside the mouth of the cave sealing the girls inside.

Chapter 42

Get Rid

They tried to outrun them, but the wheelots and kumelenjahs were skilful in pushing them closer to a cluster of rocks.

“We need to get rid of them. It’s not play time!” Rafe said.

“Yes!” Ben struck the larger of the mutants across its antennae, it fizzed and slumped.

Rafe launched his tuber with quick swipes to the hands and head of the mutants, making a quick meal of the determined creatures.

“We’ll get rid of them soon. Just a few to go!” Ben said, stunning three of them at a time. “These rocks have been more helpful - guarding our backs.”

“Watch out!” Rafe shoved Ben away from the rock side as an army of beetle bots scuttled over the rocks.

Chapter 43

Denial

It was too late for Tia and Lisa to do anything about their predicament. They yanked at the grate, but it held firm.

“You are loathsome. Absolutely loathsome,” Lisa yelled.

B33, his arms folded across his chest, with a broad grin of great satisfaction responded, “Loathsome. Is that a new word?”

“A productive day.” R37 grinned.

“Have you lost your mind?” Tia’s voice was low and disappointed. “Ray, have I missed something?” She was holding back the tears; her cousin, whom she loved so dearly, was going against every pact they had agreed on about looking out for each other. She could see a cruelty in his eyes she had never seen before. “Tell me why Ray?”

R37 glared at Tia. At first it looked as though he wasn’t going to answer, then, with disdain he said, “I don’t have to tell you anything.”

“You were getting in the way,” B33 taunted, “Too nosey, too sharp, too quick to make a mess of things!”

Lisa stood beside Tia. She could see Tia was not doing well. Lisa snapped at B33, “Typical of you to think that. You have a habit of saying the wrong thing, but you've gone too far this time."

R37 shook the grate. "It will hold. It will hold. Hold." He said this so many times even B33 had enough. He pulled R37's hand from the grate and it seemed to spark him back on track.

"Now you think you're Mr Peri, repeating yourself. Funny, very funny!" Tia's mocking surprised Lisa.

"We need to go," R37 said, "we'll be back for you later, when everything is sorted." He stormed away as though he had just had a fight with them. Tia ran to the far end of the cave.

B33 said, "Royal Languin will be pleased."

Lisa banged on the metal. "Let us out!"

"Be patient. We may return." He skipped away.

Lisa rattled the grate with frustration.

Tia curled up on one of the dusty beds, the hurt she felt from R37's actions and cruel words were so painful. It reminded her of when she was told her mother had died, and shortly after the funeral her father had to go to Jamaica as part of his work. She ended up staying with Rafe's family and was reminiscing how kind Rafe had been to her. She couldn't believe he would inflict so much pain on her knowing what she had been through. It was too confusing. Tia sobbed.

Chapter 44

Stomped Sore

“Oh no!” Ben cried, startled by green beetle spies circling them.

“Ben - they’re everywhere.” Rafe shoved Ben out of the path of the stumpy mutants. Ben was grateful because he was being confronted by pincers coming at him again. He made a quick swipe upwards with the tuber and jabbed from side-to-side to take out the beetles.

Rafe unknowingly stepped back onto a beetle, he felt it crunch under his heel. A glance downwards caught sight of orange slime oozing from the damaged beetle. Ben was more than happy to see that and stomped on them whenever he had the opportunity.

The last few remaining large mutants took turns to lead the attack.

“The one with eyes,” Rafe shouted as he jumped over the top of three beetles to get into the path of the large mutant, its eyes narrowed in on him, pincers extended in a vicious stab and rotate motion. Rafe could see that it was up to something as its motion slowed, instead of flying at him it retreated, and for a moment its clunking paused. A high-pitched zapping noise could be heard as it produced four more limbs from its side panel - the other mutants did the same. Ben and Rafe exchanged a quick glance of 'Ready' - they moved swiftly back-to-back, stomped at the beetles in quick succession to make ready the battle with the mutants.

"I can't seem to stop them."

"Keep going," Rafe encouraged as orange goo oozed unto the ground.

Ben wiped his brow. "It's the eyes, makes me dizzy."

"Yes." Rafe eyed the slow movements of the mutants "Concentrate on battering them." Rafe took a deep breath. "Cut the limbs. Aim for the eyes - avoid the glare."

Ben looked down and kicked at a beetle that seemed larger than the others. It toppled over and couldn't regain its balance, its tiny feet kicking to turn over. Multiple beetles surged to help the upside-down beetle. Ben went on a stomping rampage.

Rafe went on a torrid attack, tuber poised, then thrusting, swiping upwards, striking downwards, slashing hard along the top of the mutants. Appendages went flying. The possibility of disabling them was in their reach. Their irritating din faded.

Ben stomped triumphantly on the last beetle and patted Rafe on the back. "That was hard work."

“Steady…” Rafe stretched his back trying to eliminate the burning sensation. “It feels like they caught me where I least expected.”

“You did some damage too - loved the swipe to the right and left, you took three of them out in that movement.”

“You weren’t too bad yourself. Three in one go.”

Rafe could feel the burning sensation around his ankle and chin. He shook his legs hoping his trousers wouldn’t stick to any bloody body parts. He pulled up his trousers and saw blood running down his legs from puncture wounds. He jogged a short distance to where they had seen the dippers.

“Where’re you going?” Ben called after him.

Rafe returned with his hands full of aubergine leaves, passing a handful to Ben.

“Please say we’re not going to eat this,” Ben began to protest.

Rafe rubbed it over his wounds, grimacing at the severe burning sensation created by the liquid being expelled from the leaves. “I heard the elders speaking about the healing properties of these leaves last night.”

“You could have warned me it was painful,” Ben complained.

“Doesn’t last long. You’ll soon feel a cooling sensation.” Rafe pulled his trousers legs down as he saw the bleeding subside then cleared his hands of the remnants of the leaves.

"That's better," Ben said, "it was great. I'm buzzing. Could do it all again." He kicked at fragments of their foes.

"You may get your wish sooner than you think," Rafe said. He was standing on a boulder overlooking the scene where they had been looking for the girls. "There are more on their way. We need to get flying!" Rafe shook off any soreness he was feeling, jumped on his hover tuber, and headed towards the coastline behind a row of rocks that obscured their departure. Ben wasn't far behind.

Chapter 45

Disappointed

Lisa tried her best to hack away at the grate, but it did little damage, instead it sparked every time the tuber slammed against the metal. Fatigued, she gave up. She leant back against the cold wall, using it to cool her down. She felt bad for Tia, who had stopped crying and was curled up on the bed shivering.

"I want to go home," Tia said, her voice muted and despondent.

Lisa placed her tuber on the ground, sat next to Tia and wrapped her arms around her. "I don't blame you," Lisa said, then paused. "You never give up. You would want Meela to be safe."

"I don't think she cares. No one cares. So why should I care?" She placed her head on her knees. Lisa put her hand on her shoulder.

"Because you do care. I don't know what's gotten into Ben and co." Lisa wanted to avoid mentioning Rafe's name just in case Tia started crying again. "They're just not themselves. Well, Ben's acting like a demented cat, so I suppose no change there." She gave Tia a friendly nudge to see if she would at least smile. She didn't see her smile but hoped Tia found it amusing.

"We've got to finish what we set out to do." Lisa looked over at the fireplace. "It's getting cold. I'll set a fire then see what the boys have left us to eat. We'll be able to think better when we're not so hungry or cold." Lisa went over to Tia's rucksack removed the sleeping bag and covered Tia.

Lisa successfully started the fire by rubbing her tuber over the stones which ignited the already organised wood fragments, the embers soon got going. She was pleased with herself and especially that her friend was now able to drink something warm. Lisa had delved into the sack R37 had left and found a wooden bottle with what seemed like an herbal tea. It smelt like mint, so she heated it in the little pot and used a ragged cloth to remove it from the heat and poured the warm liquid into cups. She smelt it first, took a sip. It tasted like hot orange juice, which she thought peculiar but better than drinking mint. Lisa was a little worried that Tia refused to eat. However, Lisa helped herself to some of the food - bread rolls with a type of vegetable paste tucked inside. She believed that at least one of them should keep their strength up. She ate slowly and watched as the lazy evening sun dimmed.

Chapter 46

Calm

Rafe looked back, grateful to see that they had outwitted and outran their opponents. He slowed the tuber, allowing Ben to catch up with him. They were back in the section of the plains, heading towards the woods.

"Let's head north, see if we can get back on track."

Ben nodded. "Looks like rain."

"We'll have to find shelter soon. I was told that there are caves off the coastline which the sea people used to use."

"Who said?"

"When you were grabbing your beauty sleep, the underground people told me this, although they did say that many of the caves are in a poor condition after being used as prisons."

"We'll avoid those, I don't fancy being trapped in a cave with bats, they are one set of creatures I don't want to meet up close," Ben said.

They managed to manoeuvre through the woodlands, hoping to find the correct part of the coastline. Dark skies and purple clouds crept in behind them. Rafe jumped off his tuber. Ben rode a little way on, taking the time to try out some tricks on his hover tuber. Rafe walked behind impressed with Ben's new skills, balancing with one leg, twisting the tuber into a spin, and staying on without falling off. Ben got off the tuber once the foliage became quite dense.

Rafe said, "It looks like we'll be well covered if it rains.... These leaves are massive."

Ben jumped and pulled one of the lower leaves down, it was deep green with thick yellow veins. They heard a creak and ping sound when the leaf was released. "You could catapult someone off that," Ben laughed.

"Want to try?" Rafe grinned.

"Yeah! Let me find one that I can sit on."

"Best find one to take your weight, big boy," Rafe laughed.

Ben laughed too and ran from leaf to leaf until he found a large, thick rubbery one. Both he and Rafe hauled the leaf down into position for Ben to sit on. It was far more difficult than they had expected. The springy, spongy texture made it difficult to get a proper grip; the addition of the trickling rain wasn't helpful either. Rafe stood on the edge of the leaf to hold it in place. "This may release you into...well...over there, or there."

"I'm all in," Ben laughed with the anticipation of flying; no thought given to where he was going to land.

"Here goes. One… two..." Rafe counted, as though it was for the start of a race, with dramatic effect.

"Start from three. More exciting."

"Yes Captain. Here goes. Three… two… ready..."

"Don't say ready, just go." Ben was filled with excitement.

"Okay," Rafe laughed hard. "If you land in a nest, I'm not going to rescue you."

"Oh yes you will. You love the adventure as much as I do."

"Ok. Counting -"

Ben resettled, crouched in a ball, knees tight to his chest, eyes dancing eagerly, hoping for a soft landing. Rafe counted slowly then jumped off the leaf. The leaf creaked, swayed at the stem, and ripped away from the plant. Creamy coloured sap splattered over Ben as he rolled backwards like an elastic band in reverse motion. Rafe jumped about and howled with laughter. Ben couldn't believe it, no airborne, daredevil styled launch, just a crunch of the leaf. Tears of laughter rolled down his cheeks. He wiped the splatter of sap from the leaf and flashed it at Rafe; Rafe tried to dodge it but got caught.

Ben laughed, “It doesn’t taste of anything.” He sucked at his hand, “no, it’s actually got a slightly savoury taste.”

Rafe raised his eyebrow and grabbed a handful and flicked it at Ben. “I hope you can hold it when that muck turns your stomach.” Rafe sprinted off up a gradient chuckling. Ben jogged after him, laughing all the way. When they had managed to gather themselves, they heard a faint call. At first, they thought it was birds, or a strange animal. They both came to a halt and listened carefully.

“Is that metal? Hitting metal?” Ben quizzed.

“It’s coming from up there,” Rafe said. They cautiously headed in the direction of the noise.

“It can’t be,” Ben said.

“It sounds like Tia and Lisa?” Rafe said, still hesitant that he could be wrong.

“Why would they be calling out for help?”

“They must be in trouble!”

They both jumped on their tubers and ascended the hillside at speed.

Chapter 47

Signal

"My throat's hurting," Lisa coughed.

"I don't think there's anyone out there. It's drizzling. I suppose people, even animals take shelter."

Lisa suggested, "What if we bang the tubers on the grates or run them along the grates instead of these cups?" Lisa waited for Tia to answer.

Tia wanted to curl up and sleep for the rest of the evening, it was already getting dark.

Lisa continued, "I really don't want to damage the tubers. Goodness knows last time Ben ruined the pendants from working properly."

Tia let the comment go, knowing full well that Lisa had a hand in that disruption. "Let's try again later. I'm tired." Tia dragged herself back to the bed she had been lying on for most of the evening. Lisa looked out through the grates, searching for another idea. She took out her torch. "Perhaps this will do it." She looked back at Tia. Tia was staring into the fire, curled up on the bed that she had pulled closer to the fire.

"Tia?"

"Do what you think best." Her voice was flat.

Lisa continued, hoping her enthusiasm would encourage Tia. "I could shine my light, like Morse code. Well, I don't know Morse code, but it could work."

"Like a beacon," Tia muttered.

"Yes, like a signal. I suppose if I move it about it may mean danger than if I just shine it in one direction. I wonder if anyone will see it past the bushes out there."

Lisa glanced back at Tia. She could see a line of tears permeating her closed eyelids. Lisa felt tears welling up inside her too, for her friend's sadness. "I must do this," she said quietly, enough for Tia not to hear, but enough for her to take courage.

"Right!" Lisa swallowed hard, blinked to get rid of any tears and pulled out her torch. "Tia, give me your torch too. Two are better than one. That's what my mom would say." As the words came out of her mouth she regretted it, but Tia remained silent, however, she placed her torch on the ground without rising and rolled it along the ground towards Lisa, her eyes now open staring at the fire.

Lisa ran over to the torch. *It'll be alright. Don't worry*, she told herself, gently taking up Tia's torch and quietly returning to the entrance. She turned her torch on, shadows of the vegetation jumped about with the gathering wind. She turned Tia's torch on; the lights gave the bushes a bright, dazzling appearance. Grey insects popped up on the leaves, Lisa was relieved to see them fly into the air and disperse over foliage that was further away. She composed herself and swung the torches left to right, up and down. "Please someone, anyone, help." Lisa's voice was still tight from shouting. "Please see the lights."

Chapter 48

Warning Lights

"I can't hear anything," Ben said.

Rafe and Ben stood still and listened. They could hear the wind sweeping up the leaves, throwing them around; the large ones were hazardous, landing a couple of times right across their faces, temporarily blinding them from seeing where they were going. Rafe would peel one from his face, release it and it would, curl around Ben's head as though it were determined to hamper their progress. Ben dragged it off and threw it behind him. They eventually decided to walk and get their bearings, night was drawing in and the moon had yet to make an appearance.

"I think we must have been hearing things, we are so eager to find the girls perhaps we thought we heard them," Ben said, after listening for a while. Rafe threw a balled-up leaf away.

They paused again and listened carefully - nothing.

"You could be right. And it doesn't help that it's getting dark, and the wind is getting stronger."

"Let's find shelter until the rain goes," Ben said.

"It's only drizzling, and yet the soil feels soggy. Best move off this trail. The elders did say there were marshlands out here, I'm assuming we've found it."

"Why not head up the hillside to those trees. Looks like a safe place," Ben said.

"Let's go."

Clear light zigzagged from a hilly area ahead of them.

Ben got excited. "Look, over there. Did you see that?"

"Yes. Could be the callers," Rafe said.

"Or another trap," Ben added hastily.

"Tubers to the ready."

They moved stealthily towards the warning lights.

Chapter 49

Cold Reception

"My arms are tired. Tia, please help."

"In a minute." Tia's voice was flat.

"Please. Or I'm going to have to stop."

"I'll do it later. I doubt if anyone is around now, they're all in their cosy homes, where we should be."

"Tia. You better get up here. We need to escape!" Lisa stopped herself from saying anything hurtful, the state that Tia was in she didn't want to add fuel to the fire. She was now dismayed at her unsuccessful attempts to cajole Tia into action. Lisa reluctantly allowed her arms to take a break, she placed the torches on the ground, their beams directed towards the bushes. She sank to the floor, back against the wall she closed her eyes.

"What are you doing in there?" Rafe said, relief and panic in his voice as he realised he couldn't access the cave.

Lisa looked up, "Rafe?" Lisa's instant relief was turned sour as she remembered who had locked them up in the first place. And now that she could see Ben beside Rafe, tuber poised in his hands, grinning like a Cheshire cat, she was none too pleased.

"You can wipe that smile off your face. You two should be ashamed of yourselves; leaving us like this." Lisa picked up the torches. She saw the puzzling interchange between them, "disgusting! Don't be pleased. Be ashamed. Be very ashamed." She shook the torches at them as she delivered her scolding; the boys shielded their eyes wondering what on earth was going on.

Ben looked at Rafe, put away his tuber. "This is what you get. See what I mean."

"Don't you dare start, you Morons – Or are you going to find all this hilarious?"

"Well, it is funny," Ben said, clipping his tuber to his belt.

"Go ahead. It seems to be your new occupation," Lisa taunted.

"What are you talking about?" Rafe asked.

Lisa turned her back to them. "Makes me gag, you two acting like nothings up."

As she said this it dawned on Rafe that Tia was not responding. He could see Tia was not bothered whether he was there or not. "It's the real Rafe and Ben. Tia, TIA."

Ben caught on. "You think we're those imprint nitwits. They're the morons." Ben started laughing.

"I can't," Lisa began.

Tia refused to turn. "If you're going to be mean I'd rather stay here."

"Tia, stop being like that. It's me Rafe, RAY."

"It's cold, let us in," Ben pleaded.

Tia hesitated. She wondered if they were playing a trick on them. She slowly sat up, walked cautiously towards the grate, her sleeping bag wrapped around her. Lisa was still having a go at Ben.

"Ray?"

"Those doubles have fooled everyone so far. Well, they could because everyone else doesn't know us. But you know us. Open these gates."

Tia was still a little suspicious. "We can't, they locked us in."

"They what!" Rafe's voice sounded like thunder; he shook the bars.

Tia ignored his outburst, "What's this?" Tia showed him her bracelet a little ragged now, but the colours of the flowers were still vibrant.

Lisa stopped having a go at Ben and stared at Rafe.

"It's a – your mom's flower, from erm… national flower, Jamaica, lignum vitae - Hibiscus, Hibiscus."

Lisa whispered to Tia, “It could be programmed to say that…”

Rafe raised an eyebrow, “In the words of Auntie Sandra.” Rafe tilted his head to the right, opened his arms and said, “Tia, cum now, ah ME.”

“Ray, Ray, it’s truly you.” Tia jumped up and down. “There’s a lever out there somewhere.”

“A liguuma, what?” Ben asked.

“Look for the lever, I’ll tell you later,” Rafe said.

“To the right,” Lisa added, “keep up Ben.”

“A liguma what?”

Lisa looked to the heavens.

“I’m surprised they locked you in. The reception you just gave us should have kept you out of there,” Ben chuckled.

“Too soon Ben,” Rafe said, with a stern glance. “Find the lever.”

Chapter 50

Talk

As the rain poured down, they were all huddled around the fire, their sleeping bags wrapped around them to protect them from the bitter night wind.

They ended up sharing one of Arabella's nutritious snack bars because Rafe and Ben refused to eat the meal the imprints had left, even protests from Lisa who had eaten some of what had been provided earlier and hadn't died didn't convince the boys. They believed at some point it would take full effect and she might go into a deep sleep. Tia snuggled up beside Rafe.

Lisa finished their story. "They were really mean."

"I can't believe you thought they were us!" Ben said.

"Yours was a bit easier to believe, but Rafe's was unbelievable," Lisa said.

"That makes no sense. Mine was believable? Then how come you didn't listen to R37i, to give him his correct title," Ben boasted, "if you thought he wasn't acting right?"

Tia, who had hardly said anything, finally broke her silence. "A couple of things made me wonder why you… he had a funny twitchy neck, and they didn't have rucksacks."

"The rucksacks, I didn't think about that," Lisa said.

"All the mean things he did, didn't you even question that it couldn't have been me?" Rafe looked down at Tia and across at Lisa who avoided his gaze. "The rucksacks? Really?"

Lisa said, "Well – no."

Tia came to the rescue. "We thought you were mad at us."

Lisa nodded in support.

"Well." Rafe was dismayed.

"But I knew something was up, like I said the twitch and an empty kind of look."

Rafe raised an eyebrow. "A twitch - Not his despicable behaviour? And stupidity?"

"Don't get mad," Tia said and gave Rafe a hug.

"Yes," Lisa said, too excitedly, "like someone's licking your face and you don't like it. Like this." She stood up and demonstrated the twitch and vacant look.

"Like this?" Rafe stood and copied Lisa.

"Stop it. It's too close to the real thing." Tia pulled Rafe back to a sitting position.

"Bet that made you throw a wobbly," Ben grinned.

"It's your laugh that was so-o-o irr-i-t-a-ting," Lisa exaggerated, "not much different to now, really."

They all laughed. As the hilarity died down Tia said, “So tell us how you escaped.” Ben took the floor. By the time they had exchanged stories they were very tired. Rafe decided he would keep first watch just in case the imprints came back. Although he was tired, the score he wanted to settle with them for hurting Tia kept him alert. “Ben, you can take over from me. The girls have had such an ordeal, let them sleep first. Lisa, thank you so much for being there for Tia. I’m so proud of what you did. You’ve really come a long way.”

“That’s true sis. You tried to get out of here. I’m proud of you too.” Ben attempted to give Lisa a hug, but she quickly pulled away. “Don’t get soppy.”

Tia said, “I’m sorry I left without telling you Ray -”

Ben interrupted, “Not to worry I knew what you two were up to.”

“No, you didn’t!” Lisa snapped.

“So, what are we doing here then Inspector?”

“You had to do what you had to do.” Rafe gave Tia a hug, instead of refereeing Lisa and Ben’s quarrel. “Proud of you little T.”

“So, are they coming back?” Ben asked.

Tia shrugged, “They didn’t really say.”

Lisa said, “One of them said something like maybe?”

"Maybe - means they're trying to keep you off guard," Ben said.

Lisa agreed, "Only time will tell."

Rafe nodded in agreement. "But this time we'll be ready!"

Chapter 51

Plans

The next morning, the rain had reduced to a lethargic drizzle. Regardless, they had got up early to try out the new attachment and put on the tunics from Sam. Ben recounted how they defied the strange creatures to retrieve their attachments. And now that Rafe and Ben had demonstrated how it worked, they couldn't wait to try it out. The girls managed to balance on the platform and jump off, hold the tuber to snap back into place, they repeated this: open, jump on, close. They managed to ride around in the confined space but couldn't wait to get outside and ride in freedom.

"Try not to hold on too tight or balance like a statue, move your legs with the motion if you need to, be relaxed, or your legs will get quite stiff, and you won't be able to stay on for too long," Ben instructed, "cramp will get the better of you. Like hunger is getting the better of me."

Rafe shared out some of the snack bars so that if they got separated again, they would have an instant form of nourishment. There were a few left over for their breakfast.

Ben said, "Knowing that you had these bars, why let me spend money on our meal?"

"Why is this an issue today?"

"Cos I just thought about it, I mean, I spent money on our meal in the marketplace."

"True," Rafe said, chomping into his bar.

"I could have saved that money."

"It was impressive to watch you sort out a meal for a change," Rafe teased, "and maybe you wouldn't have that bar to enjoy now - you would have already finished your quota."

Ben thought for a moment. He knew Rafe was telling the truth. He loved the flavour of the bars as they always replicated a meal that he enjoyed. In fact, he couldn't understand how Arabella had managed to make these bars so that anyone eating them would have a very different taste experience. Ben was enjoying fried egg and the taste of well-buttered toast melting in his mouth. He would certainly have pestered Rafe for more of these bars, and he knew Rafe would have given him a hard time for it.

Lisa said, "My cereal and warm milk was delicious." She was sat at the table with Tia fiddling with the wooden plates, eventually placing them and the cups together in two neat piles.

Tia whispered to Lisa, "I enjoyed mine too. I think Ray wants to know a bit more about what happened to the

Musca, he's getting very restless 'cos we haven't answered his questions."

"But we've had so much to do this morning. You explain," Lisa urged.

"Like I said, I thought it was going to be a small fly like thing. Tiny." Tia continued the story, "It's like huge, a hughamungus wasp-like thing, purple and blue with feathers at its tail end..."

"With little followers - mean looking things, I thought they were going to sting me to death. I don't know why they didn't sting T-so when he captured the Musca," Lisa added.

"I knew there was something off about T-so," Rafe said, "and if I wasn't sure, the attack of those wheelots and mutants made me know for sure he was behind it. He told us we'd find you over the rise, and before we knew it, we were surrounded."

Lisa got up. "Let's not keep harping on about that." She stacked the plates and cups on the shelf. She did this slowly keeping her back to the others as much as possible. Ben couldn't believe he'd ever see Lisa spend so much time tidying up.

Lisa said, "One minute T-so's helpful, and then the next he's hard to place, or believe." Lisa avoided facing them, shuffling the items around unnecessarily.

"Helpful?" Rafe wasn't having that. "He's shady. After all you and Tia have told us about him, what has he really done?" He looked to Ben for confirmation, but Ben had other motives.

"I think Lisa has a little crush," Ben sang.

Rafe sighed, "Really?"

"Shut up Ben." Lisa gave him a stony stare and plunked herself next to Tia. "Keep your nose out of it."

"What's there to keep my nose out of if there's nothing in it?" Ben taunted.

"Well, don't let him get the better of you," Rafe said, with a stern look. "Now, let's get back to what we need to do. We're all certain that they'll come back, right?" Rafe looked to them for confirmation.

Lisa was eager to answer. "Yes. Because I heard Ben say…"

"Not me. Call that dumb, rock-head another name or B33, not mine."

"Anyway, moron said something about tomorrow, which means they'll be back."

"They provided food for us which means they want us to be ok," Tia said. She picked the sack up from under the table. "We'll have to hide this or get rid of the contents."

"I'll eat it," Lisa said, sheepishly. When the others frowned, she said, "I hate to see good food go to waste."

"Who said it was good food – T-so?" Ben winked.

Lisa ignored him, grabbed the sack, and looked around for a place to empty the contents.

"So, we need to hide." Rafe looked at Ben. "One of us needs to pose as the imprint, trap the other one here, find out where the Musca is hidden, scupper their plans."

"Well, the other moron did laugh a lot." Lisa stared at Ben, as if he didn't know she was talking about him. "I think you could play that part really easily."

"You mean my impression last night wasn't very good?" Rafe asked.

"No, I didn't mean -"

Rafe chuckled, "It's ok Lisa, I'm pulling your leg."

"I think Ben could play the part well," Tia said, as she walked around to Rafe. "Because Ben finds it easier to goof around, but Ray's not like that, they may catch him out. Although, a couple of times, your robot kept repeating his words like he had a blip. We might be able to capture that one, whether you could pull off the blip Ray, that's another story."

"It's malfunctioning. That's not a good sign. It may mean it'll need to go back to the rejuvenation facility just as Meela described," Rafe said.

Tia slipped her arm through Rafe's and rested her head on his shoulder.

"Don't worry. It will be okay," Rafe said.

"I'm happy to do it," Ben said proudly, "besides, I'd like to find out what's really going on. I'll find a way of getting out of being tested if needs be. I'm not scared."

"So how are we going to capture your moron?" Lisa asked.

"We need to separate them," Rafe said.

"I could tell your moron that I need to speak to him in private, take you aside or something, you guys catch the other one," Lisa said.

The others nodded as they thought it over.

*

By the afternoon, the rain had stopped, and their plan was almost complete. They talked it over again and kept a watchful eye for the imprints' return. Lisa dashed back into the cave. "They're on their way."

Chapter 52

Instructions

They all took their places. Rafe released the lever to put the grate back in place, then concealed himself in the foliage and kept an eye on the entrance of the cave. Ben had pushed himself between the two beds at the furthest area of the cave. Tia arranged the blankets over him as though the blankets had been left in a messy pile. Lisa shoved a bed against him. She heard him give a sharp cry, but she paid no attention. Tia stood, staring into the warm but fireless hearth. Lisa lay back on the bed, watching the entrance. Once the imprints appeared she jumped up as if in surprise. “About time! Where have you guys been?”

The grate juddered as it gave way. The imprints didn’t wait for the completion of the rise they lowered their heads and entered.

“Hope you had a good sleep,” R37 said. Lisa now knowing it wasn’t Rafe felt at ease being rude to him.

“And what do you care?”

R37 shrugged, dumped a sack of food on the table, viewed the cave. They hoped he didn’t want to know what the lump was in the corner.

"Where's T-so?" Tia asked, as a distraction, she really didn't care about his whereabouts.

"He's waiting for us -" R37 replied, his twitch interrupting the rest of his sentence. Tia stifled a giggle as she now knew that the imprint was malfunctioning. "Does your neck hurt?"

"What, -hat, -at, you me- mean?"

Lisa joined in. "You keep doing this, this. This." She clicked and flicked her head in an exaggerative ploy.

Tia couldn't hold the laugh, she half laughed, half coughed.

Ben wanted them to stop playing games and get on with the plan, he was already aching from the cramped conditions.

R37 paused.

"We need to go," B33 said.

R37 grabbed Tia's arm. "Time to go." Tia didn't resist, she kept up with his pace, wishing she could zap him with her tuber and dislodge his circuit.

"We don't need them," B33 said. R37, who was about to leave the cave with Tia, looked down and shoved her away as though he was holding something disgusting. Tia fell to the ground with the unwarranted force.

"We don't need them," B33 said again, but didn't leave the cave. R37 reached down, twitching, and yanked Tia up and out of the cave, up the trail and round the corner. Tia noticed that B33 wasn't following, grabbed her tuber and slapped the back of R37's knees. He released her and buckled, unable to get up he remained on his knees repeating,

"I need to stand. I need to stand."

Tia ran back and stood at the mouth of the cave, glad that B33 couldn't see her as Lisa was speaking to him.

"Don't want to seem ungrateful for all this hospitality." Lisa knew the excuse was weak but didn't know what else to say to keep him there a bit longer. She was amazed as the imprint stared intently at the beds, as though it was computing that the beds were incorrectly positioned and needed adjusting. Tia beckoned to Rafe who slipped into the cave, "He looks nothing like me!" Rafe muttered. Tia smirked at Rafe's denial then quickly took her position as look out, just in case R37 returned; it was up to her to keep him out of the way while they disabled B33.

B33 and Lisa pulled the bed back to its original angle. Rafe snuck in and knocked him out with one swift crack of his tuber. The imprint collapsed to the ground with a long groan and started to hiccup. Ben was relieved to take the pressure of the bed away from his ankles and sprung out. He threw the tangled blankets on the ground.

“Thank goodness for that. I thought you were having a Saturday afternoon chat with your friends. After all that practice, what a lame excuse.”

“It got the job done.” Lisa rolled her eyes.

“Get going you two. Save the sniping for later.” Rafe bound the arms and legs of the imprint. Ben made sure he kicked the imprint as he ran out of the cave. “That’s for doing a poor imitation of me.”

“Don’t forget to laugh, he was always laughing,” Lisa said.

“He’s not laughing now.” Ben started lowering the grates. Lisa gave him a telling look to say: *we’ve already gone over this.*

“Ok. Is there anything else?”

“Be bold!” Tia said, as she ran under the grate before it hit the ground. “Your imprint is always bold even when laughing.”

Ben jogged up the slope, where he met R37, who had recovered from the blow to his legs. He was sat in a small cart with a long-benched seat, led by two horses. The small storage area held an open wooden crate with a silver net, coil of ropes and a colourful blanket. Ben jumped up onto the seat, R37 handed the reigns to Ben, Ben noticed how muddy his trousers were and wondered what R37 had been doing.

"No thanks," Ben said, "you best do this." He hoped that was enough for the imprint to follow instructions, because he had no idea of what or where they were going. How he wished at that moment that Rafe was the decoy because Rafe had a better sense of direction. R37 shot him a defiant look and flung the reins in Ben's direction. Ben wasn't sure if this was a malfunction or if R37 had worked out what was going on and was going to foil the plan.

"Where to?" Ben said.

R37 scowled, "The Palace!"

"If all else fails," Ben said, and started to laugh.

R37 stared at him not amused. Ben continued to laugh and tossed the reins into the air, the horses charged forward. This did the trick. R37 grabbed at the reins as they landed loosely across the rear end of the horses. Ben continued to laugh through sheer terror, as the horses galloped off the cart jolted uncontrollably. R37 got hold of the reins and set the horses back on track. Ben watched carefully as they travelled along. He wanted to make sure he knew his way back, so he managed to snap a few branches along their route, until R37 growled at him to stop.

It didn't take long before they were entering the marketplace, along its main route. Ben looked out for Sam or Alamo, but there was no sign of them. They passed the passageway where Ben and Rafe had previously fled the palace. Guards waved them through an adjoining trail.

"I hope the Royal Highest Languin is happy with us," Ben said.

The imprint grunted.

"The Musca is safe?" Ben hoped R37 would give him some information about where the Musca was being held.

The imprint grunted, then said, "Underrated, underrated."

Ben sighed in disbelief; this was worse than he had feared. The plan would only work if he managed to get information out of the imprint. Now that it was having another melt down, Ben didn't know what to do.

Chapter 53

Unsatisfactory Situation

They entered a field, where all the work horses were given their temporary freedom. R37 negotiated their carriage in between the line of carts and carriages lodged in front of a brick wall. Ben looked over his shoulder to see T-so sprinting towards them. '*Put on your best act,'* Ben said to himself.

"You took your time. The Languin is getting impatient." Ben could see T-so was clearly anxious about the situation. "So come on." T-so pulled at Ben as he jumped down. Ben wanted to say how unhelpful it was but noticed that the imprint hadn't moved.

"He needs a helping hand," Ben said.

"Not now." T-so growled and marched on.

But the imprint remained seated, staring into the distance, mouth agape. By this time T-so had made it past the carriages. Ben, stood by the cart, not knowing whether to encourage R37 to get down or follow T-so without him. When he saw T-so turn and shout, as though he were the carer of two disobedient teens, he started laughing, but soon stopped when T-so threatened to get the guard and throw them both into the rejuvenation pods. Ben ran round to R37 and pulled his arm, “Get down. You’re not going to get me in trouble. I refuse to be fried.”

R37 leapt out of the seat, “underrated!” he shouted and started doing cartwheels.

“Stop it. Stop it!” Ben tried not to raise his voice, “just, follow T-so.”

R37 stopped for a brief moment, he looked over at T-so and started dancing. Ben couldn’t believe what he was seeing. He heard T-so shouting, but Ben refused to turn around, he had to get R37 under control.

“Click, click, click.” Ben’s tone was harsh as he stared at R37, “click!”

R37 stopped dancing, the word somehow made his eyes brighten, he ran towards Ben.

“That’s the spirit.” Ben was relieved, jogging alongside the imprint. T-so continued on his way.

They ran alongside a high, imposing stone wall. Ben could hear the sea beyond the wall; he could taste the salt in the air. They left the greenery behind them as they headed towards the palace walls, brown and chalk coloured stone under foot. They weaved through a long open pathway, blue-grey skies above. Finally, the coastline was revealed through two monstrous rocks, a pebbled beach, and pink sands. Ben caught sight of boats out on green seas and people wading into shallow waters, scooping something out of the sea with baskets, others standing inland on sandy shores with large baskets at their feet.

Hidden between rocky pillars was a steel door embossed with a large flower head; a guard showed them in. Ben could see a myriad of corridors, each one dimly lit. The smell of something citrus mingled with the dampness of the corridors.

"Be respectful when you see her Royal Highest Languin," The guard said. Ben listened but didn't pay attention to any of the other instructions they were rapidly being given. He was trying to work out where the smell was coming from, but when he finally arrived at the place where the Languin was waiting, he realised it must be her perfume. Ben could see the relief on T-so's face once they entered the room. Guards flanked the outside doorway.

There was an elaborately carved chair in the room, on which Elleba was perched. Her fabulous gown of white and yellow pearls rode atop her black boots. A purple and blue flowered brooch added the final touch to her outfit. She sat comfortably in the empty room. The tall, narrow windows revealed the nautical scene Ben had observed on his way to the palace. Ben didn't know whether to stand in front of her as T-so had done or against the wall opposite her as R37 had done, legs apart and hands behind his back. But when he saw her wave T-so out of the way, Ben quickly shuffled beside R37 with the same stance. T-so stood to the side of her, staring out at the sea.

Elleba seemed in high spirits. "You have done well to capture the Musca and place her in my capable hands."

Ben wasn't impressed when T-so bowed, as though he had done this single-handedly.

"And I am very happy to inform you that she is in good spirits. Thank you so much for doing as I commanded."

"The pleasure is all mine." T-so stepped up beside Ben and bowed again. As the Languin turned away, Ben nudged T-so in the back before he could straighten up.

T-so stumbled forward, missing the Languin by centimetres as she stood to take in the outside view, her boots squeaked against the dreary flagstones.

T-so regained his balance and shoved his fist into Ben's side. "I'll get you back for this," He sneered out the corner of his mouth, glad he was the same height and similar build to Ben. Ben stared ahead as if he had no clue of what had just taken place. Elleba turned, T-so quickly placed his rolled palm behind his back.

"Now, just to make this clear, try your best not to be seen. I have ordered the Shobi people to have a time of rest tomorrow. They are delighted. The rest period starts at sunrise and finishes at sundown the following day -"

She was interrupted by R37, a long groan, twitch and groan. "Sunset, Sundown - Sunset Sundown - Sunset Sundown." His head flopped forwards, "underrated."

"Not again!" She cursed and stomped over to the imprint.

Ben watched as the Languin examined R37. His head flopped forward, she pushed it back, tried to hold it in place. "This shouldn't happen now." She said this more as a plea than an observation. "Hold your stance," She commanded, "Hold your stance!"

"Underrated."

"Hold your stance." T-so was at her side shouting at the imprint.

Ben thought *is there anything this guy won't do for a bit of recognition*.

"Call the guard." The order was for either of them; however, T-so moved quickly to dutifully carry out the instruction.

"You were to last until this operation was over," She sighed and released his head. "Take him to the rejuvenation room. Have him ready for tomorrow morning - early."

The guard led the dancing imprint away. Ben felt a pang of regret, then remembered it wasn't really Rafe and on reflection was glad to see him go.

The Languin coughed politely, turned to T-so. "You will take Musca to the marshland basin."

"I'll need help. The imprint you've sent to the rejuvenation room was going to help me," T-so said.

"B33 will take his place."

Ben stood to attention.

"But he's not as strong as R37. Besides, he can't deal with the bothersome girls."

Ben really wanted to smack T-so.

Elleba was about to sit, she paused, removed a long black hair pin from the back of her head, a plait dangled loosely. She made her way to T-so, slow and measured, her eyes raised to the grey ceiling, then casting her severe glare on him. She stood in front of him and dug the hair pin into his sash.

"You are a perfect ally." She smiled when she saw T-so wince as the hair pin pricked his skin. "Who would suspect you? Cheeky, loveable. Who would suspect you of anything?" T-so knew better not to answer. She balanced his chin in the palm of her hand, and slowly closed each well-manicured finger around it until she had it firmly in her vice-like grip. Ben could see T-so grimacing.

"Remember you have a lot at stake. Your opinion is not required." She brushed the top of his shoulders with the hair pin, as if there were lint on his garment. "The fine people of Gakinde should never know what you're doing." She applied pressure to his shoulders. Ben was horrified to see how strong she was as she pushed T-so to the ground with one hand. He lay there knowing not to get up. She looked down at him and spat her words out. "I don't want to hurt you. You can be assured of that. But you have one more thing to do for me and I will stick to our arrangement." She took her time to replace her loose plait with the hairpin, raised her foot to stomp on T-so but stopped short of his hands, the tip of her boot clipping his fingers. T-so scrambled to his feet holding the injured fingers.

T-so's voice was clearly shaken, "I'll do as you say, your Royal Highest - Languin."

Ben wondered what kind of hold she had over T-so. He felt a little sorry for him, so he said, "I'll get the girls."

Elleba stepped to Ben, glared at him. Ben tried his best to avert his gaze to the floor, he thought he was helping to calm the atmosphere. Her eyes seemed to burn a hole at the top of his lowered head. “Do you need the rejuvenation facility too?”

Ben thought it best not to say anything. It was T-so who jumped in to save him, Ben wasn’t sure if it was because he didn’t want to do all the work on his own or he genuinely didn’t want him to get rejuvenated.

“He’ll be fine. Like you say, the agreement is the agreement. Your - Royal, Highest, Languin. He can go to the rejuvenation facility after we carry out our duties for you.” T-so feigned a contented smile.

Elleba held Ben’s chin, tilted it so that it faced the ceiling. He felt as though his neck would crack in two. She peered into his eyes. He tried not to swallow. She slowly tilted his head back in place. He did his best to swallow slowly, as if he were a robot, and wondered if they were supposed to swallow. She placed her hands on his neck then shoulders as if checking for something. He waited for the pressure, but relieved when she took a step back, still scrutinising him.

“As soon as he gets back, he’ll need a re-formation. Or perhaps a little zap. What do you think B33, no? Don’t you think a little zap would be helpful?” She gazed into his eyes as if searching for the answer. Ben slowly released his breath as she stepped away with a side gaze.

“I could use a guard?” T-so suggested in a mutter.

“Don’t be so stupid.” She flashed her hand in the air dismissively, and elegantly perched herself on the chair and contemplated.

Ben gave a quick glance at T-so who looked as though his idea was being thought through.

She finally said, with a light-hearted tone, “I can’t have anyone see a guard, let alone see the Musca being taken into the marshlands. It will incriminate the palace and I can’t have that.” She narrowed in on T-so, her tone once again urgent and severe, “Now listen carefully. Bug will meet you at the marshlands once he secures these lovely ladies at the cave. Remember to provide him with the tail feathers. When they are found the villages must see evidence that they were involved with kidnapping the Musca. And don’t forget you have to inform your people of the kidnapping.”

T-so nodded rapidly in confirmation.

Ben didn’t like the new name - Bug, he felt as though she meant she could squash him at any time.

“I will reward you for coming to the rescue. The girls will be publicly banished from our land, and I will organise a kingdom-wide search for the Musca. Of course, the Royal Lanquis will be back in time for the Musca to be found, but, unfortunately, she will have had a fatal accident -”

“Accident? I thought you said…”

"I will complete the details. You carry out what we agreed," she said, with a nonchalant nod and a little jig. She removed the time piece from a secret pocket in her gown, studied it, then said, "now go, collect the feathers for Bug."

"I was to collect them tomorrow."

"Now!" The Languin yelled.

T-so scampered out of the room.

A guard marched in. The Languin greeted her warmly and lowered her voice. "The Musca must die. The little fool is too anxious to allow it to survive. So, make sure you're not seen with the others. Once it's in place, make it look like an accident, his accident."

She turned to Ben. "Isn't it lovely to share secrets among friends." She didn't smile, she didn't laugh. She sighed. "Now, my little imprint." She played with Ben's fringe. "Don't forget, spread the feathers in the cave, a few outside, to make it look like a struggle. Bend, break, tear them make it look like a terrible struggle – add this." She took a small bottle from the guard.

Ben nodded and received the bottle trying not to look too closely at the red substance.

"Please sit." She tapped the top of the chair. "I'll provide refreshments. I don't know why I made you all capable of eating. I must look at the program. Alternatively, if I didn't, you wouldn't be human enough." She gave Ben a cold stare and laughed heartily.

Chapter 54

Dismantle

"What's taking them so long?" Lisa sighed.

"Ben has to be careful. If he gets found out we're all in trouble. Maybe rot away in this place with no return to our real lives."

"Don't be so morbid Ray. We're going to get out of here." Tia turned around on her hover tuber. "I'm getting better at this."

Rafe smiled, happy that Tia was back to her normal, playful self. However, he still wanted to get hold of his imprint to dismantle it so that it couldn't hurt Tia again.

"Do you think we should get rid of that thing?" Lisa pointing at B33 who had been shoved in the corner, seated, nose to the wall with the beds as a mini fortress hemming it in. They had taken turns to guard the imprint just in case it tried to escape.

Rafe was sat at the end of one of the beds, watching as the imprint's head slowly rotated from left to right. "We didn't think this part of the plan through," Rafe said.

"I'd hate to know we've got to sleep with it in here, gives me the shivers." Lisa hopped off her tuber and snapped it to her waist. "I did it!" She beamed then looked at the imprint. "I think we should dismantle it."

"You read my mind, although I was thinking of doing that with my imprint," Rafe chuckled.

"I was wondering whether it had an alarm system," Tia said, as she hovered in a static position facing Rafe.

"B33, do you have an alarm?" Rafe asked.

Its response was flat yet audible, "No."

Tia did one more lap around the cave, clipped the table; a cup tipped off the edge and rolled along the ground. "Ooopsee," she said, sheepishly, and hopped off her tuber.

"Glad that wasn't me," Lisa teased. She picked up the cup. "Oh dear, it's got a split."

"Split! Split!" The imprint yelled as it shook uncontrollably.

Chapter 55

Night Life

Ben was grateful to leave the palace without T-so or anyone shadowing him. He was provided with clear instructions from the Languin on what he needed to do that evening. He had driven the horse and cart through the market, stopping at Sam's cousin's stall, pretending he was purchasing supplies so he could pass on a message for Sam. Vizam provided him with food and drink for all of them. Ben was chuffed with his achievements so far and even resisted the temptation to sample the food.

Ben had followed the track as far as possible; the rising wind had stirred up the trees and vegetation and this had confused him as to which way he should go. It all seemed to look the same to him. Ben continued a little further and then decided as the wind subsided to leave the horse and cart. He found a secluded area where the horse could shelter. He stroked and spoke gently to the horse, as Alamo had taught him.

"Now you know I'm not supposed to do this, but I'm relying on you to stay here. Here… don't wander off." He secured the reins to a tree then wandered around to the crate. He opened it up and looked past the metal ropes, nets and all the other regalia that was to help T-so with his plot for the Musca. He would come back for them later. Ben pushed the food bags into the large sack that held the feathers of the Musca. The feathers were large, and smelt of something sweet, they stuck out of the top of the sack. Ben used the cord around the neck of the sack to swing the sack onto his back; it was very uncomfortable. So, he separated the cord with his tuber to make the necessary adjustments, he placed one section over his right shoulder, down his front, to his left side, and the other around his waist anchoring the sack on his back. He knotted the cords across his stomach. He went back to the horse. "See, not bad huh?" He patted the cord. "My delivery will be made. Now I'm sorry I have to leave you here. Stay put, stay here. Don't let anyone take you away – that's an order." He stroked the horse. "I'm relying on you." Ben could feel the weight on his back and hoped the cave wasn't too far away. The horse started gnawing at the foliage. "That's it, have something to eat – keep your strength up until I get back."

Ben opened his tuber, hopped on, and hovered slowly around the area, checking to make sure he could remember where he had left the horse. He stopped and started as he got used to the weight he was now carrying, the late afternoon sky turned from blue to hues of red and orange. Ben saw broken vegetation, believing it must have been the way he had previously travelled. He followed this trail until he came to a branch of a tree that he had snapped to indicate that the cave was down on the left. His heart leapt for joy as he sped away.

Chapter 56

Cave Life

"What's your name?"

"B33. At your service."

"Tia, will you stop asking it the same questions." Rafe was getting impatient, looking out from the cave mouth, waiting for Ben.

Lisa and Tia had been asking the imprint questions, as they knew it was slowly malfunctioning, because Rafe had disabled its arms, preventing it from attacking them. They laughed every time its reply ended with; 'I'm at your service'. Lisa would then ask it to complete a stupid action like touch your nose with your tongue, lick your hand, twist. Rafe wasn't happy with having the imprint freed but the girls enjoyed the entertainment.

"Thank goodness!" Rafe shouted. Excited to see Ben return, the girls left the imprint dancing on the bed. Rafe quickly ripped away a shabby bed sheet, the imprint fell, landing on the ground still twisting. Rafe tore away a section of the sheet. The grates opened. Rafe stuffed the rolled-up piece of bed sheet into the lever gap to stop the grate from shutting down. They all gathered around Ben.

"Hello inmates!" Ben grinned.

Tia looked at the feathers sticking over his head. "Why have you got some of the Musca?"

"I can smell her," Lisa said, sniffing Ben.

"There's so much going on." He was glad to be the fount of information; he started to untie the knotted cord.

"Do you need a drink?" Lisa asked.

"No. I'm fine. I've got us news, and food too."

"From the palace? No thanks," Lisa said.

"About the news or the food my dear sis?" Ben asked.

"Enough. Get to the nitty-gritty." Rafe helped to free him from the weighty sack, which dropped to the ground.

"Well," Ben began as Tia took the food bags out of the feather sack and handed them to Lisa. "What's this?" Tia looked at the small bottle.

"It's for later."

Tia put it back and laid the feathers carefully on the ground. Ben flexed his back as he spoke. "The Musca is going to be moved tonight. You, I mean your double was supposed to help T-so do this, but because you're in need of rejuvenation… sorry Rafe, your antics of cartwheels and dancing didn't help. I think that was the final straw."

"Cartwheels?" Tia laughed, "I wish I'd seen that!"

Rafe was glad his imprint was out of operation, even for a while. “He could stand on his head for all I care.”

“I won’t be surprised if he did,” Ben smiled. Finally, he noticed his imprint on the bed, “What’s that doing free?”

“We were testing B33,” Lisa laughed.

The imprint stirred. “At your service.”

“I really don’t like looking at it. It’s unnerving, looking so dumb,” Ben sighed.

The girls laughed.

Ben looked over at B33, “Tie it up and keep it quiet.”

Tia and Lisa ran over and secured the imprint back in the corner. Ben was surprised at how quickly they reacted, especially Lisa.

Ben said, “I’m feeling rather cold.”

“Get yourself warmed up,” Rafe started the fire.

“I could live like this.” Ben stretched out on a chair with his feet on the table.

Lisa came over and flung his feet off the table. “Manners.”

Rafe said, “Come on big boy tell us what’s going on.”

Ben gazed cautiously at the imprint as he spoke. “Where was I…?”

Rafe replied, “I’ve got to meet T-so in the marshlands.”

"No, you can't, you're getting fixed. I have to do it, but first I have to scatter the feathers and make it look like a terrible scene, that's where that blood bottle comes in and they are the cause of the mayhem." Ben nodded in the direction of the girls now unpacking the food.

"This food smells delicious. Are you sure it's from the palace?" Tia asked.

"It's from Vizam," was Ben's quick response as he saw Rafe's scowl. "I was getting quite scared, it felt as if the Languin knew I wasn't the real imprint."

"What do you mean?" Rafe was surprised at this, but more grateful that Ben had made it back in one piece. Rafe helped the girls.

The food was now spread out on the table.

Tia happily said, "Dig in when you're ready."

"Tia, please!"

"No need for meanness Ray."

"It's not.... Can we hear what's going on - please?"

"Why?" Lisa asked

Rafe stared at Lisa.

"I mean why the feathers and -"

Ben interrupted Lisa, "Because you are the scapegoats. They're going to blame you for the kidnapping of the Musca."

Tia jumped up. "The devils!"

"T-so's a moron!" Lisa stamped so hard she agitated the old ankle injury, she had to rub her ankle to calm the ache.

Rafe raised his eyebrow. "To what ends?"

Ben was enjoying this. He couldn't wait to explain what T-so didn't know. "They want to publicly banish you guys from Pershee, the Languin will make it look like she was the one who found out that you were traitors. I think it's called treason?... Anyway, she'll send out a search party, her guards, to find the Musca."

"Is she related to Evelyn?" Tia asked, "she may not be the same colour, but she's as evil as he is."

"She's clever," Rafe said, pondering everything Ben had said.

"And she's going to look like the saviour, or the highest whatever she is," Lisa said with disdain.

"No, you haven't heard the best." Ben leaned in, lowered his voice as though someone was going to steal the information. "She's going to kill the Musca." Ben was happy to see the horror on the girls' face, and Rafe's contempt for the spitefulness of the woman.

Ben held his hand up, to add dramatic effect to the last part of his information. "T-so has no idea that the Musca is going to die. Elleba has made sure of that."

"That's despicable," Rafe said.

"I only came to see if Meela was alright, and it's led to all this," Tia gasped.

"Don't be hard on yourself," Lisa said.

Tia brushed it off. "I'm not sad about it. I think it's a good thing that we're here. We can help, and then go home. I don't want to come back to this place again. It's too much."

"I think we need to get some rest, eat, and set out to help Ben with this thing. Hopefully, we can grab the Musca before the guards get to her." Rafe stood. Now let's see what food you've bought. I hope it tastes as good as the food from that market stall, you know Ben the one you bought."

"By the way, I managed to slip a message to Sam via Vizam. I said - A situation like Sanguel, we need the group – marshland basin. Sunset. Soon as possible."

"Are you sure that will work?" Lisa asked.

"Sam and I go back a long way; he'll understand what I mean. Chuck me one of those parcels, I'm really hungry all of a sudden. In fact, I'm quite proud of myself."

They looked at him. Lisa finally said, "What did you do?"

"Elleba gave me refreshments and I didn't eat it or drink anything."

"Give him a break Ray, your eyebrow can rest assured that after having one poisoned drink he could resist another."

"Thank you, Tia." Ben bowed towards her and sat back down.

*

Rafe and Ben watched as the evening sun dipped behind dark orange clouds. They whispered to each other as the girls tried to separate the Musca's feathers, packing a few of them in their rucksacks.

"If you extract mine, I'll do yours."

"How can you say that so easily?" Ben looked over his right shoulder, Tia and Lisa looked deep in conversation.

"Because, if she knows, she'll give you a shock. I want mine out cos it makes me mad that she could do this without my permission."

"Okay. When they're fast asleep we'll do it. I may not feel a thing if you do mine when I'm asleep," Ben grinned.

"You'll probably kick me out of the way, Mr Deep Sleeper."

*

Rafe woke the others, it was still dark outside, but they knew they had to be ahead of T-so. They packed their sleeping bags carefully so as not to damage the Musca's feathers. Rafe carried Ben's rucksack.

The brooch fell out of Tia's rucksack.

"Tia, remember this?" Lisa held out the brooch.

Ben snatched it from Lisa's hand and took a closer look at it. His arm throbbed, but he refused to complain. "Where did you get this from?"

"It's a long story, but it was on a trip with T-so to see something amazing. By-the-way, no need to snatch; next time I'll give you a dead arm."

Ben flinched. Rafe felt sympathy for him knowing that they had removed a small plastic implant from each other's shoulder last night, and their arms felt quite sore.

"We were supposed to see the Musca, we had no idea -" Tia yawned.

"This must belong to Elleba. She was wearing one just like this, only the flower was a different colour, but the crest was exactly like this."

"So, Elleba may have been tracking the Musca," Rafe mused.

"Or got T-so to do it. I remember Zee saying he was always going off when he wasn't supposed to," Tia said.

"They must have been plotting this long before we got here," Lisa said.

"I think you're right Lisa." Rafe gave an affirming nod.

"Well done sis," Ben said and patted Lisa on the back.

Lisa took the brooch and said, "Next time don't snatch!" And handed it to Tia.

*

They walked out to a moon lit sky, vigilant to make sure no one was spying on them. Tia saw a mutant stumble into the bushes caught by surprise at their appearance. She dashed into the bush and jabbed the mutant repeatedly until it stopped moving. She heard its motor slowly grind to a halt.

"That'll teach it to spy on us!" she whispered, holding her tuber triumphantly. The others silently applauded.

"Do you think we should take that imprint with us?" Lisa asked

"It seems to have run out of energy," Tia said.

"You teased it so much, it gave up the ghost," Rafe smiled.

"I know what that feels like, don't I, Elisabeth?" Ben almost nudged Lisa then thought better of it.

"And so, you should, brain-less." Lisa fired back, with a jovial spirit.

"The cave is locked; it can't get out," Rafe reassured them. "Best put that mutant in too." Rafe started to pull it out of the bushes. He grimaced as a pain shot up his arm. He had caught hold of the tangled severed wires and dropped the mutant. Lisa kicked it towards the grate. Tia opened the gate and Lisa kicked it into the cave. Tia sealed the entrance and dusted her palms.

Ben uttered his last instructions. "Remember once you see the pink cliffs you know we'll be around that area, it's part of the marshland, but it's sandy more than boggy. Further up is the marshland basin okay. I'll try to delay T-so as much as possible. I really don't want to be the one to imprison the Musca or T-so. Because one thing I know, warrior girl can kick my butt." He waved them off cheerily, but deep inside Ben wanted to make sure he wasn't the one to ruin this mission.

They were soon on their way, Ben finally on the horse and cart, the others down the hillside towards the coastline, to find the pink hills.

"Who's Warrior girl?" Tia asked.

"Zee," Rafe said.

Lisa chuckled, "She's tough. I'd laugh if Ben had to come up against her. I think he'd surrender before being embarrassed."

*

Their conversation ceased as their descent met with cold air from the sea. They got off their hover tubers, as their legs were getting stiff. Tia led the way down the slippery slopes, followed by Lisa and then Rafe. They found it slightly warmer weaving through long grass and sandy mounds. By the time they got to the bottom of the hill, the cold air clawed at their faces and seeped through their layers of clothing.

"Let's use our sleeping bags before we get going on the hover tubers," Rafe suggested.

They kept their rucksacks on their backs, each one helping the other, undoing each other's rucksack and pulling out the sleeping bags, without damaging the Musca's feathers. The wind whipped at the rocks across the coast, the dark seas lashed the shoreline.

"Be careful when you start off, if you go too fast, the wind will knock you back." Rafe said, "As we both learnt, I mean, Ben and I learnt. The feathers have made it even more difficult." Rafe, waited as the girls, controlled their tubers against the blustery wind. Once they were steady, they rode side-by-side, every so often one or the other would thrust a little further, propelled by the wind. The moon disappeared behind deep purple clouds, it reappeared to throw their shadows long and lean.

The wind gave way as they entered the steep rugged hillside. It was difficult, at first, to see if the hillside was pink, but on closer inspection they were able to identify the pink soil. Rafe got off his tuber and signalled to the others. They dismounted and followed weaving past the rocks and bushes as Rafe was doing.

Tia pulled Rafe's arm. "Ray, this looks like the area where we were thrown out of the palace."

"It makes sense now, how T-so found us there. We thought it was a coincidence, but he clearly knew what was going on," Lisa said.

"The marshlands are over there. We know where it is. We passed this area and T-so didn't want to stop, he just said to avoid that place." Tia pointed to the slope that would lead to the plains of the marshland basin. Should we wait for them here?"

"Good idea. I don't envy Ben's task of getting the Musca up here, because these feathers are heavy, I can't imagine how heavy the Musca will be," Rafe said.

"A mechagribea pulled her away last time." Lisa was still disappointed at the capture of the Musca.

"I'm surprised we haven't seen any of them tonight." Tia eyed the shadowy landscape.

"We have to be ready for anything," Rafe said. He placed a calm hand on Tia's shoulder.

Chapter 57

Bad Company

Rafe, Tia, and Lisa were hiding in a crevice overlooking the final curve of the slope that T-so would have to pass to enter the outer perimeter of the marshlands before getting to the marshland basin. They hid their rucksacks behind a cluster of rocks.

Deep blue hues radiated from the sky with dark clouds threatening rain. They were fortunate to be out of the wind, so they were able to listen keenly for any impending movements. Tubers now in weapon mode, a strong wind whipping around the slope, they heard Ben cry out, and T-so yell. They tucked themselves snugly in the crevices to avoid being seen.

Rafe poked his head out as he heard the approaching, grunting beast. Its snorting reminded the girls of the chukkans. Rafe signalled to the girls to get ready. The shadow of the large beast crept along the crevices. The sweet smell of the Musca drifted over them.

"Move on, move on. We're nearly there, Chug-chug." T-so prodded the animal along.

Ben had a thick rope over his shoulder, attached to the side of the Musca's cage. His arms felt totally useless. He believed what he was doing had little effect on the movement of the cage, but he had to pretend to be the imprint, so he grimaced and huffed, at intervals.

They passed Rafe, Tia, and Lisa, without so much as a glance. The chukkan seemed to want to stop and explore them, but the stick being prodded in its side, was enough of an irritant to keep it going.

Rafe checked that no one was following the small convoy. "That's as far as you're going tonight," Rafe shouted.

T-so jerked around; surprised to see them, but the look he gave Rafe was enough to tell him that he wasn't going down without a fight. Rafe didn't want to hurt T-so, he wanted him to listen.

"Don't do anything stupid," Rafe said, "or I'll have to hurt you."

T-so was not deterred. "You best leave me to do this, or you'll be sorry."

"No, you'll be sorry," Tia said, lowering her weapon. Lisa still held hers in combat mode, she wouldn't have minded taking a strike at him.

Tia stepped forward, in front of Rafe. "We haven't come to harm you. We've come to help."

T-so looked at her suspiciously, glanced over at Ben and said, "Terminate them!"

Ben gratefully released the rope and charged towards Rafe as if he was about to attack him, then stopped, his legs apart, almost ready to pounce, suppressing a laugh. He stood still, as though he had a glitch.

"Attack. Attack. Attack." T-so surged forward, angrily wheeling his stick. Now that he held it as a weapon, the rest could see that it wasn't a stick at all, it had several prongs protruding at the top of it that looked like razor-sharp teeth. Before he could get to Rafe, Tia raised her tuber. T-so laughed and tried to land a strike at Tia, who returned with a smack to his hand and weapon. T-so felt the pain vibrate though his fingers, he had no option but to release his weapon. Tia gave a final blow to sweep his feet from under him, T-so landed heavily, rendering him helpless on the ground. Groaning from the pains now running through him, "What, did…you… do...?"

Rafe patted Tia on the shoulder. "Good little T, made mincemeat of him."

"Tia is no push over!" Lisa hissed over him.

The chukkan yawned, its rancid breath released about them. The children covered their noses, not even the sweet smell of the Musca could save them from the putrid air, which seemed to last for far too long.

Rafe was the first to speak, “Let me help you up.” He extended his hand to T-so who batted it away. Rafe stepped back, as T-so tried to grab his legs. “T-so? What’s wrong with you?” Rafe sighed, “We’re trying to help you.”

T-so curled into a ball, shut his eyes tightly and moaned.

Tia had enough of T-so’s antics and turned her attention to the Musca. “How are you?” Tia’s tone was low and warm, “We’re so sorry it’s taken so long to rescue you, but now we need to know where to take you to make sure you’re safe.”

Lisa and Ben stood with Tia, they both marvelled at the beauty of the Musca.

The Musca opened her eyes, they were filled with water.

“Don’t cry.” Lisa also felt tearful. “We’re here to help.”

“Yes. We are. Although I pulled you up here, it was to rescue you. Please stop crying,” Ben said.

“TRAITOR!” T-so yelled at Ben, his voice raced down the hillside. “When the Languin hears what you’ve done she’ll dismantle you!”

“Chill!” Rafe said, and shoved T-so back on the ground.

The Musca opened her mouth - silence.

She opened her mouth again, this time she was able to say, “I’m not crying.” She closed her eyes and continued to speak. “I’m not normally in this cold place for too long. I need warmth. I need my food and all my little ones.”

“Come with me,” Lisa said to Ben, and tugged his arm to follow her.

“Where do we need to take you?” Tia asked hastily, she didn’t want the Musca to die.

Ben and Lisa came back with the Musca’s feathers. They pushed them through the bar, laying them on the floor of the cage. The feathers floated to the Musca’s lower body and connected back in the right position.

The Musca opened her eyes, they believed she smiled at them and closed her eyes again. “Where you found me. Shelter leaves in the marshlands.”

“Where?” Ben asked.

Lisa nudged him hard in the ribs, “Don’t make out like we’re all dumb.” She quickly turned to the Musca, “WE know where that is.”

The Musca said nothing more, although she opened her mouth to speak several times. They could hear a low hum as a small swarm emerged and landed on the returned feathers.

"Come on Rafe, we need to move the Musca," Tia said.

"You can come with us, or you can remain here, tied up until the Languin or her guards find you." Rafe pulled T-so off the floor but didn't manage to make him see sense.

"Tied up, please," T-so said with a sarcastic tone.

"I don't know if you're being stupid or are just stupid," Rafe said shaking his head.

"Don't you understand? Elleba is not on your side," Lisa said, "get it into your…"

"Okay. He doesn't want to listen. My mom would say those who can't hear must feel. So, leave him here for Elleba to deal with him and he'll learn," Tia said.

Rafe had already retrieved two rope ties to bind T-so.

"I think we should take him with us," Tia said.

"Dead weight," Rafe said, and tied T-so's hands behind his back.

"The guards will be on their way soon, too," Ben said.

"Then we'll see who will be sorry," T-so sneered. "HELP! HELP!"

"I need a gag," Rafe said

"No gag," Lisa cried, then composed herself. "He can lead us out of here."

“I can remember part of the way,” Tia said, “after that I hope the Musca will have enough strength to tell us.” She looked over at the Musca hoping they weren’t too late.

They heard crunching sounds resonating from the long grass, they jolted around.

“GET THEM,” shouted a female guard as a set of guards charged out of the long grass.

*

The children lined up against the cage of the Musca. The band of five Ellebanites wore dark green apparel. They had empty sheaths on their backs, their swords now placed on the ground. They laughed at their captives, wielding their batons in jubilant display. They danced around their swords energetically.

“The Languin will be pleased,” The leader announced haughtily at the catch of the night. “All the runaways … and the traitor!”

“Traitor?”

“Yes, you!” A male guard was happy to say and danced past T-so.

T-so was aghast he thought they were going to point Ben out. “I’m on your side!”

Another guard held her side and released a hooting belly laugh that echoed into the night sky, all the Ellebanites joined in.

Their amused leader waited until they calmed and said, "Her Royal Highest Languin is correct. You are no better than… these." She jabbed T-so in the stomach with her fist, he doubled over, gasped for breath. Rafe helped him up. This time he didn't refuse the assistance.

A scraping noise, like a spade being dragged across flag stones, could be heard coming up the slope. Two more guards appeared, pulling a long silver mesh between them.

The leader drilled out orders, the Ellebanites scattered into action. "And finally..." she howled; the four adventurers thought she looked like a headteacher handing out prizes. "You… my friends will be cosying up with the Musca for the prosperity of our kingdoms."

T-so shook, trying to remove the hand ties Rafe had bound him with. "That's not true. I'm to go home."

"Of course you are." Another guard laughed louder than needed.

The leader continued, "And this is how you'll go home…with this special wrapping."

T-so looked on in horror as the Ellebanites continued merrily to spread the lengthy mesh across the ground.

Another guard began to untie the Musca from the cage, with only one guard to keep an eye on the children. Rafe signalled to the others; they all slowly readied their tubers. T-so was kicked towards the mesh. Tia pushed her pendant, dropped to the ground, and rolled under the chassis of the cage. The leader immediately shouted, “Come out or I’ll make it painful for you.”

The guard set with the task of watching them, jerked around when Lisa and Ben charged at the guards holding the mesh in place. They were taken by surprise by the youngsters’ sudden attack. Rafe tried to knock out the guard with a strike to the back of his head, but his strength fizzled away as he lifted his arms, his elbows connected with the guard’s back. The guard stumbled against the cage, face-first. The small Musca swarm instantly surrounded his face. He darted away down the hillside screaming from the stings. The large guard tried to follow him, but Rafe was determined that he wouldn’t get away too. Rafe managed to apprehend him with three swift strikes to his legs, he fell backwards onto the mesh.

Tia was now invisible; the leader searched for her. Tia snuck behind her and whacked her across the back of her knees. She went down shrieking in agony. A guard leapt out of the cage, after being stung by the Musca. He fell to the ground, excruciating boils growing over his body.

Lisa and Ben wrapped the six Ellebanites in the mesh who were unable to escape as the children stunned them into submission. Rafe untied T-so who was suffering the after-effects of the large guard falling on top of him when Lisa struck him down. Rafe hoped that by now T-so had got the message that the guards were not there to rescue him.

Chapter 58

Reconciliation

With the frantic goings on, the chukkan had slumped off to sleep. Its snore whistled into the air, a sour smell in its path.

"What are those weapon things?" T-so asked.

"As my grandad used to say - never you mind," Rafe said, "look at your so-called friends." He used his tuber to point to the mesh that now imprisoned the debilitated guards.

"They're certainly not my friends."

Lisa smiled far too widely for Ben's liking, he leaned into Lisa and whispered, "Be careful, he may just be saying it."

T-so looked across at Ben, "I don't know what you've just said, but I have to warn your friends that you are an IMPRINT."

They all laughed, only Rafe subsided with a chuckle to say, "He's the real deal. This is Ben not B33."

T-so turned to them mouth agape. "The Languin has a whole army of those things. All dedicated to her… willing to kill if needs be."

“You mean there’s more like me?!” Ben didn’t like the idea of that, although the idea of an army of Bens seemed quite appealing.

“Not more of you. More imprints, strange things.”

“We know,” Rafe said.

T-so hesitated - his eyes filled with tears. He exhaled deeply, then words flowed out in a steady, low torrent. “She said she would release them on my people if I didn’t do as she instructed… And if I didn’t capture the Musca, she would make sure that the surrounding kingdoms would not trade with us, …take our resources, even… kill us. I couldn’t let that happen.”

Ben put his arm around T-so’s shoulder. “When we were in the palace, she hinted at that when you left the room.”

T-so quickly wiped his eyes, staring back at Ben in shock.

Rafe said to Ben, “It would have been useful if you told us this before.”

“I forgot. Besides, I left the message for Sam, I hope he’s got it.”

“Isn’t the marshland near the Shobi people? So, isn’t she afraid that they’ll see the Musca being moved and killed?” Tia asked.

"No. She's given the Shobi special time off, for all their hard work. They normally come inland to the towns and villages to visit family and friends. With this special time-off there'll be so few of them around, if any," T-so said, gloomily.

"Now do you believe us?" Rafe asked.

T-so nodded in agreement. "I'll show you the way back to the Musca's hiding place, and I'll show you where Meela is."

"Ok. Time to get the Musca back," Rafe said, and rubbed his arm. "How do we get that chukkan up?"

"Now that it's had a sleep it will move more quickly, I hope you'll be able to keep up." T-so ran over to the chukkan.

"Don't worry about us," Lisa smiled.

T-so picked up his weapon. "It will need a start though; it's not used to travelling so long at night. I'll give it a good feed and rest when we get home."

Rafe chuckled. They all looked at him. "What? I just thought it reminded me of two people I know."

"Who?" Ben asked.

Tia giggled, "I think you and Lisa know the answer to that."

Lisa was too busy watching T-so climb up the chukkan to see Ben give Rafe a friendly tap. “Yep, you know me far too well,” He grinned.

“Easy.” Rafe rubbed his arm.

“What’s up with your arm?” Tia asked, worriedly.

Ben jumped in quickly, “He’s fine, I’m getting stronger.” Ben flexed his arm to release the pulsating tension.

Chapter 59

New Outlook

The small entourage followed the chukkan and the Musca on their hover tubers, except Lisa who travelled with T-so on his chukkan. She felt that T-so needed company after witnessing and realising the truth about Elleba's plans, but if he was tempted to stray, she would knock some sense into him.

They made it to the Musca's resting place and settled her back into her circle of shelter leaves. Once there, she pointed out some blackberries they could consume before they slept.

"I forgot," Tia said, as she rushed out of her sleeping bag, removing the smaller feathers from her sleeping bag and placing them around the Musca. The feathers glowed and returned to their rightful place on the Musca.

"How did you miss those, Lisa?" Ben asked.

Tia answered, not wanting a quarrel to disrupt the calm atmosphere. "I thought that if we were caught, the large feathers would be easily seen and these little ones could be better hidden, and, well..., here they are." She crawled back into her sleeping bag and snuggled down.

As they settled down Rafe said, "When the Ellebanites don't return to the castle, the Languin is bound to send out a search party and she'll know her plan has gone awry."

"Don't forget the one that got away," Tia added.

Rafe continued, "Yes, so we need to be up early to warn your people, T-so."

"I don't think I can sleep. I'd rather go back now and warn them." T-so was anxious. "You can guard the Musca, should they try to find her."

"Ok, I'll go with you," Rafe yawned, "but I need just twenty minutes of rest; just in case we meet any mechagribeas on the way, I'll be ready." Rafe could see T-so wasn't happy with this decision, but he nodded anyway,

"Thank you, Rafe, it's been a long night." T-so lay back on his bed made of large leaves, staring at the dark canopy not willing to sleep, well, not quite yet.

Chapter 60

Asa

The early morning air had a cold tinge to it. Rafe made his way, following the depression of the undergrowth, where he believed the chukkan had trod. Rafe had suspected that T-so would leave without him, but he hadn't anticipated that T-so would have been able to raise the chukkan without making any noise to alert him. Finding out that they had already gone while everyone lay sleeping gave Rafe a sense of respect for T-so, that he wanted to warn his people of the possible up-coming dilemma. Yet he hoped he hadn't done anything stupid.

Rafe caught them in his sights heading through a dense part of the woods. Rafe decided not to sidle up beside him but followed at a safe distance. The chukkan was travelling at a brisk pace which surprised Rafe. Once they left the woods behind and saw the splattering of red earth, Rafe was relieved T-so was heading home.

Rafe slowed down as he saw T-so dismount, almost losing his balance as he jumped down instead of running down the animal's extended front leg. Rafe returned the tuber to its original state and circled just inside the woods, making sure he wasn't seen. The herd of chukkans lumbered out into the open, Chug-chug joined them. Rafe watched as these heavy creatures entered the space so quietly, he realised how T-so had left without anyone noticing. A large man came into view from amongst the chukkans, Rafe realised it was T-so's uncle Asa. T-so ran to him and stopped a little distance away, adopting a humbled stance. Rafe crept through the woods to a point where he hoped to listen to the exchange. The words gushed out so quickly from T-so that Rafe just about caught what he was saying.

" ….. I was so stupid to believe her. Elleba wants to create problems between us and the Shobi people. It's all my fault. I'm so, so sorry uncle." were T-so's last words, before his uncle grabbed him firmly then pushed him away, shaking his head in disgust.

Rafe rushed out of the bushes to T-so's side.

"It's okay Rafe. I've bought disgrace to my household. My uncle has every right to express his displeasure at the shame I have brought to my people."

"And what do you know about this?" Asa asked, his tone severe.

"Elleba has created this problem…" Rafe began, searching for the right words. But Asa continued,

“The Languin is a problem all on her own. We, as a people know this. So, we keep away from her and deal only with the Royal Lanquis. He and his wife are supporters of our people working together. T-sodon had no right to include her in our business. If he was dealing with his responsibilities around here, he would not have got caught up in her agenda!”

T-so hung his head in shame, speaking to the soil as much as to his uncle, “She made it my business. I tried to make it go away.”

“And in so doing you made it worse.” His uncle gave a sharp tut, raised his eyes to a beautiful dawn sky. “We must now prepare for something we hoped would never happen. Why?” He looked at Rafe, who thought he wasn’t asking a question but thinking aloud.

Rafe cleared his throat, with an uncomfortable cough. Asa stared at him and asked, “Have you seen the Shobi’s territory?”

“No sir,” Rafe said.

“It’s mainly sea, a whole territory of homes and businesses, all based around the sea, accessed by boats or rocky pathways at low tide. When they were fearsome people, they would garner monsters from the depth of the waters to stop anyone getting to the shores, even inland.

The Musca has been said to come from their territory. They have calmed over the years due to the Lanquis' hard work. Can we allow this to be ruined?"

T-so began to attempt an answer, but Asa held his hand up.

"There is nothing more for you to say. Your actions have been foolish." He turned to Rafe with an agreeable stance. "What do you know?"

"Elleba hasn't managed to raise suspicions with the Shobi people as yet, but her plot is to do so… So far, we have ruined her attempts at leaving the evidence to implicate your kingdom. T-so helped with this."

T-so nodded eagerly. Asa gave him an approving side glance.

Rafe continued, "We know that Elleba will bring, I mean, we are aware of what she plans to do, to distort the truth, to say that this kingdom killed the Musca…."

"Her guards of course, the Ellebanites, I have heard of them," Asa said.

"Yes, but also she has her regenerated strange creatures,"

Asa wasn't astonished by this revelation. "We have heard of such things, Evelyn introduced her to more than what we were led to believe. But I've seen sightings at night.

She uses the mechagribeas to keep the plains and woodlands free, so she can train her spies and mutants."

"We are prepared to fight. We have defeated them before." Rafe was confident.

"You say we, who is this we?" Asa opened his hands as though he were welcoming guests.

"There's, Ben, Lisa and Tia." As Rafe said this, he realised it didn't sound very impressive and thought T-so's uncle might disregard them.

"The last time you were here, you mentioned Sanguel. You come from Sanguel?"

Rafe nodded.

T-so nodded enthusiastically.

"Who do you know in Sanguel?"

"Arabella Marquelleth, and…"

Asa put one hand on Rafe's shoulder. Rafe knew he wanted him to stop, and Rafe was ready to hear what he had to say about Arabella.

"You're in good company." His voice warm with a triumphant quality. "Were you the ones that helped her defeat -" he glanced over his shoulder towards the woods, lowered his voice, "Evelyn?"

Rafe gave a confident nod.

"That's amazing!" T-so shouted, jumping and punching the air. Some of the chukkans raised their heads from grazing, looked in their direction, as though interested in what was happening, then returned to their grazing.

Asa's face brightened. "Then you're not merely children! You can truly help us. You will fit in well with our units." He took Rafe's hand and shook it delightedly. "Anything you see from here on, you'll not repeat to anyone."

Rafe nodded confidently, silently pleased that his arm had stopped aching.

T-so's eyes grow large with acknowledgement that these were the children who thwarted Evelyn.

Asa smiled at T-so, "Go tell you sister and Kai what you have told me. She will know what to do." T-so began to walk away, Asa called after him, "Time to be a man, T-sodon, duty calls."

Chapter 61

Detour

"It's good of the Musca to let her swarm lead us back to the homestead," Lisa said.

"It's hardly a swarm. It's a small group, minuscule, if you will, in comparison to what we left behind," Ben said.

Lisa mimicked Ben, putting on her best voice, as though she had a plum in her mouth, "Minuscule, if you will! You're not Rafe you know."

"Rafe wouldn't use a word like that, besides, you're only jealous you didn't think of it. Fortunately, Rafe left with T-so, so they don't have to listen to you yapping on and on." Ben revved ahead to avoid Lisa's comeback.

Tia was hardly listening to Lisa and Ben in their argumentative mode, she was thinking about the kindness of the Musca, and how she had survived against the odds. She was pleased that she was able to help rescue the Musca. "Did you notice that her feathers were all back in place? I'm glad we did our best - it all paid off," Tia said.

"What was that?" Ben slowed his hover tuber, waited for the girls to catch up and put his finger to his lips. 'LOOK!' Ben mouthed and pointed. Tia and Lisa couldn't see what

Ben was pointing at. They held their breath briefly then exhaled slowly, steadily, listening intently, leaves fluttering, subtle birdsong.

The snapping of stalks grew louder. It took Tia and Lisa a little while but sure enough they saw why Ben looked so anxious; the undergrowth was moving. They caught glimpses of an army of mutants creeping through the undergrowth, determinedly, pushing forward in stealth-like manner, an army heading in the direction of the Gakinde people's settlement.

Chapter 62

War Rooms

The underground dwellings were a hive of activity. From children to adults, they all had their duties set out for them; for decades, this drill had been rehearsed. Those outside, were busy securing the necessary animals, preparing the hardy animals, and making ready the weapons around their perimeter. Anyone from the outside would believe it was business as usual, the façade of peaceful fields and labour in the hills continued without any sign of concern. Underground, it was a hive of activity, orders being shouted out, men, women and children taking weaponry, some getting dressed in protective clothing, others pulling metal grates across entrances and walls.

Indiscriminate clattering noises surrounded Rafe as he observed the rows of weaponry and protective clothing that were displayed along a myriad of secret corridors.

"All this time, I thought these vests were for the cold weather," Rafe said. He pulled on a woven vest made of blue flax reeds, the silver threading was the special technology in this piece, as it provided a sturdy coil that made the whole vest a defence against attack, providing a shield for the body.

"We weave many things here, servicing many kingdoms, but this is solely for our protection," Zee explained.

Rafe said, "Have you got anything similar to the leggings that can go over the arms?"

"Not really." Zee went over to a wooden box; fragments of fabric lay undisturbed. Rafe came over, searched the box, and found a short tubular piece. "This will do." He stretched it over his upper left arm, satisfied with his discovery. Zee showed him the territory map, engraved in the red wall and the weaponry linked with each area.

"We, the Gakindes, are the only users of this special armour." Asa walked in. Rafe had been studying a long metal spear with a serrated tip. He put it back with an uncomfortable look as though he had been caught out.

"Please, continue. These quarters are here for our protection. Unfortunately, this is one of those times." Asa paced into the larger weaponry space; he was already dressed in battle apparel. Rafe was impressed with how easily he moved with the top-to-toe adornment of dark clothing overlaid with the vivid blue protective vest and trouser, his hammer and pincer spear strapped to his back in a cross mesh covering.

Asa handed Rafe a metal pincer, which looked like a spear with a crab's claw at the top. "This is a fine weapon..." He got close to Rafe, "but, you have a weapon far superior, one that only Arabella's descendants used, and it is kept as a closely guarded secret."

They exchanged a knowing smile and nod.

"Rafe, come and talk with our warriors and allies, they will need to know as much as you can tell us about the wheelots and those mutant kumelenjahs. We need to know how to destroy them effectively. T-sodon has done well by letting us know what they look like and how they function."

Rafe was glad to be of service, providing as much information as possible.

"Their strange appearance won't bother us, what we need to know is: are they brave?" Asa asked with a tone of scepticism.

Rafe explained, "They are more than brave! They are vicious creatures."

"It's about time we had a good fight. To defend our grounds is an honour! We will match their vigour with cunning and righteous bravery!"

Chapter 63

Warning

Tia, Ben, and Lisa tore through the woods on their tubers, leaving the mutants at least ten minutes behind. They believed that this surprise morning attack was to catch the Gakinde people off guard. Thin branches and foliage slapped at their faces and bodies as they crashed through the woods not wanting to be caught.

Ben shouted across to the girls, "We need to create a diversion, we can stop and fight, but one of us needs to keep going to warn the others."

"I'll fight!" Tia said.

"I'm on my way!" Lisa zoomed ahead as Ben and Tia slowed.

Ben said, "When we've done enough damage we'll jet off."

Tia agreed.

They both hopped off their tubers. Ben hoped his arm would hold up.

"Let's put something in the way," Tia said, and sliced at a tree with the tuber. Ben ran to another tree and did the same thing. They pushed the trees in the same direction and got out of the way as the trees tumbled together. They continued creating the blockage for about two metres, stood back, and waited for the enemy.

Lisa didn't look back, even when she felt cramp trying to take over her legs. She shook it loose and relaxed but pushed on until she saw the underground settlement in sight. She could see the fields dotted with people, the chukkans and iggogos were nowhere to be seen. A group of older children were hanging silver fabric over the entrances to their dwellings.

Lisa started shouting, "Get inside, Get inside!"

The children jerked their heads around and watched her enter on the tuber. A deathly silence settled around her, they were all interested in what Lisa was riding. Lisa jumped off her tuber as she got to them, "Hide, get inside!" They were still more interested in the tuber; she was glad to see Rafe and Zee appear.

"They're coming Rafe!" Lisa said, with staggered breath.

"Welcome." Rafe grinned and hugged Lisa.

Lisa pulled away "No Rafe, you don't get it. They're on their way. NOW. NOW. LIKE NOW."

"We know." T-so was proud to give such a calm response.

Lisa stared at them, not knowing whether to relax or shout at them, to make them understand the urgency of the matter.

“We’re ready!” T-so said.

Lisa felt a little deflated. “Do you mean to say, I didn’t have to travel at breakneck speed?”

“Steady Lisa, you did a good job, ok.” Rafe looked at her, held her shoulders to confirm they had it under control. “You did a good job. Where’s Tia and Ben?”

“They’re creating a diversion.”

“Intelligent, strategic children.” Asa came out to find out what the shouting was about. He turned to Lisa. “We are proud to have you all on our side.”

Lisa felt pleased and allowed herself to relax, she quickly scanned everyone in their protective garments, admiring the way it looked.

“Come with me,” T-so said, “you’ll need armour, and I’ll tell you how we know.”

“Can I get something to eat as well? I lost every bit of my breakfast on the ride over here.”

“Give our young guest whatever she wants,” Asa said.

*

Rafe, Zee and T-so waited outside, motionless in the peaceful surrounding of the homestead, listening for the warning signs of the oncoming attackers. Zee had repeatedly instructed T-so to secure his ossula, for some reason he was having problems doing this. Rafe hoped Ben and Tia would get back safely. He was relieved to see them crash out of the woods and hop off their hover tubers.

As they got to them Tia hollered. “They didn’t have a chance!”

“We heated up the trees without setting them alight. The heat caught them off guard and they scattered in different directions, some retreating all together!” Ben matched her excitement.

“The mutants dispersed so quickly, we managed to get rid of a good batch of them,” Tia grinned.

“I heard the howls of some of those creature imprints and well…”

“We legged it!” Tia said. “They’re about twenty minutes behind.”

Ben noticed Rafe’s new attire. “What’s this?’”

“It’s impressive huh?” Rafe smiled, displaying his body armoury with a swift point at the arm band. “It’s added protection.”

Ben's eyes bulged with envy. "As much as I'd love one, those things are on their way."

"We can fit you up before they get here. Everyone knows what they need to do." T-so patted Ben on the back.

Rafe hugged Tia tightly, they walked in together.

"Glad you're back," Rafe said.

Tia squeezed his arm. "Back at ya!"

Chapter 64

Units

The sky dulled; a light wind swept through the homestead. The Gakinde people were all in position, ready for battle. An unsettling silence descended throughout the myriad of underground corridors. Rafe was positioned in one of the hideout tree trunks, carved out to house three people; Rafe, Ben and T-so, spied through the peep holes. The holes were positioned around the circumference of the tree, to provide a good all-round view. Rafe looked up to the hills where a sizeable unit had the advantage of air attack, a group of eagle-eyed citizens feigned working in the field. They were all awaiting the sound of the battle horns.

Zee's unit were teenagers, all vested and armed with either special metal spikes, hammer head batons or their ossulas with a metal cord running through them. Lisa and Tia now wearing protective armoury joined the unit.

"They're attempting to get in through the north passage," Zee said. They sprinted through a short corridor. Two lads rapidly opened the multiple bolts on the large metal door. Zee ushered the group through into a long dimly lit passageway, the door securely bolted behind them by a child who ran back to report that Zee's unit were on their way.

As they neared the end of the passageway scraping noises could be heard above them, fragments of soil fell from the ceiling.

Zee instructed, "Don't wait, commence battle immediately."

They nodded quickly.

"Remember what you were taught," Zee said.

Tia and Lisa exchanged glances, unclipped their tubers as the others held their weapons ready for battle. Zee still had her weapons strapped to her back, her ossula attached to her hip.

Zee signalled for silence, then unlatched the narrow door and cracked it open, hoping not to alert anything on the other side. Shrubs concealed their exit, on the other side, they could hear the grunts and squeals of whatever was attacking the soil. Zee carefully drew out her pincer, crept forward and peered out, the others gathered behind her. She signalled with four fingers and pointed to the left, five fingers to the right and three to the front of her. Zee charged forward; her weapon positioned for battle. She jabbed it into a winged imprint that was burrowing into the soil. The creature screamed and wheeled backwards, its face a mass of decaying teeth and a long yellow tongue. She sunk her pincer into its body; it collapsed. Lisa and Tia knocked the other two aside, while the unit spread into two groups to battle the creatures to the left and right. Once all these creatures were disposed of, the teenagers kept a sharp eye on the woods for any on coming attack as they circled the area.

*

Twelve green wheelots roamed around the main area of the settlement as if disinterested.

"We need to do away with those things, trying to look innocent." Ben was anxious to get started with the battle.

"Not yet. They'll survey the area and inform Elleba and her guards. So far, they think it's all peaceful, they can't see the battle at the back of the homestead yet. Wait until we see what's coming out of the woods." T-so was calm, knowing how strategic the Languin would be to try to catch them off guard. "She'll have something to -" T-so was interrupted by thunderous reverberations a short distance away from them, the ground was being attacked by red-grey birdlike creatures with spades for upper limbs and sturdy legs, flurries of soil being thrown in the air.

"Rafe look, those nasty things we had to destroy before we could escape from the palace." Ben gave way for Rafe to look through his spy hole.

"We need to stop them." Rafe was getting ready to charge when T-so grabbed his arm.

"Not yet," T-so said.

"Look, Rafe, it's Tia and Lisa!" Ben said, excitedly.

Zee's group had circled around and were taking out the creatures with great precision. A group of the creatures flew in, swooping low. Zee and a few others with ossulas went into action, pulling them out of the air with skill, the others dismantling them with their batons and spikes. The creatures kept coming, diving at the teens, their hard bills pecking, claws ripping relentlessly. Lisa and Tia used their tubers to remove claws and zap them out of the air. Slow cackles could be heard as they were defeated.

"It's time," T-so said, as he heard the warrior alert - a deep drumming sound resonated through the corridors before horns were blown on the outer perimeter.

Rafe smiled patted Ben on the shoulder. "Ready?"

"Ready!" Ben said and off they went, joining with the others piling through the various exits.

Chapter 65

Battle Cry

Fighters riding iggogos, positioned on the hillside, battled a second wave of flying creatures; while on the ground, the villagers fought with the vast army of creatures and multiple-limbed kumelenjahs.

The injured were taken to two designated areas where they could be treated, while young children created piles of stones and rocks to be used with spring action catapults to defend the entrances. In the meantime, large wheelots whizzed around, picking up all the dismantled limbs and shattered devices, depositing them in wooden boxes disguised as foliage.

Rafe spotted his imprint brandishing a spiked baton. Rafe couldn't wait to get even, smashing his last opponent, clumps of sparking wires exposed; without looking back, Rafe made a beeline for his imprint who had also spotted his rival. Tia glanced over her shoulder to see the two face-off, a loud din and chaos about them. She quickly demolished her opponent and swung around, shouting to Lisa. Lisa saw the first clash of weapons between Rafe and R37 and cried out with excitement and fear. Lisa ducked as her adversary, with a wooden box for a head, and rubbery large limbs, jabbed at her stomach, missing her both times as Lisa slipped out of the way and crashed her tuber into its limbs, removing them in a volley of strikes. The body crumbled to the ground.

“So, we finally meet!” R37 gave a sly grin at Rafe after a momentary pause to regain their footing.

“Talk is cheap!” Rafe swung his tuber towards its side. R37 blocked it with a swift downward strike of his own weapon. Rafe felt the force of the imprint’s strength. Eyeballing him, the imprint held his baton forward trying to weigh him up. Rafe side-stepped, pretending to go in another direction, then leapt back. The imprint, not sure how to respond, straightened up. Rafe sprinted towards the imprint then circled it. The imprint twisted. Rafe kicked him off balance. The imprint hit the ground. Rafe knocked the weapon out of his hand. A chorus of vicious roars threw Rafe off his battle stride; he jerked his head around to see four mechagribeas storm out of the woods. This sent the whole battlefield into a frenzied panic; some villagers ran, leaving weapons behind. R37 launched himself at Rafe and pinned him face down on the ground. A mechagribea sailed over them and landed with a thud, leaving Rafe disoriented.

Villagers on the hillside rained down boulders to knock out the mechagribeas and block their path to underground homes. Ben, who had just pulled a colleague to safety into one of the safe enclosures, heard a welcomed voice.

“How did they get here?” Sam yelled, surprised to see mechagribea outside of Sanguel.

Ben was relieved to see the Sanguel entourage, weapons strapped to their backs.

“The mechagribea are taking charge!” Izzy looked to the others.

“Let’s give them something to think about.” Alamo gave a welcomed smile as he and Sam grabbed a discarded mesh blanket. Izzy and Evan followed suit and dashed to the aide of the remaining villagers who had the courage to continue fighting.

Alamo and Sam sprinted with the mesh between them, opened wide as the mechagribea charged towards them. They pulled out their double spiked spears with their other hands, defending themselves against the beast’s claws as they threw the mesh over its head and shoulders. This covering confused and disoriented the mechagribea. Now up on its haunches, it released frightening bellows. Alamo and Sam shouted to T-so and Zee’s units to bind the beast’s legs with the ossula. The mechagribea hit the ground with a tremendous crash. Evan and Izzy pinned the mesh to the ground with metal stakes. The beast was rendered motionless.

They headed after the other rampaging beasts. Evan took a detour back to Ben. "Rowhan and Safia are here. They'll help to slow the mechagribeas but we'll need to defend them so they can get the job done."

Ben swiftly followed Evan to stand guard on the edge of the homestead where Rowhan and Safia sat cross legged on the ground feverishly, adjusting their equipment to subdue the mechagribeas in their attempt to aid the Gakinde people.

Tia's tuber smacked the head of R37 as he was about to strike Rafe again. She pounded R37. Sparks flew. R37 stopped, sat still, wobbled then toppled side-ways, releasing Rafe from his confinement. Rafe coughed uncontrollably, spat out soil and rolled over, sitting up with Tia's help. "Th…anks…"

"No probs." Tia stood quickly, watching for any oncoming attack. Within minutes Rafe was back on his feet, happy to see the Sanguel entourage in action. Without warning, R37 sprung to his feet. Rafe, glimpsing the shadow lurching towards him, swung around with a forceful strike of his tuber to R37's torso. It crumpled to the ground with a sizzling sound. Rafe made a final blow, "Stay down!" The imprint was made obsolete. Burnt metallic vapours filled the air.

No one noticed a guard, hair and face hidden under a dark scarf, sneak out of the woods following T-so's progress. Two kumelenjahs pursued T-so around the back of the homestead. The guard followed too, battling anything in the way, demolishing them. T-so was thankful for this assistance, until he recognised the black boots. He froze. She wielded her long pincer, skilfully grabbing his ossula. She snapped a metal ring on his arm. T-so turned and fled towards the woods. Two mutants appeared from the woods and grabbed T-so, removing his protective wear.

She grinned and with a quick release of the ossula she shouted, "Apologise!"

T-so refused.

She launched the ossula, it tightened around T-so's body, she pulled him towards her tightening the loop with each tug.

"Apologise!"

With his failing breath he murmured, "No."

A cold ring of ice ran from the metal ring down the rope rendering T-so powerless.

Chapter 66

New Beginnings

The battle raged on through the afternoon. The sky dimmed as the evening clouds gathered, cascading soil flowed like waves through the homestead, throwing everyone off balance. The fading din of the battle was eclipsed as ferocious roars echoed through the woods. Metal lions, larger than any of the creatures in the kingdom, emerged from the woods and formed a semi-circle in the middle of the homestead, their large scorpion-like tails ready to sting anything that came their way. The battle gave way to the intimidating sight of these imposing lions. Trees to the north of the homestead parted like curtains being flung apart, as the royal guards, mounted on horseback, entered the semi-circle and formed another protective arc. A defining hush fell over the area at the magnificent sight of Lanquis Levi his long greying locks held back with a gold metal band studded with diamonds, and his wife, Languin Ziba, striding in on black, furry mechagribeas, their triangular white ears turning like sails, alert to any impending danger. The royal entourage's purple and gold attire matched the reins and harnesses on which they were seated.

Lanquis Levi's strong voice punctured the still air. "How is this possible?" He looked about him. The sun slipped from behind the clouds and shimmered over his brown skin. "Fighting in my kingdom? This is never to be repeated!"

Four members of his troop flanked a guard who had tried to escape on an iggogo. They marched straight to the royal party. The royal mechagribeas sniffed at the offender.

"Reveal yourself!" Levi demanded.

They unwrapped the dark green cloth that covered the person's head and face. Astonished murmurs erupted in the crowd.

Ziba gasped, "Mother!" Her gold headband with two lines of ruby studs, almost slipped from her hair. She quickly managed to push it back in place.

Levi's voice softened as his mechagribea obediently lay down for him to dismount. "Why are you dressed in guard apparel?"

Everyone listened keenly to what was being said. At first Elleba's demeanour was one of submission. Then she raised her head, nose in the air, and in an audible voice she began. "I heard there's a traitor in these parts. A slippery Gakinde called T-sodon Leumason. He stole the Musca in your absence."

Levi's eyes searched the crowd. "Where is he? Come, I will give him a fair hearing," He demanded. Some of his troops ran through the crowd to fulfil the Lanquis' request.

"Is he from nobleman Asa Leumason's family?" Ziba asked.

Elleba hid a smirk and nodded.

Wailing came from the back of the homestead. Tia and Lisa exchanged puzzled glances. Tia managed to slip away without being seen. A guard spoke in whispered tones to the Lanquis, he responded with concerned nods.

Asa could be seen moving through the crowd carrying someone.

Whispers ran like rippling waves. "T-so, it's T-sodon."

"He's dead."

"He's breathing?"

Cries came from friends and loved ones.

"Not dead. Not breathing."

Rafe and Ben were stunned in disbelief.

Elleba shouted. "So, the traitor who stole the Musca has been delivered the same fate that he wished for her." The Ellebanites ran forward to substantiate their concocted story.

The crowd were astonished

The crowd gave way as Asa, in despair, departed to his underground home with his family to make T-so comfortable in his final moments. Ziba followed with her guards, their heads lowered as a sign of respect to the family of the ailing child.

Chapter 67

Welcome

“That’s not the truth!” Rafe stepped forward, bowing confidently.

Elleba swung around. “Don’t let him speak! He was with that fool too.” She stood defiantly. “There’s another one and another one.” She glared as she pointed out Ben and Lisa. She became mystified when she couldn’t see Tia.

Lisa stepped forward, gave a clumsy curtsy. “Dear Royal Lanquis. We were imprisoned by this woman. She wanted the Shobi to blame the Gakinde for the death of the Musca.”

“Yes,” Ben interjected, “she made doubles of me, - and him,” He pointed at Rafe, “imprints, to carry out her dishonest plans, but we didn’t…. here look.” Ben reached into his pocket and fortunately he still carried the small bottle which he handed to the Lanquis. A guard blocked Ben’s path to Levi and took the bottle carefully and examined it. He whispered to the Lanquis. Rafe, Lisa, and Ben tried their best to explain everything to the Lanquis, who listened intently, the crowd whispered and gasped at intervals as the story unfolded.

Elleba listened, with a spiteful look, and nose in the air, she announced, "These children are deluded. I've done everything to help. I've never been anywhere near the Musca! We all know she's hard to find."

The crowd parted for a teary eyed Ziba and her guards, Tia at her side. Elleba's eyes darted nervously from Tia to her daughter.

Ziba blinked tears away, shame building in her chest as she opened her clenched palm. "It's our duty to guard this with our life."

"Your crest," Tia stated, staring at Elleba.

Elleba offered a meek gaze to her daughter and Levi, glancing maliciously at Tia, "She stole it! Little thief." As she snatched at Tia, one of the time pieces slipped from her pocket, the chain swung like a glittering trail. Ziba grabbed onto the time piece as Elleba wasn't quick enough to hide it away. Levi extended his hand for Elleba to hand over the other one. Only shame and disgust passed between them as the crowd watched aghast.

"These should never leave the sacred place at Reverie. You of all people should know this!" He took the time pieces and safely secured them in a black velvet pouch on his mechagribea's saddle.

"Those children confused me. Made me do things I would not have done. They took the Time pieces, I had them for safety." Elleba pointed in turn at Rafe, Tia, Ben, and Lisa. Before they could respond, Arabella emerged out of the crowd and announced,

"It isn't wise to accuse someone of something they haven't done." Arabella presented herself to the Lanquis and Languin. Her healing fleece draped over her shoulders. Cheers rumbled through the crowd.

Arabella extended warm greetings from Sanguel, then said, "These children alerted me to the disturbance in your kingdom. Elleba's assignment, like Evelyn's was to disrupt the peace you have established over these many years."

The crowd gasped in disdain. Arabella continued, "I arrived as quickly as I could. Unfortunately, I fear, I maybe too late."

The crowd quietened to a deathly hush.

Ziba whispered to her husband, he nodded. Ziba led Arabella away to see Asa.

Levi turned his attention to Elleba, "Bind her!" Levi commanded his guards.

Elleba tried to resist, shaking and protesting angrily.

"Your fate will match your betrayal,"

*

Tia, Lisa, Rafe, and Ben were allowed to follow underground to where T-so's lifeless body rested on his bed, his family around him. The door was closed as they waited outside.

Zee briefly joined them in the corridor and said, heartily, "He's already asking for something to drink." She sped down the corridor to fulfil the request.

"What does that mean?" Lisa whispered to Rafe.

"I think Arabella's fleece has come in handy and T-so is healing!"

Chapter 68

Almost Home

The following day, the evening sun welcomed the festive crowd through the front doors of the palace. The Lanquis and Languin had previously arranged a festive celebration for their return from their peacekeeping mission, so this celebration was even more special after finding out what had happened while they were away. The Gakinde people, the Shobi people, and representatives from Sanguel were all invited to the gathering and were thanked for working together. Then Rafe, Tia, Lisa, and Ben were given special commendations and provided with blue and purple royal robes for the event.

They were seated on a long table surrounded by their companions from Sanguel and their newly found Gakinde friends. Tia noticed that Zee and T-so seemed to squabble nearly as much as Ben and Lisa. Tia was overjoyed when she saw the Peri's all sat together on a special table, Meela beckoned to her. Mr Peri pulled up a chair for Tia beside Mrs Peri.

"This is the person we have to thank for our family being reunited." Mr Peri patted Tia on the shoulders so hard that

Tia winced, he was about to continue when Mrs Peri cut in to save Tia any further pain and embarrassment.

“That’s enough Omar. I believe Tia is well aware of our gratitude.”

Mr Peri was trying to hide his embarrassment for making the wrong decision in agreeing with Evelyn to use his daughter as a bargaining tool between the Kingdom of Clover at first and then Pershee. “All’s well that ends well,” He cheered.

“Fortunately, Tia and Meela made great decisions. Omar, we need to talk about making sure this never happens again,” Mrs Peri said.

“Of course, of course Reena. You enjoy, enjoy this festive occasion.”

Tia spoke happily with Mrs Peri and Meela about the future as Evan and Alamo went over to speak with the others at Rafe’s table. They were in deep conversations about Elleba’s fate.

“I’m so glad she’s locked away in the rejuvenation facility, like we were. Perhaps they’ll be able to rejuvenate her!” Ben sipped his drink.

“I’d love to get a look at those facilities,” Sam said.

“Let me know when you do, I’ll come with you. It may help us to deal with Evelyn more effectively,” Evan said.

“I’m sure Levi and Ziba will find a fitting punishment for her, but it won’t be easy,” Rafe said.

They all agreed that the imprints and the crazy creatures should be reprogrammed and put to good use.

Rafe moved away from the group to have a quiet word with Arabella, “When Levi said, the sacred place, what did he mean?”

Arabella gave a wry smile, “The Lanquis mentioned that?”

“Yes. He said it when he took the time pieces away from Elleba.”

“It’s difficult to explain to those who don’t know or understand… but, in time you will.” Arabella gave Rafe a knowing smile and went back to the festivities.

“Ray, why do you look so puzzled?”

“Nothing.”

Tia felt hurt, “It’s something, but you don’t want to tell me.”

“No, it’s not that. I asked Arabella a question and she answered, but…”

“She did what Arabella does. Left you guessing?”

“You’ve got it in one!”

*

Meela approached the group as they were about to say their goodbyes in the great hallway. She introduced them to Lanquint K-dee. Evan and Alamo were honoured to say that they liked their soon-to-be brother-in-law, admiring his integrity and adventurous spirit. Mr Peri was relieved that everything had worked out well, his wife more relieved that her daughter was finally back to herself, although she was saddened at what her daughter had to go through.

Meela took a little time away from the small gathering to present something to Tia.

"This is the best present, ever," Tia gushed, as she kept looking at the silver bracelet with purple-blue flowers Meela had presented to her.

"Does that mean you'll let me off the hook for not getting you any presents?" Rafe grinned as he came up behind Tia, Izzy at his side and Ben close behind.

"And me," Ben said.

"You don't give me presents."

"Well, if I did…" Ben grinned.

Lisa patted Ben on the shoulder. "You're too mean. I hardly ever get a gift from you."

Meela was amused by the youngsters' witty exchange. She turned to Tia, "Lisa explained why you love our crest flower so much."

"That's so kind of you." Tia could feel tears pricking her eyes, "so thoughtful of you." Tia hugged Lisa and brushed her tears away.

"Spare a thought for me will you sis, when you get me prezzies."

"You'd be lucky if I buy you anything this year," Lisa teased.

T-so and Zee wandered over to them as Meela and K-dee returned to the festivities.

"How are you feeling?" Lisa asked.

"A bit sore," T-so said.

"T-sodon is fine. He's just trying to get out of his chores for the next few years!" Zee gave him a friendly push.

"For all he's been through he could do with a break," Lisa said, as Ben nudged her. Lisa waved his attention away.

"Thank you, Lisa, all of you for helping me. I didn't realise how bad things were." T-so shook their hands and before he returned to the festivities he said, "Although, I would have sorted it out eventually." He walked away with a bounce in his step. Zee followed unimpressed.

Rafe stared at him. "Really?!"

*

Moonlight confirmed the way to the rocky pathway. Sam, Alamo, and Izzy waved from the horse drawn cart at the base of the hilly terrain.

Rafe, Lisa, Ben, and Tia made their way up the rocky path, this time enjoying the peaceful surroundings. None of them spotted the owl, Tulisa, circling high in the sky observing their re-entry to the library. Tia closed the door behind them. Tulisa settled close by on a ledge, awaiting her master. Once inside the library Rafe and Ben listened out for the security that had pursued them. The reading room door was open, the library empty, the aroma of fish and chips lingered in the air.

"They must have been shocked when they didn't find us, so had a fish and chips supper instead," Ben whispered.

"Let's get out of here. I just want to go home!"

"Tia, you couldn't wait to get here. Now you can't wait to get home."

"What's your point Ray? Or should I say R37?" Tia giggled.

"I won't live that down."

They all agreed.

They hurried through the main space of the library, the girls dashed to the toilets for their belongings, and left via the side door.

"I can't believe I left my kit in such a mess." Lisa moved her belongings around to close her bag.

Rafe looked over at Ben. Ben winked. "You shouldn't be so messy."

"I'm not!"

"Are you missing your friend, Lisa?" Ben teased.

"What are you talking about? Tia's here." Lisa swung her bag to smack Ben in the side.

"T-so, T-so where art thou?" Ben sang, as he sprinted off down the road, Lisa swinging her bag after him.

"Ben's in for a rough time if he ever owns up to Lisa about her kit." Rafe chuckled.

"I'll never forget this adventure," Tia sighed contentedly, admiring her gift from Meela. "It was worth it."

End

Acknowledgements

My sincere thanks to Bigjayart for the fantastic cover and the supporting illustrations on my Instagram, and to Sue Johnson for your editing skills, advice, and insight.

I couldn't have completed this project without the dual roles of many of you: Moji Balogun, Jason, Warren, and Michael Davis, Sue Nicholls, Patrick Mattis, Oliver and Nicky Smith, Omari Hutchinson, Valarie Sinclair, and Chevon Lindsay.

To Brandon Watson – special appreciation for influencing the development of T-so's character, I hope you like him.

My gratitude and thanks to the Jamaican discussion team led by Mafuta Sam and Mrs. Joyce Sam, and the others who offered lively discussions about the Jamaican national plant.

To Bear Bookshop – thanks Jenny for championing authors and providing a space for writers and readers to enjoy. It's more than just a bookshop!

For all those not mentioned who have provided support and encouragement, I am forever grateful.

Recipes

The youngsters enjoy their food in the Kingdom. Here are a few recipes to try out ...enjoy!

Flatbread

Ingredients
2 teaspoons Basil
2 teaspoons Parsley
½ teaspoon Salt
½ teaspoon Black Pepper
2 cups (300g) organic self-raising flour
3-4 tablespoons organic sunflower oil (or your oil of preference)
175 litres of water

Method
1. In a bowl, combine the flour, herbs, salt, and pepper with a fork.
2. Slowly add the water, stir until the ingredients form a dough. If the dough is a bit sticky sprinkle a small spoon of flour over the dough and bring the dough together with your hands.
3. Divide the dough into 7 pieces and form into 7 balls
4 Sprinkle flour over your pastry board or clean work surface and roll out each ball (approximately 0.5 cms)
5. Add your oil to the frying pan (depending on size of your pan, the oil should coat the base of the pan) and turn on to medium heat sprinkle a little flour into oil to test if it's hot enough; it is ready when the mix sizzles.
6. Once oil is ready, carefully place one flat dough into the pan. Watch small bubbles rise as the dough cooks. Allow it to cook until golden brown. Turn over with a spatula.
Cooking time approximately 2-3 minutes.

This can be added to any meal, especially soups and stews. You can try them with a salsa dip. You can also try a variety of herbs for a different flavour of flat bread!

<u>**Ginger Bakes** – with natural sweeteners</u>

½ cup (UK) 75g (organic) Self-raising flour
½ cup (UK) 75g Spelt flour (or Plain flour)
100g Butter
A knob of fresh root ginger (approximately 5cm)
2 Teaspoons of ground Ginger
1 Teaspoon of Cinnamon
1 Teaspoon of Nutmeg
Pinch of salt
1 ½ Teaspoons Vanilla
2-3 Teaspoons Maple Syrup
10 Dates or ½ cup Currents (75g)
50ml of water

Method

1. Peel ginger and chop into small pieces, add to a saucepan of water and bring to the boil, turn off heat.
2. Add chopped dates to the pan, mix and allow both to cool and soften.
3. Place the flour, ground ginger, cinnamon, nutmeg, and salt into a bowl and mix with a fork.
4. Dice the butter and add to the dry ingredients. Use a pastry blender, fork, or fingers to create a crumble.
5. Add softened ginger and dates, vanilla, and maple syrup to the crumble, combine with a fork until the ingredients form a soft dough ball. If dough is sticky, sprinkle a little flour over the ball.
6. Dust pastry board and rolling pin with flour.
7. Roll out dough to approximately 1cm thick and use pastry cutters to form your biscuits. If you haven't got a cutter, roll into small balls, and flatten with the base of a mug or jar (dust the base of the item with flour). This should produce approximately 16-20 individual bakes.
8. Place shaped dough on baking parchment or a greased tray.
9. Bake in pre heated oven 180°C (fan assisted), gas mark 4, for 15 min or till golden brown.
10. Allow to cool (on cooling rack) before consuming or store in an airtight container.

Enjoy a sticky taste with honey, Agave syrup or Maple syrup dip (intensify the sweetness!)

Contact the author:

Email - davis.fiction@outlook.com

Instagram - @alex_lee_davis

Printed in Great Britain
by Amazon

10866286R00237